# FINDING MONICA

SEAL Team Hawaii, Book 4

## SUSAN STOKER

# CHAPTER ONE

Stuart "Pid" Hall wasn't surprised their carefully laid-out plans had gone to hell almost the second they'd touched down in Algeria. Rescue missions like these never went according to plan, but that hadn't kept the SEAL team from hoping maybe this time would be the exception.

Dealing with people whose emotions were high, as well as those who loved to incite a crowd into violence just because they could, tended to mess up even the best plans. The sitting president had been in power for twenty years and the citizens of Algeria were fed up with the corruption in his government. Protests had broken out. At first they'd been peaceful, but as time wore on, more and more violence had begun to creep into the country.

The government had begun to crack down on the protestors, but that didn't quell the enthusiasm and desire of the people to fight for change. It only fanned the flames. Certain groups were also inciting the protestors for their own agendas. In addition, reports indicated that rival political parties, representatives from foreign countries, and even private groups had joined the protests and were

1

purposely turning peaceful gatherings into violent, out-of-control mobs hell-bent on destroying everything in their path.

Homes and businesses were being broken into, then burned down. Murders were up 403 percent. And there had even been three kidnappings of foreign nationals. It all added up to one hell of a powder keg.

Which was what had brought Pid and his SEAL team to the area. They'd been tasked with evacuating US Embassy employees until the country and the situation stabilized.

They'd flown into the city of Algiers on the coast of the African country just as the sun was setting. Fires from the current protests burned vividly against the night sky as they flew toward their target building.

The evacuation on the roof of the US Embassy had gone smoothly so far...until a small boy had brought up the possibility of his nanny being missing.

Normally, Pid wouldn't have been so concerned. The woman could have simply been evacuated on an earlier transport, or maybe the child was wrong about his nanny's nationality—in which case it was out of his hands. They were only allowed to evacuate American citizens. But something about the child's urgency had dinged Pid's radar.

They had a bit of a wait before the next chopper would arrive. Not much...but some. The ambassador's home wasn't far from the embassy, a few blocks at most. Pid was sure he could get to the house, check for the missing woman, and make it back before the last chopper left.

Slate volunteered to go with him, and after a brief conversation with Mustang, their team leader, and getting his approval, they set off into the dark night to find the woman. The boy had said her name was Monica. They'd verify her identity and nationality, then get back to the embassy and get the hell out of there.

What should've been an easy snatch and grab, so to speak, turned out to be anything but. The mob outside the embassy had grown in numbers in the relatively short time since the team's chopper had landed on the roof. Currently, their actions had nothing to do with democracy or protesting the current president, and everything to do with destroying things for the sake of destruction, by the looks of things. Looting was rampant; people were running everywhere, arms full of whatever they could carry. No building was immune. And it wasn't just businesses. Homes were just as vulnerable to the lawless men and women.

From what Pid could tell, many of the most destructive looters didn't look like Algerians.

Shaking his head at the blatant violence and of the depths of depravity he was witnessing, he and Slate did their best to avoid the worst of the crowds. It took them longer than they wanted to reach the ambassador's residence, where the little boy had been certain Monica would be waiting for the family's return.

By the time they got to the house, the sounds of rioters getting closer and closer from all sides made the hair stand up on Pid's arms. Mustang had already radioed and said there was no way they'd be able to get back to the embassy safely. It was fully surrounded by the unruly mob and was no longer safe. Mustang ordered them to stay in touch and let him know when they'd made contact with Monica. They'd figure out a time and place for them to be picked up by the chopper in a safer location once the rescue was made.

Pid and Slate silently crept up to the ambassador's house. There were no lights on inside, which didn't bode well for their chances of finding the target still there. They approached from the back, away from the street.

"Shit," Slate said as they neared a sliding glass door. It was shattered into a million pieces. The shards crackled as the two men slowly moved forward, their weapons at the ready.

Stopping to listen, Pid didn't hear any sounds from within. His heart thumping strongly in his chest, he took point and entered the dark house ahead of Slate.

They cleared the living area and the kitchen, with no sign of Monica or anyone else. Aware of the unruly crowd getting closer, and that their window of time to find the elusive nanny was slipping away, Pid and Slate headed for the stairs.

At the top, Pid gestured for his teammate to check the rooms to the right while he took the ones to the left. He checked a bathroom and what was obviously a child's room before entering the master. It was dark, like the rest of the house, and there was still no sign of the nanny.

After clearing the bathroom, then looking under the bed and in the closet, Pid lowered his weapon a fraction. No one was here. The house was empty.

So why did he feel so uneasy? Why was the glass door downstairs broken from the outside? Had someone broken in, forcing the woman to flee?

Looking around the master bedroom, Pid frowned. Nothing seemed out of place. The bed was made, the drawers were shut, and the clothes in the closet still hung neatly. No signs of a break-in. Yet...something still niggled at the back of his brain.

He stepped closer to the nearest dresser and opened the top drawer.

Bingo.

While at first glance, the house looked neat and orderly, someone *had* been here. The clothes in the drawer were in disarray, as if someone had rifled through looking for something. Opening a few other drawers, Pid saw the others had also been gone through as well. Whoever did it had been smart enough not to leave outward signs that anyone had been there.

A noise from behind him had Pid spinning around, his weapon at the ready.

"The rest of the house is clear," Slate said quietly.

Nodding, Pid forced himself to relax. Taking a chance just in case, he took a deep breath and called out, "Monica? If you're in the house, it's safe to come out! I'm a Navy SEAL and I'm here to get you to safety."

Pid's voice echoed in the room, and there was no response from Monica or anyone else.

Slate shrugged. "It was worth a shot," he told his friend.

They heard an explosion coming from outside, then cheering from a crowd of people.

"Shit, we need to get the hell out of here before they firebomb this house," Slate said.

Pid nodded. He followed behind his teammate as they headed out of the master bedroom—but something made him turn and look behind him one more time.

"Wait," he said urgently.

Slate turned. "What? What's wrong?"

"Something's off," Pid said. "Look at this room. It's... uneven...?" He couldn't believe he hadn't noticed it the moment he'd entered the space.

The window on the far wall wasn't evenly centered, which normally wouldn't be surprising...except in each of the other bedrooms, the window on the front-facing wall was perfectly centered. In the master, there was about five feet to the right of the window, but only two feet on the left. Maybe the builder did that on purpose...but Pid didn't think so.

His eyes scanned the room. He didn't know what he was looking for...

Then his adrenaline spiked when he saw a spot on the wall that wasn't completely flat.

He wanted to think he would've noticed it first thing if there had been adequate lighting. And now that he'd seen it, the fact that there was no furniture against that wall—when almost every other one in the room had bookshelves, a dresser, even an armchair against one wall —was an obvious sign there was some sort of space behind it.

Pid gestured to Slate and his teammate nodded as he raised his weapon, pointing it at the part of the wall that wasn't quite flat. As he crept closer, Pid thought he could make out the outline of an almost imperceptible door.

This would be tricky. Pid wasn't exactly sure how to open the door, and fumbling to find the mechanism would alert anyone hiding behind the wall to his intentions.

"US Navy SEAL," he called out once more, hoping like hell it was Monica hiding behind the wall and not anyone else. As he stepped closer, he had the momentary thought that maybe it had been the nanny herself who'd rifled through the ambassador's belongings.

To his surprise, he didn't have to figure out how to get into the hidey-hole. The crack in the wall that had caught his eye widened...

And suddenly Pid was staring down the barrel of a pistol.

"Don't come any closer. I have no problem blowing your head off," a woman's voice said.

* * *

It was all Monica Collins could do not to throw up. Time had no meaning while she'd been holed up in the safe room. The ambassador had it installed right after he'd moved in. He'd stocked it with a bit of food, some blankets—and most importantly, a handgun.

After running up the stairs when the SEAL had shown up at the back door, she'd headed straight for the room. The walls wouldn't stop bullets, but the ambassador hoped the space would keep his family safe and hidden if someone ever broke in looking for valuables.

Monica had always thought it wasn't the best idea. Her dad had taught her that the worst position to be in was one in which you allowed yourself to be cornered. Her childhood had been hell, but one thing he'd instilled into her brain was never to give up. *Never*.

She'd watched as the SEAL searched the ambassador's home. Someone else had soon joined him, and Monica heard their low, increasingly frustrated curses when they couldn't find her. She silently waited behind the wall, watching the tiny security screens, observing as they opened drawers and stole whatever valuables they could.

She saw them leave the house, and thought she was finally safe...until someone appeared yet again on the screens in her hidey-hole. But as she studied the video, she realized these men weren't the same ones who had been searching the house before.

Hearing him call out that he was also a SEAL made Monica's skin crawl. She could only assume they were with the other two men claiming to be US Navy, maybe sent in to search once more. It seemed they weren't going to leave until she was found.

Fine. If a confrontation was what these men wanted, that was what she'd give them.

She wasn't stupid. She knew her odds of making it out of the house unscathed were low. Especially since there were two of them and only one of her. But if she could take one out immediately with a bullet, maybe, just maybe, she could get out of the house and disappear. Walking the streets of Algeria in the dark wasn't her idea of a good time, but beggars couldn't be choosers. As long as she could get away from these obviously corrupt military men, she'd figure things out from there. She was her dad's child. And he'd taught her well.

*Trust no one but yourself.*

*Protect what's yours.*

*Don't hesitate to pull the trigger.*

Shivering at the "lessons" her dad had taught her, Monica tightened her right hand around the pistol.

Light footsteps came closer to her hiding spot, and Monica knew this was it. Somehow the SEAL had figured out where she was. Still, any element of surprise would give her a much-needed advantage in this situation.

The nonexistent fingers on her left hand throbbed. They'd been amputated twenty years ago, but the phantom pain lingered to this day. The safe room was mostly dark, but she didn't have to see her hand to know what it looked like. Four stubs were all that remained of her fingers. They'd each been amputated at the second knuckle. Doctors had tried to save them, but the damage had been too extensive and by the time her parents had brought her to the hospital, it had been too many days since the "accident."

Hearing a noise on the other side of the wall, Monica forced herself to concentrate. She brought her left hand up to balance the gun, took a deep breath—and pushed the door open far enough for him to see the barrel of the pistol. She said in as menacing a tone as she could, "Don't come any closer. I have no problem blowing your head off."

Monica hadn't thought too much beyond this moment. She figured the SEAL would do his best to convince her to put the gun down. Maybe even laugh at her. Over the years, people had consistently underestimated her. At five feet three inches tall and not much over a hundred and ten pounds, she was definitely petite. Her dad had always told her she could use her pipsqueak stature to lure the enemy into thinking she wasn't a threat. Then she could strike.

Hating that her thoughts constantly turned to the man who'd made her life a living hell for sixteen years, Monica squinted, trying to see the SEAL through the crack in the door.

Her moment of being lost in her head cost her.

Between one heartbeat and the next, the SEAL moved.

Monica cried out in pain as the door flew open and he knocked the gun right out of her hand so quickly, she didn't have time to pull the trigger. Before the weapon even hit the floor, he'd pulled her out of her hiding space and spun her around, wrapping one huge arm around her chest and trapping her own against her body.

She did her best to squirm her way out of his hold, but it was no use. He'd disarmed her and rendered her immobile in less than five seconds. If Darren Collins was alive, he'd be disgusted.

"I'm assuming you're the nanny," the man behind her drawled.

His amused tone pissed Monica off. He didn't even seem fazed that she'd almost shot him. "Let me go!" she ordered as forcefully as she could.

He didn't loosen his hold even a fraction. If he had, she might've been able to somehow get out of his grasp. But where would she go?

"Weapon secured," a second deep voice said from behind them.

Shit. She'd already forgotten about the other SEAL. Panic flooded her body.

As if he could read her like a book, the man holding her said, "Easy. You're safe. Did you not hear me say I'm a SEAL?" he asked.

"I heard you," she said, knowing the bitterness in her tone was loud and clear.

"We need to go, Pid," the other man said.

Monica frowned. She had no idea what kind of name Pid was, but she didn't like it.

"If I let you go, are you gonna fight me?" the man holding her asked.

"Depends," she told him honestly.

"On?"

"If you're going to try to rape me or not," she answered bluntly.

"What the fuck?" the man behind them swore incredulously.

"My name is Stuart. Stu for short. My friends call me Pid," her captor said.

"Your friends aren't very nice," Monica retorted, suddenly understanding how he'd gotten his nickname.

"Unfortunately, you can't pick your nickname. Your nickname picks you," Stuart replied.

"Seriously, Pid—we need to go," the other guy repeated.

"In a second. The man behind me is Slate. His real name is Duncan Stone. Slate, Stone...get it?"

"I know what you're doing," Monica said. She wished she could see the face of the man holding her, but he had too firm a grip for her to even turn her body enough to catch a glimpse of his face.

"What am I doing?" he asked.

"Trying to get me to trust you by making you and your friend seem harmless. It's not going to happen. Ever. Especially not after your *other* friend shot the door downstairs."

"My other friend?" he asked.

Monica clenched her teeth. She couldn't stand his ridiculous innocent act. "Yeah."

"I hate to disagree with a lady, but that wasn't anyone I know. What makes you think it was?"

Monica snorted. "Of course you know him! How many other people go around knocking on doors, claiming to be Navy SEALs?" she asked.

"Fuck," Slate muttered again.

"He wasn't with me," Stuart repeated calmly.

Monica snorted. "Right."

"How long ago?"

"I don't know. Half an hour maybe? He left just before you got here." She didn't know why she was humoring this asshole.

"Right. Half an hour ago, Slate and I were standing on the roof of the American Embassy. We met the ambassador and his family, and a little boy begged me to find his nanny. Said she was waiting at his house for him and his mom, dad, and brother to get home. I promised him I'd find you and make sure you were safe."

Monica stilled, swallowing hard. That sounded just like something August would do. He was a sensitive little seven-year-old. And the fact that he'd been worried about her almost broke her heart.

"So you see, we were busy half an hour ago and nowhere near here. And there aren't any SEALs to spare, considering everyone—except for us—is currently doing their best to evacuate the embassy. You're sure he said he was a SEAL?"

Monica snorted again. Why did men always think she was so stupid? Was it because she was short? A woman? Blonde?

"Right. Of course you're sure. Slate?"

For a second, Monica thought he was still talking to her, but when his friend started talking low and fast, she realized he'd somehow asked his buddy a question while only saying his name.

Before she could concentrate on what Slate was saying, Stuart spun her around. He had a firm grip on her forearms, so she couldn't reach out and grab one of the many weapons the man had strapped to his chest. Now that she was face-to-face with him, she was even more positive he wasn't one of the men she'd seen earlier. But just because he didn't shoot the door out, that didn't mean he wasn't working with the SEAL who had.

This man had a five o'clock shadow...which didn't detract from his looks. It only enhanced them. He was tall, although everyone seemed tall to Monica. She guessed he was at least six feet. Maybe more. He had dark eyes that were currently fixed on her and his nose was crooked, as if it had been broken at one time. He also had a furrow in his brow as he stared down at her.

"What?" she blurted, uncomfortable with his scrutiny.

"Can you describe the man who called himself a SEAL?"

Monica thought about that for a second. Could she? She sighed. "Not really. He was older than you. Had on green camo pants and a shirt. His mouth and nose were covered by a cloth or something, and he creeped me out."

Stuart frowned. Monica had the feeling he wasn't frowning at *her*, so much as thinking about something.

"We've got about three minutes before that mob gets here," Slate warned.

The man holding her didn't look away as he nodded. "Here's the deal," he said calmly. "We need to get the hell out of here. But I have to make sure you aren't going to shoot me or my friend in the back of the head as we do it. We're the good guys. I don't know who the fuck that other guy claiming to be a SEAL was, but he wasn't with us. We're here because a little boy loved his nanny enough to get up the courage to approach us. I'd like to keep my promise to that kid—and I need your help in order to do so."

Monica pressed her lips together, her mind racing. If he hadn't brought up August, she would continue resisting...but the last thing she wanted to do was traumatize the little boy more than he probably was already. The fact that August had even thought about her in the midst of a rescue made her give in.

"I won't shoot you," she said honestly. She didn't mention the fact that he'd disarmed her of her one and only gun.

"Trust me," Stuart said quietly.

"I don't trust anyone," Monica shot back.

He stared at her for a long moment, as if trying to read her mind, or somehow get her to change it simply by gazing into her eyes.

Wasn't going to happen. Monica hadn't lied. The only people in her life who'd never let her down were the children she'd looked after throughout her career. They hadn't been jaded or corrupted by life yet. They were open and honest.

Every single adult in her life had let her down in one way or another. Starting with the two people who were supposed to protect and shelter her from everyone else. Her parents.

Her dad had only taught her that military men were scary and untrustworthy, and her mom taught her that she was completely on her own.

"You might not believe it, but you *can* trust me," Stuart told her. She couldn't think of him as Pid. It was a ridiculous nickname. Despite knowing after he'd delivered her to wherever they were going, she'd never see him again, she refused to use the name his military buddies used.

"They're at the front of the house," Slate said.

Monica was amazed not to hear any panic in the other man's voice.

Without another word, Stuart let go of her arms and turned slightly, tucking the fingers of her right hand into the waistband at his back. "Whatever you do, don't let go," he told her. "If the shit hits the fan, stay right with me. No matter what."

"Aren't you afraid I'll take that big K-BAR out of its sheath on your side and use it against you?" Monica asked.

Stuart shook his head. "No."

"Why?" she insisted as they quickly headed out of the master bedroom and down the stairway toward the back of the house.

"Because if you do, we're both dead. You worked hard to stay alive this long, I figure I'm safe at least until we get out of the house and away from the mob closing in."

Monica sighed. Damn the man. He was right. She might not like soldiers, or the fact that she needed Stuart and Slate's help, but she didn't have a death wish.

*Use the assets you have at your disposal.*

It was something else her dad had drilled into her head. And right now, as much as she hated it, Stuart and Slate *were* assets. Time would tell if they continued to be of use or if they'd morph into liabilities. Monica wasn't convinced they weren't with the other SEAL who'd shot out her door. Maybe the two pairs of men were working together, taking advantage of the unstable situation in the city to steal whatever they could from the American Embassy households while the occupants were evacuated.

Without a word, Monica held onto Stuart's belt as he and Slate led the way out of the house, over the broken glass from the door. She shivered as she remembered the look in the other SEAL's eyes as he stared at her from the other side of the pane.

She suddenly realized why he'd freaked her out so badly. He reminded her of her father. There was something simply...unbalanced in his eyes.

She hadn't seen anything in Stuart's eyes that reminded her of her father, but that didn't mean much. Her dad had been able to hide his crazy from the world most of the time. It was only when he was home with his family that he'd let his true self show through.

"Hold on," Stuart reminded her. "No matter what."

Monica nodded. She could hear the shouts of what sounded like hundreds of people. They were close. Too close. There were no fences around the houses in this neighborhood, and she'd never been so glad for that as Stuart and Slate led her into the darkness, away from the house where she'd lived for the last year.

Less than a block away, a loud whooshing sound made Monica turn her head as she stumbled after Stuart.

If they'd been even thirty seconds later leaving the house, they would've been inside when someone threw the Molotov cocktail into the living room. She saw dozens of people cheering and jumping up and down in glee as the beautiful house caught fire.

All her belongings were inside. Her clothes. The pictures August and Remington had drawn for her. But she'd started over with nothing before. She could do it again. She had her IDs with her; she *always* had them on her. She even had a bit of cash too.

Darren Collins had been an asshole, a horrible father, a paranoid and abusive man, but he'd taught her a few useful things over the years. The biggest lessons of all: never let down your guard, never trust anyone, and always make sure to have identification and cash on hand, just in case.

Monica had no idea what would happen in the future, but she'd manage. She was a survivor.

Flexing the stubs on her left hand, she took a deep breath as Stuart led her into the darkness of Algiers. It was only a matter of time before she could say goodbye and good riddance to the man and his teammate. The farther she could get away from anyone and anything related to the military, the safer she'd feel.

## CHAPTER TWO

Pid was ultra-aware of the woman at his back, though she hadn't said a word since they'd barely managed to slip out of the house before it went up in flames. Even though he'd told her he wasn't afraid she'd take his knife and use it against him, he honestly wasn't one hundred percent sure she wouldn't.

He'd never been in a situation where he and his team had gone in to rescue someone who was so openly hostile. Some were scared out of their mind, others were distrustful at first, but normally loosened up once they realized they were about to be rescued. Others were demanding.

In this case, he one hundred percent believed Monica would've shot him if he hadn't moved as fast as he had. And it seemed the longer she was around him and Slate, the more her distrust grew. It was baffling.

It didn't help that whoever had shot out the door of the house had claimed to be a SEAL, but he suspected her antagonistic behavior went beyond that event. How Pid knew that, he had no idea, but when he'd looked into her eyes, he'd seen a level of fear he'd rarely encountered before. She had bravado in spades, but someone had treated the woman like shit—and it pissed him off. Pid wanted to beat the hell out of whoever had taught her to be so distrustful.

He also hadn't missed her disfigured left hand; it was the reason why he'd grabbed her right to hook to his belt.

He found himself wanting answers. How had she injured her hand? Who'd made her so distrustful of military members? Why had her attitude changed instantly at the mere mention of the boys she was in charge of?

But she was a mission; nothing more, nothing less. As soon as he and Slate met back up with their team and deposited Monica with the rest of the people they'd evacuated, the SEALs would be on their way home to Hawaii.

Sounds of the out-of-control mob at their backs spurred Pid to walk a little faster. Slate was several paces ahead of them, his head constantly on a swivel, looking for trouble. Monica maintained her silence as they walked through backyards and down alleyways to avoid the main streets.

Just when Pid thought they were home free and would be able to make it to the meeting spot without trouble, Slate stopped in his tracks, then turned and headed back toward them. The look on his face told Pid all he needed to know.

"We can't go that way," he said.

Pid heard the shouts from another group of rowdy protestors getting louder and louder as the crowd neared their location. He turned to reassure Monica that he and Slate would keep her out of harm's way. Her gaze was fixed to the middle of his chest and she had absolutely no expression on her face.

"It'll take longer, but we'll circle around to the east," Slate said.

Pid nodded, and once more they were walking at a fast clip, trying to outmaneuver the protestors. Monica tripped once, but her grip on his waistband kept her upright. Pid reached back and took hold of her arm to try to assist, but she shook off his hand.

"I'm fine," she told him, her tone resentful.

Many men would take her attitude personally. Would let it affect how they treated her. But Pid wasn't one of them. The more standoffish she was, the more he wanted to know why. She was acting so differently from how most people would in her situation, he was sure there had to be a reason.

He was also honest enough to admit to himself that regardless of her prickly attitude, he found the woman attractive. And noticing someone's looks in the middle of an op wasn't like him *at all*. He was always professional, and had never felt one iota of attraction toward someone while on a rescue mission.

But there was something about the contradiction between her vulnerable looks and her fierce attitude that got to him. Pid didn't have a type when it came to women. He'd been with brunettes, redheads, blondes...tall, short, curvy, athletic, slender...artistic, analytical, liberal, conservative...he'd dated them all.

But from the moment Monica had threatened to shoot him, something in his psyche had inexplicably stood up and taken notice. She was around a foot shorter, but he could feel the muscles in her petite frame when he held her. Her hair was pulled back in a no-nonsense ponytail and the light strands had clung to the stubble on his face. He saw intense emotion in her ice-blue eyes, though the rest of her face had been largely expressionless, save for the slight flush of her cheeks betraying her anger.

He suspected she had more passion in her little finger than some people had in their entire bodies. She did her best to bank it, but Pid saw it simmering behind her eyes. He had a feeling when she let loose, truly let loose, she'd be a sight to see.

One thing Pid was certain of—whoever broke through her extremely thick barriers would be a lucky man.

Even though it was inappropriate as hell, he thought that he might want to be that man.

Then he shook his head at his own ridiculousness. The second they rendezvoused with the other citizens being evacuated, she'd be gone. And he had no doubt she wouldn't look back.

Reminded of that fact, Pid did his best to turn his concentration back to the mission at hand. Namely, getting the hell out of this neighborhood and safely evacuating the nanny and themselves.

But it didn't seem that was going to be as easy as they'd hoped. The number of protestors in the neighborhood had risen since they'd crept into the streets. It was as if someone had decided it was open season on the houses in the upper-class neighborhood.

As soon as the thought entered his head, Pid knew that was *exactly* what had happened. And with mob mentality, all it took was a few people to start the looting and raiding before others followed.

"We need to find a place to hunker down for a while," Pid told Slate.

His teammate nodded. The trick was finding somewhere that wouldn't become a target for the opportunists currently looking to steal anything they could get their hands on. The air was already thick with the smell of smoke as houses were set on fire after they were cleaned out.

"There's an abandoned factory of some sort a few streets over," Monica said.

Both Pid and Slate turned to look at her. Her chin came up, as if she felt the need to defend her suggestion. "I like to take walks on my time off. It relaxes me and gives me space to think. The building seems safe, there aren't any machines or anything in there anymore. Just a bunch of empty boxes and old wood. When the weather's bad, some of the neighborhood kids use it for pickup games of football...soccer...because the main floor's completely open, without a bunch of walls breaking it up."

"Which way?" Slate asked.

Monica let out the breath she was obviously holding. She'd clearly expected them to dismiss her suggestion. She lifted her hand off his belt and pointed to the right.

Slate nodded and headed that way. Monica started to follow, and Pid reached for her hand. He wasn't paying attention and realized as soon as his fingers closed around her hand that he'd taken hold of her left one. The one without fingers.

Monica lashed out so quickly, Pid was unprepared. She jerked her hand out of his and hissed, "Don't touch me!"

Pid held up his hands in surrender. "I'm sorry."

"I mean it. No one touches my hand. *No one.*"

He nodded. "I'm sorry again."

They stared at each other for a heated moment before Monica dropped her gaze, her cheeks flushed once more.

"I was just trying to help you grab hold of my waistband again."

"You don't have to manhandle me. All you have to do is use your words," she said caustically.

Surprisingly, her words and tone didn't turn Pid off. But he didn't dare smile. He had a feeling she'd incorrectly assume he was laughing at her. He wasn't; that last statement just sounded as if she was talking to one of her kids. He wasn't seven, but she had a good point.

"You're right. Sorry. Please grab hold of me again, Monica. I need to know you're at my heels at all times."

She stared at him with a look of confusion.

"What?" he asked.

"I just— You apologized."

It was Pid's turn to be confused. "Yeah. I shouldn't have grabbed you like that. Especially since I don't know you. Hasn't anyone ever told you they were sorry after doing something they shouldn't have?" He meant his question to be lighthearted, but when she didn't immediately roll her eyes and say "of course"...he realized perhaps no one *had* ever apologized to her.

"It doesn't matter," she mumbled. "Can we go? The last thing I want is to end up in the middle of a crazed mob." She reached out her right hand and lightly took hold of his belt once more.

There was so much Pid wanted to say at that moment, so many questions he wanted to ask, but she was right. They needed to get off the streets and to safety. He headed in the direction Monica had indicated and quickly caught up to Slate, who'd been not so patiently waiting for them.

"If I'd known you were going to stop to have a chat, I would've left your ass," Slate grumbled.

Pid shook his head. "Always so impatient," he chided.

"Whatever," Slate said under his breath.

The threesome continued through the streets, moving

away from any sounds of crowds before finally arriving at the back of a dark cinderblock building. It was on the edge of the upscale neighborhood, and with one glance, Pid knew it would be the perfect place to hole up for a while.

There were scraggly looking weeds all around the building and most of the glass in the windows had long since been broken out. The doors were missing and the vibe of the place was actually quite creepy.

"Kids come *here* to play?" Slate asked in disbelief.

To Pid's surprise, Monica actually looked amused. "That's what I thought the first time I saw it. But when you want to play soccer and the weather's crappy, it's pretty perfect."

"I bet it's haunted," Slate said.

"Now that you mention it, I did hear strange noises when I was here, but I dismissed them," Monica said.

The look on Slate's face was priceless. Monica obviously thought so too, because she giggled. The woman actually *giggled*. Pid didn't even care that he wasn't the one to make her laugh. He was too blown away by how the smile on her face changed her whole countenance. And for the first time, he realized she had a dimple in one cheek.

A fucking *dimple*.

Fuck. He was such a sucker for dimples.

"Shit, woman, please tell me you're kidding," Slate begged.

"I'm kidding," Monica said obediently, but it was clear she was humoring him.

An explosion from a street over spurred them into action. Slate immediately entered the menacing-looking building, with Pid and Monica at his heels.

"Which way?" Slate asked.

Pid heard Monica's subtle snort before she said, "You're asking me? You're the big bad Navy SEALs."

He couldn't help but smile. There was that prickly attitude. He didn't think her lightheartedness would last, and he'd been right.

"A big bad Navy SEAL who's never been in here. You have. Which way?" Slate asked again, no irritation evident in his tone.

"There are a bunch of boxes to the left. Last time I was here, checking to make sure the local kids were all right, I saw a young boy who wasn't playing soccer making a fort with them," Monica said.

Without another word, the threesome headed that way.

Monica had been right. The old factory building was a perfect temporary hiding spot. Rioters would have no interest in the place because it was abandoned, nothing of value inside for them to steal. Their attention was focused on the houses of the government workers.

Within five minutes, Pid and Slate had rearranged the empty boxes to give all three of them space to sit, protected from being seen at first glance if someone decided to enter the building. They wouldn't be protected from bullets, but Pid was fairly confident they were safe from that sort of threat at the moment.

Monica had taken a seat about four feet away from him and Slate. Pid didn't like that she wasn't within easy reach, but because he didn't sense any immediate danger, he kept his mouth shut.

"So...Monica. What's your story?" Slate asked.

Pid held back his chuckle. Slate had never been one to beat around the bush. He liked getting right to the heart of things. He supposed it went along with being impatient.

Earlier, Pid had lamented the fact that the moon was almost full tonight, as it hindered their ability to walk around undetected, but now he was glad for it. The light coming through the pane-less windows allowed him to just make out Monica sitting against the wall nearby. Her knees were drawn up and her arms were around them, as if she was holding herself together. He didn't like the defensive position, but he and Slate were strangers, so he couldn't exactly blame her for being uncomfortable.

"No story," she said, not cooperating with Slate's attempt at conversation.

Slate harrumphed. "Right," he said sarcastically. "What's your last name?"

"Collins."

"How old are you?"

"Thirty."

"You aren't very tall; you can't be much above five-three or four."

"Five-three."

Pid smirked. This wasn't going well. But he had a feeling he knew what to talk about to help her loosen up a bit. "How'd you get the job with the ambassador?" he asked.

He could literally see her muscles relax a fraction at that question, her shoulders dropping. "I applied and was hired," she said, but there was a bit less animosity in her tone now.

"You like being a nanny?" Pid asked.

"I love it. Once upon a time, I wanted to be a teacher, but that didn't work out since I couldn't afford college. I started babysitting to earn money to live on, and I found that I enjoyed it. I click with kids, more so than with adults. They're honest to a fault. They'll always tell you what they're thinking and feeling."

After a beat, even Pid was surprised when she continued.

"I had a string of long-term babysitting jobs and then someone asked if I'd be a full-time nanny for their two-year-old. That lasted two years, until the couple moved out of state. I took a few other nanny positions before someone connected me with a couple who were moving to Israel for an ambassador position. They wanted to hire someone to homeschool their three kids, and I was recommended. When the family was preparing to move back to the States, they asked if I'd consider going to Algeria to work for Desmond Laws. I jumped at the chance. And here I am."

Pid mentally nodded to himself. She'd been so happy to talk about being a nanny, he had a feeling she didn't even realize she'd answered his original question about how she'd gotten the job with the ambassador.

"You're obviously very good at what you do," Pid told her. "That boy was extremely concerned about you, and even though he was scared, he mustered up the courage to approach and ask me to find you."

A small smile formed on Monica's face, and once more Pid caught a glimpse of her dimple. "We've talked a lot about safety and doing the right thing," she said. "I don't remember where I heard the saying, but it stuck with me, and I taught it to the boys. 'Being scared means you're about to do something brave.' I'm sure August—who I'm guessing is the one you talked to; his older brother is Remington—was nervous about approaching you, but hopefully he remembered that saying and was proud of himself afterward."

Pid heard the confidence in her tone as she talked about her charges. She sounded almost friendly, which was quite the change from her standoffish attitude since the moment they'd found her.

He opened his mouth to ask her more about August and Remington, just as Mustang's voice sounded through the radio in his ear.

"This is team leader one. Got your ears on?"

"Ten-four," Slate responded.

Pid pointed to his ear and said softly to Monica, "It's our team leader checking in."

She nodded.

"We've got you on the map, good choice to hole up for a while. It's a fucking mess out there," Mustang said.

"It was Monica's idea," Slate said.

"Well, no one's gonna mess with a hollowed-out building, not when there are houses to loot one street over. Stay put as long as you can. As soon as the fucking mobs break up, we'll send a helo for you both."

"Ten-four," Slate said.

"Mustang?" Pid asked.

"Yeah?"

"She said someone else came to the house claiming to be a SEAL. Gave her bad vibes, and she hid while he shot out the back door."

There was silence on the radio for a beat before Mustang said, "Fucking hell. Seriously?"

"Yes."

"I'm assuming he didn't find her?" Mustang asked.

"You'd assume right. But there was evidence that the house was searched. He was smart, didn't trash the place, left everything as clean as he could."

"Was anything taken?"

"We didn't have time to stick around and check things out."

"Is he asking if the SEAL stole anything?" Monica asked.

"Hang on," Pid told Mustang, then nodded at Monica. "Yeah. Did he?"

"Yes," she said without hesitation.

"How do you know?" Slate asked.

"Desmond had camera monitors inside the safe room. They weren't expensive, just a cheap system he bought off the internet and installed himself. But I watched as the SEAL and his accomplice went from room to room. There were a few guns Desmond had stashed around the house that they took. They also grabbed jewelry and cash, and even broke into the safe the ambassador had in the back of his closet."

"Someone else was with him?" Slate asked.

"Yes. But it didn't look like they were partners...if that makes sense? They didn't really talk much. The SEAL guy kind of looked annoyed that the other guy was even there."

"Shit. All right. What was in the safe?"

"Passports, birth certificates, and a lot of money."

"How much?" Mustang asked through the radio in Pid's ear. Slate had obviously opened the mic so their team leader could hear Monica.

"How much money? Do you know?" Pid asked, since Monica couldn't hear Mustang.

She shook her head. "I'm not sure, but probably several thousand. Desmond was a fan of keeping a stash of money on hand for emergencies."

"Didn't help him much, did it?" Slate muttered.

It was a rhetorical question, but Monica didn't seem

to realize. "No, it didn't. He would've been better off keeping other, more important things on him at all times."

Pid had an epiphany. "Like you do?" he asked.

Monica looked surprised, but quickly blanked her expression. "I don't know what you mean."

"I'm just thinking, it would make your life a lot easier if you had your passport on you right about now," Pid told her.

No one spoke for a long moment before Monica shrugged and said as nonchalantly as possible, "I've got my passport."

"Smart," Mustang said through the radio once more. "But at the moment, I'm more concerned about this asshole claiming to be a SEAL and going around ransacking houses."

"Same," Slate said.

Pid kept his gaze glued on Monica. She fascinated him. The more he found out about her, the more he wanted to know.

"Seems fishy that an area of town that wasn't the site of the main protest is suddenly ground zero for the rioters," Slate said.

"I thought so too," Mustang agreed.

"As if someone spread the word that the occupants had fled and their houses were ripe for the pickin'," Slate mused. "That asshole's partner was probably a local, happy to get first crack at looting houses in return for helping to incite violence."

"Possibly. I'll talk to the commander," Mustang said. "If someone is out there pretending to be a SEAL, that shit needs to be nipped in the bud."

"Agreed," Slate said.

"Keep your heads down. I'll be in touch when things calm down. Might be a few hours," Mustang said.

"Ten-four."

"Over and out."

Pid hadn't looked away from Monica. It was more than obvious not much got by her. Many people would dismiss her because of her size and gender, but the intelligence and perception in her gaze were easy to see...if you were looking.

"So we're staying here for a while?" she asked.

"Yeah. Mustang knows where we are and he'll send in a chopper as soon as it's safe," Slate said.

"How?"

"How what?" Pid asked.

Monica looked at him. "How does your friend know where we are?"

"We've got trackers," Slate said.

Her eyes nearly bugged out of her head. "You let the government put trackers inside you?" she asked in disbelief.

Pid chuckled. "Hell no. But when we're on a mission, we've learned the importance of our teammates knowing where we are at all times if we're separated." He reached into a pocket of his vest and pulled out a piece of metal about the size of a quarter. "Tracker."

"What if your vest comes off? Or is stolen?" she asked.

Slate pointed to his boot.

"And if your boots are taken?"

She was like a dog with a bone. But she was dead right. Someone had taught her to not only be wary, but distrustful...and a bit about military tactics as well. "We have a friend who's somewhat of an expert with trackers. He works independently from the government, and we're more than happy to let him track us when we're deployed."

Monica sat forward, curiosity obviously getting the better of her. "How?"

"We'd tell you, but then we'd have to kill you," Slate joked.

Every muscle in Pid's body tightened. He was going to beat the shit out of Slate for saying something like that. The woman already distrusted them, and that comment wouldn't help.

To his surprise, Monica chuckled once more.

Shit. Slate had made her laugh twice now.

*Pid* wanted to be the one to coax that dimple out.

"Injected or swallowed?" she asked with uncanny insight.

"Swallowed," Slate admitted without hesitation.

"But it'll only stay in your stomach a day or so. That's not going to be much help in a long-term deployment," she said.

Pid sat back and listened as she and Slate talked. Monica was turning out to be utterly fascinating.

"True. But this tracker doesn't stay in our stomachs. It gets into our bloodstream and swims around for up to two weeks before it dissolves completely. I don't understand the science behind it, but our friend's a genius."

"And you have a backup in case your mission takes longer than two weeks?" she asked.

Slate nodded.

She breathed out a sigh and leaned back against the wall. "That's scary smart," she observed.

"Yup," Slate agreed. "Tex is one guy who I'm glad is on our side."

"You're *sure* about him being on your side? He could

sell you out. There are lots of people and governments who would love to get their hands on a SEAL team."

"One hundred-thousand percent," Slate said without hesitation.

Monica didn't comment.

The three sat in silence for a few minutes, listening to the distant shouts of the rioters in the neighborhood nearby.

"So...your nicknames are weird," Monica said after a few more minutes.

Pid wasn't offended. On the contrary, he was thrilled she'd initiated some sort of conversation. "They could be worse," he said with a shrug.

"Worse than Stu-*pid*?" she asked, emphasizing the second part of the word.

"Yup," he insisted.

"Like what?" she asked.

"Twinkie," Slate offered.

"Pig," Pid said.

"Fart," Slate added.

"Shut up," Monica said with a shake of her head. "You're making those names up."

"I'm not," Slate insisted. "A guy I went to bootcamp with was saddled with the name Fart, and deservedly so. The kid passed gas so much, something had to be wrong with his innards. I'm talking silent but deadly farts too. Ones so awful, the entire barracks wanted to throw up."

There was that dimple again. Pid was coming to terms with the fact that he sucked at making her smile, too fascinated by the small feature to care.

"Remember Slug?" Pid asked Slate.

"Of course. That asshole was the laziest son-of-a-bitch I've ever met."

Pid turned to Monica. "I was actually relieved when Pid caught on. Growing up, I'd been called Little and Mouse so much, I learned to loathe them both. I'm not sure I could've stomached being called either of those for the rest of my life."

"Stuart Little?" she asked.

Pid winced and nodded.

"But it's such a cute movie," she protested with a small twitch of her lips. It wasn't enough to bring out that dimple, but Pid was counting it as a win anyway.

He purposely shuddered, shaking his head. "No. Just no," he said.

"Well, I don't think there's anything wrong with Stuart," she said. "I refuse to call you by that *stupid* nickname."

And just like that, Pid wished things were different. Wished they'd met at the grocery store back in Hawaii. Or maybe on the beach. Hell, he even wished she'd jumped on his head, like Kenna did to Aleck when they'd first met.

But in a few hours, he'd say goodbye and most likely never see Monica Collins again. It was really too bad; she was the first woman in a very long time to catch his interest. There were so many layers to the woman, he'd need a lifetime to peel them all back. Which made him mourn for something he'd never had in the first place.

"What?" she asked, using the belligerent tone he'd first heard from her.

Pid shrugged. "You can call me whatever you want."

She stared at him for what seemed like an emotionally charged moment before quietly saying, "Whatever."

"What happened to your hand?" Slate asked in the awkward silence that followed.

Pid held his breath. For once in his life, he was damn glad for Slate's lack of social skills.

"You're kind of rude," Monica told him.

Slate shrugged. "Think of me like one of your kids. Straight to the point, sayin' it like it is."

She snorted. "Right. You're *nothing* like the kids I look after. You're a military guy."

"You say that with such disdain," Slate said. "I might get a complex."

"Uh-huh, sure," Monica retorted with a roll of her eyes.

"So anyway, your hand? You get hungry one day and gnaw off your fingers?" Slate asked.

Pid wasn't surprised at his friend's silly joke. He was trying to bait her into talking.

"No. My father wanted to teach me a lesson, so he made me hold a doorjamb and he slammed a steel door on them." Her voice was almost monotone.

Pid gasped in surprise. Anger closely followed.

Monica kept talking in the same unemotional voice, as if it didn't matter one way or another how it had happened. "My fingers were shattered and the skin had broken open. The next day, he told me to stop being a baby and took me hunting. Told me we'd stay out in the cold until I shot a deer. No eating. No going home. It took two days, since I was left-handed and had to shoot with my right. Then he made me skin and dress it before we went home."

"Holy fuck," Pid breathed, too appalled to say anything else. He literally couldn't imagine anyone doing that to their own child.

"How old were you, and what lesson was he trying to teach you?" Slate asked quietly.

"Ten. Earlier that day, he'd been running me through

the obstacle course he'd built on our land, and when I couldn't get up the vertical climb, I asked him for help. He went to the top and helped me up and over it, but later, after he'd crushed my hand, he told me that asking for help came with consequences. Always. And my consequence was my dominant hand getting smashed.

"Anyway, not surprisingly, after field dressing the deer, my hand got infected. But Dad taught me well. I didn't ask for help. A month later, he told me to get in the car. I didn't ask why. He took me to the hospital. There were lots of questions, but Dad deflected them all. My fingers were amputated...and that was that."

"I don't like your father," Slate said after a long pause.

Monica snorted. "Join the club."

There was so much more Pid wanted to know. Where was her father now? Where had her mother been while her dad was abusing her? Did she have siblings? Why did her dad make an obstacle course? Where had she grown up?

Her hatred for all things military was beginning to make sense. Pid assumed her dad had some connection to the military. Which branch wasn't clear, but he supposed it didn't matter.

He wanted to reassure Monica that she could ask him for help and there would never be any strings attached, but he had a feeling now wasn't the time or place. Besides, the clock was ticking on their acquaintance. Dammit.

But he couldn't just sit there and say nothing.

"I give you my word, I'm gonna get you out of this country safely," he said, his voice a low promise.

Monica merely shrugged.

Pid wasn't happy. Not at all. He'd never felt as frustrated as he did right that moment. He didn't know what to say to make this woman feel better. He wanted to comfort her, reassure her...wanted to beat the shit out of her father. But all he could do was give her the space she so obviously wanted.

It stung. A lot.

He wasn't so conceited to think that everyone he came into contact with would look at him with admiration in their eyes. He might not be able to make Monica Collins trust military men again, but he'd be damned if he'd do anything that would perpetuate her uneasy feelings toward him or anyone else who fought for their country.

That thought brought him back to the asshole who was pretending to be a SEAL. The man who'd scared her earlier that night. Who'd taken advantage of the current instability to pillage. There was even a good chance if he'd found Monica's hiding spot, he might've assaulted her. And *that* was fucking unacceptable.

Pid was proud to be a SEAL. He'd worked damn hard to earn his Budweiser pin. He might not be in Monica's life for long, but he'd do what he could to prove to her that at least one military man was honorable.

# CHAPTER THREE

Monica mentally kicked herself for saying as much as she had to the two men. She'd been taught to never give out more information than was strictly necessary. And she'd sat there and blabbed on and on about herself. For a second, the sick feeling she got every time she knew she'd done something her dad would disapprove of welled in her belly and throat. But she pushed it down.

She was an adult, and he didn't have any control over her anymore. It was ridiculous that fourteen years after escaping from his iron fist, she still made decisions based on the warped lessons he'd taught her. She'd been to therapy. Intellectually, she knew she was letting her father "win" by continuing to live by his tenets. But the fear he'd instilled, the control he'd exerted, was seriously hard to break.

Though she had to admit, the outrage the two men felt after hearing what had happened to her hand made her feel...good. It was a lame word, but it fit. She didn't hear pity in their voices, only fury on her behalf.

Her childhood had been hell. Absolute *hell*. It was a

miracle she hadn't turned out to be a serial killer or something. She'd left home as soon as she'd been able to at age sixteen. She'd managed to get her GED while working minimum wage jobs and staying at crappy motels. Oddly, her dad hadn't even tried to find her after she'd left.

She babysat for money during that time, then lucked into her first live-in nanny job. And she'd never looked back. Not even when she'd heard her father had died. He'd been hunting and had fallen out of his deer stand. Since they lived in Wyoming, and it had been January, he'd frozen to death before anyone found him.

Good riddance.

As for her mother...Monica had never understood her at all. Not even a little. Why had she stayed with that man? Why hadn't she protected her daughter when he turned on her? Her mom hadn't shown her an ounce of affection, but she'd remained loyal to her husband to the very end. The last Monica had heard, she'd remarried a man exactly like Darren Collins.

The last therapist she'd seen had of course pointed out that not all military men were like her dad. Most were upstanding men and women who would never hurt their children. The woman had even suggested that maybe being around other military members would help her heal...which was why Monica had begun nannying for ambassadors. They weren't actually in the military, but worked closely with them enough to count. It was one of the most difficult things Monica had done, purposely putting herself in a situation where she'd occasionally interact with military members...but she'd done it.

Some days she thought she was making progress at not immediately being terrified of anyone in a uniform, and other days it was more of a struggle.

She wanted to leave everything her dad had taught her behind. Wanted to move on with her life, to heal...to not immediately suspect anyone in the military was out to get her. But she still struggled to block her dad's voice and hard lessons from dictating her actions.

Stunningly, after overthinking everything she'd told the two SEALs, when the men remained silent, Monica fell into a light doze.

She jerked when Stuart spoke in a low, easy tone. "You ready to get out of here?"

Monica was asleep one second and completely awake the next. That *never* happened. She never let down her guard like that in front of strangers. Something else her father had drilled into her head.

She looked over at Stuart. He'd promised to get her out of the country safely. He'd been so serious, so sincere, that she was tempted to believe him. She'd come to terms with the fact that the first man who'd claimed to be a SEAL and had broken into the house probably wasn't actually in the Navy. But a niggling feeling of doubt remained. He'd *looked* military...and it wasn't just his clothes. It was the way he carried himself. The way he'd methodically searched the house. It was the way he'd easily broken into the ambassador's safe.

She'd grown up around men like her dad and his friends, and Monica had a feeling if the man wasn't a SEAL, he'd definitely been in some branch of the military. But she kept her mouth shut. That guy was no longer her problem, and in a few hours she'd be back with the ambassador and his family and doing what she loved.

"Monica?" Stuart tried again.

She took a deep breath. "How long have I been asleep?"

"A couple of hours."

Monica's eyes widened. "Seriously?"

"Yeah. You obviously needed it. How do you feel?"

She felt much better than she had earlier. Less jumpy. But she didn't want to talk about that right now. Didn't want to think about the fact that she'd managed to let down her guard enough to actually sleep.

"I'm fine. And yes, I'm ready to get out of here," she said.

Stuart studied her for a long moment. She was sure he was going to ask a few more questions, until Slate stood up and wandered over to one of the windows to peer out.

The night was completely silent now. Monica couldn't hear any of the shouting and cheering that she had earlier. She pushed herself to her feet and swayed a bit. Stuart was next to her in a heartbeat. He didn't touch her, which she appreciated, but it was more than obvious he would help her if she needed it.

She didn't need assistance. Asking for help brought back too many painful memories. She flexed the stubs of her fingers on her left hand and took a deep breath. The day she voluntarily asked for help again was the day she grew horns and learned how to fly.

She straightened her spine and lifted her chin, staring at Stuart, daring him to say something about her momentary weakness.

He just stared back, then nodded, turning to join his teammate at the window.

Letting out a long breath, Monica mentally shook her head. She knew she was too defensive. Too quick to judge. Even with all the therapy she'd had, it was why she preferred to spend her time with children.

Stuart walked back toward her. "It looks clear, but we

still need to be very cautious. If the rioters are still around, the second they hear the chopper, they're gonna zero in on it. They could shoot at it in the hopes of bringing it down and adding even more chaos to the area."

"Is that possible? I mean, these aren't terrorists, they're just people taking advantage of the turmoil to get their hands on stuff to make their lives easier," Monica said.

"Maybe, maybe not. But even though the situation isn't the same, I can't help but think about Mogadishu," Stuart said.

Monica shivered. Yeah, she knew all about what happened to the American soldiers in Mogadishu.

"They've probably all slunk home to rest up for another day of destruction," Stuart said, obviously attempting to put her at ease.

Monica could've told him there was no need to baby her, but she simply nodded. The threesome headed for the same door in the back of the large empty building. Slate exited first, while she and Stuart hung back, letting him check out the immediate area. He reappeared two minutes later and nodded at his teammate.

Stuart nodded back, and Monica expected him to lead the way out of the building immediately...but instead he turned and held something out to her. It was a knife. The one she'd seen strapped to the side of his vest earlier.

She looked at it, then up at Stuart, but she didn't reach for the K-BAR.

"Take it," Stuart insisted.

Still Monica didn't move. "Why?" she asked.

"Why?" Stuart echoed in confusion.

"Yeah. Why now? What aren't you telling me?"

"Nothing. But after thinking about what you said, and after seeing how you handled that pistol back at the house, it's obvious you have some knowledge of weapons. If I was in your shoes, I wouldn't want to be unarmed. I can't give you a gun, but I can at least let you have this. Just in case."

Monica was conflicted. She wanted that knife more than she'd wanted anything in a long time. She wanted to be able to protect herself if they ran into any stray members of the mob. But she didn't want to be indebted to a SEAL. It went against everything she'd ever been taught.

As soon as the thought entered her brain, she heard one of her many therapists in the back of her mind telling her she wasn't under her father's thumb anymore. That he wasn't representative of everyone who wore a military uniform.

"No strings," Stuart said quietly, proving that he'd definitely listened closely to her babbling earlier. "But I'd appreciate it if you didn't stab me in the back."

Monica's gaze whipped up to meet his. Was he kidding? He was staring back at her without even a hint of a smile on his face. He definitely wasn't making a joke. She didn't know if she should be offended or satisfied that he thought she might hurt him.

Reaching out slowly, she took the knife from him with her good hand.

"It's sharp," Stuart told her. "I recommend you keep it in the sheath unless you need it."

Monica pulled the weapon from the leather sheath and tested the blade. He wasn't kidding—it *was* sharp. Deadly sharp. Feeling an uncomfortable surge of gratitude toward the man standing in front of her, Monica nodded her thanks. She didn't have a fancy vest to strap the sheath to, but she hooked it in the waistband of her jeans, making sure it was secure before looking back up at Stuart.

He hadn't moved from his position in the doorway, and his gaze was fixed on her. "Good?" he asked.

"Yeah."

"Like before, hold onto me and don't let go. Not for any reason. Okay?" he asked.

Irritation rose up within Monica, which was a relief. She was used to being irritated with people. It was more... comfortable, than the gratitude she felt seconds ago. Pressing her lips together, she nodded.

"I'm not trying to treat you like a child," Stuart said with infinite patience, proving that he could somehow read her mood. "I just have no idea what we're going to run into when we leave and if you're holding onto my belt, I know where you are and can act accordingly."

That made sense, and Monica appreciated him taking the time to explain. That was one thing her father never did. When he said something, he expected her immediate acquiescence, never bothering to explain the reasons behind his orders.

"With any luck, we'll be inside the chopper in less than ten minutes and you'll be reunited with your charges as soon as it can be arranged. Grab on and let's get out of here."

Monica wasn't sure why she suddenly wasn't more excited to see August and Remington. Maybe because along with seeing them, she'd have to talk to their parents. Deep down, she resented the fact that they'd left her in the house. And it hadn't been the ambassador or his wife who'd notified the authorities of her whereabouts. It had been their son. She knew she was just another hired helper, but it still stung that they hadn't immediately raised the alarm that another American citizen was alone and vulnerable in their home.

The walk through the streets was eerie. Almost completely silent except for the occasional barking dog. Monica could see flickering light from the random fires still burning in the distance, in all directions from where they were walking. The mobs had been busy.

She could also hear Slate talking to someone through the radios he and Stuart had in their ears. He was constantly updating their location and pinning down where the chopper should pick them up.

After ten minutes or so of walking, they came to the edge of a large park. Monica had been there with August and Remington in the past. There weren't many trees, and the open space where children could play soccer was the perfect place for a helicopter to land.

She heard Slate confirming their coordinates as Stuart urged her to squat down next to some sort of shed on the edge of the field.

"Things are gonna go hard and fast in a few minutes," he warned.

Monica took a deep breath and nodded. Instinctively, she looked around for potential dangers. It was late...or early, depending on how she looked at it, and while most citizens in the area should be locked safely behind doors, considering what had been happening all around them, the possibility that there were still some people out and about looking for trouble was high.

Slate's gaze was fixed to the sky, searching for the chopper and listening for its arrival, while Stuart did the same as Monica...looking for trouble on the ground.

Within three minutes, which seemed much longer, Monica heard the distinctive sound of a helicopter in the distance.

"We'll wait until we have a visual before we leave cover," Slate said.

Monica wanted to say "duh" but kept her mouth shut. It was never good to antagonize a soldier when their adrenaline was up.

When Slate gave the signal to move, she still couldn't see the chopper in the inky black sky, but she could definitely hear that it was almost on top of them. Even with the full moon, the black helicopter was difficult to see until it was directly overhead.

The threesome ran for the center of the field—and for a split second, Monica thought she saw something moving on the far side of the open space. It was just a dark shape, but she didn't hesitate to bring it to Stuart's attention.

"Movement at one o'clock," she told him as they ran, using the terminology her father had taught her for giving directions in battle.

Stuart looked in the direction she'd indicated. She saw the movement again, and opened her mouth to update Stuart when he called out urgently to his teammate.

"Slate! Two o'clock!"

No sooner were the words out of his mouth than gunshots rang through the quiet night.

"Fuck!" Slate swore. "Shots fired, shots fired!" he yelled.

Monica assumed he was telling whoever was on the other end of the radio, because she and Stuart had obviously heard them.

Quicker than she'd expected him to move, Stuart shifted, grabbing her around the waist and practically throwing her down. He didn't hurt her, easily controlling their descent so she didn't slam onto the ground. Then, to her surprise, he crouched over her, his chest to her back, his elbows on the scraggly grass on either side of her head, cocooning her under his body as he scanned the edges of the field.

The helicopter was directly over them now, the rotor blades kicking up dirt and making it almost impossible to hear anything other than the machinery whirring above their heads.

"Get her inside!" Slate yelled as he went down on one knee and held his rifle at the ready.

Monica couldn't tell if someone was still shooting or not. She also had no idea if they were trying to hit them or the chopper. She supposed it didn't really matter at this point. If the helicopter went down, it would crush the three of them like bugs. A bullet to the head or being crushed under tons of metal and steel would have the same outcome.

She didn't have time to think about what was happening. A ladder suddenly appeared in front of her, and Stuart jerked her upright. He had a tight hold on her biceps as he reached for the metal ladder with his other hand.

Then, to her surprise, he let go of her and climbed up a few rungs.

Monica was positive he was leaving her to save himself, and not altogether surprised. Until he stopped, her head level with his knees. The ladder was swinging with the movement of the chopper twenty or so feet above them. He fiddled with something on the ladder before he leaned down and held out his hand.

Monica stared at his fingers—and literally couldn't move.

Another day...another person's hand...and the consequences of taking that hand flew through her brain.

"Monica! Grab on!" Stuart yelled.

But she didn't move. Couldn't. Her muscles wouldn't

cooperate. If she accepted his help, something bad would happen. She knew it.

As if from the far end of a long tunnel, she heard Stuart swear, then he was back down in front of her once more. He took hold of her chin and tipped her head up so he could see her eyes. In a distant part of her mind, Monica knew there was no time for this. Someone was out there shooting, and they needed to get into that chopper and leave the area.

"You need to get on the ladder," a deep voice said. "Can you do that?"

Monica nodded without thought.

"Okay, I'll hold it still. Here. One foot up...good job. Now the other."

Monica followed directions without hesitation.

"Grab onto the sides, yes, like that. Step up one more. Good." He quickly but calmly encouraged her up two more rungs. "Hold on. Whatever you do, don't let go. No matter what. Can you do that?"

Could she? Yes. She was her dad's little soldier, she could hold on like he told her to. She didn't want to know what the repercussions would be if she didn't.

A part of her knew that this man wasn't her father. She wasn't ten years old and she wasn't back in Wyoming on her dad's "training grounds." But the vision of that hand reaching down to her wouldn't leave her mind. Was making her remember too much, and her brain had turned off in order to protect her from reliving the pain that had come as a result of accepting help.

"Now don't freak out, but I'm coming up behind you," Monica heard the man say a second before she felt his body heat against her back. He was so much taller than her, even standing on the rung below her own. She watched him clip a carabiner onto the side rail to her right, then a moment later did the same on the left. His left hand curled around hers, holding her tightly to the ladder.

"Secure," he said.

And just like that, Monica snapped back to the present. Stuart was behind her, talking into his radio. The wind from the rotors continued to whip around them as the chopper rose a few feet higher.

Looking down, she saw Slate step onto a rung below them. The ladder had been long enough that part of it was lying on the ground when she and Stuart had strapped in.

"I'm on. Go!" Slate yelled loud enough for Monica to hear him, even without a radio in her ears.

The helicopter immediately rose at a fast clip and began to head out of the area.

Monica squeezed her eyes shut as they flew through the air. It was dark, but the burning houses she'd glimpsed were more than enough for her to see how high up they were.

"You're doing great," Stuart said as he pressed closer, speaking into her ear. "Hang on for just a minute or so longer and they'll pull us up."

Even as he said the words, Monica could feel the ladder shuddering under them as people in the helicopter hauled them upward.

There was so much she wanted to say to Stuart, but it was just as well, talking was next to impossible as they flew toward safety, because the words were stuck in her throat.

She'd choked. Bad. Any one of them could've been shot by whoever was lurking in the shadows along the edge of that field. She realized now that Stuart had gotten onto the ladder first to stabilize it before assisting her, and she'd made everything more complicated by refusing his help. The position he was in right now couldn't be comfortable, yet he hadn't berated her or become impatient. He'd simply pivoted to another plan.

Monica felt sick. It had been years since she'd suffered this intense feeling of dread in the pit of her belly. Stuart would have every reason to chew her out when they were finally safe. She'd put them all in danger, and there was no way he could overlook that.

It took a bit of maneuvering to get both her and Stuart inside the chopper. Monica realized another reason he'd gotten onto the ladder first, climbing a bit higher than she'd been—it would've made it much easier to get into the helicopter. Now, the men inside had to awkwardly haul both her and Stuart together over the edge of the open door and into the cabin.

He pointed to a corner, and Monica gladly crawled toward it, trying to make herself as small as possible as she watched Stuart turn back to the opening and help bring Slate inside as well. The second the door slid shut, the noise level dropped considerably, but not enough to have a normal conversation.

Stuart took a set of headphones from one of the crew members and brought them over to her. He started to put them on her head, but stopped himself at the last second. He gestured to them with a nod, then lifted an eyebrow.

Too tired and off-kilter to reach for them, Monica merely nodded.

Stuart gently placed them over her ears, and she sighed in relief as the noise from the engine reverberating all around her was immediately silenced.

Stuart kept his eyes on her for a long moment before nodding and turning back to grab his own set. Monica kept her gaze glued to him as he settled himself nearby. He began to talk to someone through the headset, but she was too shaken by her flashback to pay attention to what everyone was saying.

Ten minutes later, Monica felt a change in the helicopter's engine. They'd throttled back or something. Looking over at Stuart, she found his gaze on her. He gave her a thumb's up and a small smile.

Then she felt a thump as the chopper landed.

Blowing out a sigh of relief, she waited for the helicopter to shut down so she could take off the headphones. The door slid open, and she saw four men dressed exactly like Stuart and Slate standing there.

"Good to see you!" one of the men exclaimed.

"If you wanted a ride, I would've approved some time off so you could go to Disney World," another quipped.

The others simply smiled as Slate hopped out of the cabin.

Stuart followed, then turned back to her. "Come on, you're safe now."

Monica noticed that he didn't hold his hand out to her. A part of her was grateful, and another part hated that he was so observant, he knew exactly how badly she'd freaked out earlier.

She scooted over to the door of the chopper and dangled her legs over the edge, somewhat disgusted that because of her height, she was still quite a ways from the ground.

"You got this?" Stuart asked.

Monica nodded and hopped out. Her legs almost gave out under her, probably because adrenaline was still coursing through her veins, making her unsteady. But Stuart was there to ensure she didn't make a complete fool of herself by falling on her face. He grabbed hold of her arm, letting go as soon as he was certain she wouldn't fall.

Again, a part of her was glad he was so perceptive. Oddly...another part wished he'd held on longer. To say she was confused was an understatement.

"Monica Collins, I assume?" one of the men asked.

"That's me," she said. Looking around, she saw that the helicopter had landed on what could only be an airport runway. There were stretches of blinking lights and she could see a well-lit building in the distance.

"There are two little boys who will be very glad to see you," another man said.

Monica felt her muscles loosen at knowing August and Remington were obviously safe.

"These are my friends," Stuart said. "Midas, Aleck, Jag, and the guy with the phone to his ear is Mustang, our team leader."

"Nice to meet you," Monica said, shocked that the dread she always felt when she saw men in uniform was currently absent. She didn't have time to figure out why before Mustang turned to Stuart with a frown, holding out the phone.

"It's the commander. He wants to talk to you."

"Now?" Stuart asked.

"Now," Mustang confirmed.

Butterflies began to flutter in Monica's belly again when she saw Mustang's gaze dart to her, then slide away, as if something was wrong.

Stuart accepted the phone and took a step away from her, but Monica impulsively reached out and grabbed hold of his sleeve. "If that's about me, I want to hear it."

He shook his head, but Monica took a step closer.

"It's my right," she insisted.

Something passed between them as they stared at each other, and just when she was sure Stuart was going to deny her, he nodded.

"I don't think—" Mustang started, but Stuart held up a hand, cutting off his friend.

Stuart glanced at the phone and hit a button before saying, "Pid here. Mustang said you needed to speak with me, Sir?"

# CHAPTER FOUR

Pid had a feeling he wasn't going to like what Commander Huttner had to say, so he braced.

"I've ordered Mustang to bring Monica Collins back to Hawaii."

"Come again?" Pid asked.

"It's a matter of national security that I speak with her," his commander said.

Pid was shocked. And he knew Monica *definitely* wasn't going to be happy with this development. He looked at her and, sure enough, her mouth was hanging open as she stared at the phone in his hand.

"She's a civilian, Sir," Pid said.

"I'm aware of that. She's also the only person able to describe this asshole claiming to be a SEAL. I need to know everything about what happened and what she saw. I also need her to sit with one of our forensic artists to create a likeness."

"Um...I'm sure she'd be willing to do a video chat and tell you everything she knows."

"Not good enough. Hall...we have prior intel on this man. He's been doing this for a long time."

"Doing what, Sir?"

"Taking advantage of conflicts around the globe. He enters countries dealing with civil unrest and incites protestors. He spreads rumors and flat-out lies to prolong the riots. Once he's stirred the pot and things get out of control, he breaks into certain buildings to steal whatever he can find. And the man somehow knows exactly who to hit. He's taken millions of dollars in cash, weapons, stocks and bonds, and jewels. He's damn good at what he does... too good...and he needs to be stopped. As far as I know, that woman is the only one who's come face-to-face with the man and lived to tell the tale. I want her on base by the end of the day tomorrow. Is that clear?"

Pid swallowed hard and kept his eyes on Monica. She wasn't happy, and he couldn't blame her. She hadn't been asked if she was willing to cooperate. There were other ways his commander could get the information he needed without resorting to hauling her all the way to Hawaii to interrogate in person. Hell, Commander Huttner could fly out to wherever Monica was going.

"And if she doesn't want to come?" Pid couldn't help but ask.

"She doesn't have a choice," Huttner responded flatly.

Pid pressed his lips together in frustration. "So you want us to force her if she doesn't agree," he couldn't help but say.

"Yes," the commander said without hesitation, surprising the hell out of Pid. "This is a matter of national security. That man's been a thorn in our side for longer than we care to admit."

"How come we've never heard about this?" Pid asked.

"Because it's an embarrassment. To the Navy and to the United States."

"So he really *is* a SEAL?"

"I'm not willing to talk further particulars over the phone," the commander said. "Mustang tells me you took fire as you were extracting the woman."

Pid didn't like how his boss referred to Monica as "the woman," but he confirmed.

"And how do you think anyone knew where the chopper would pick you up?" The commander didn't wait for a response. "Because he knows our tactics. Knows that you would've hunkered down until it was safe, then find the nearest available space where a helicopter could land. He's smart. And again—he needs to be stopped. To date, Miss Collins is our best chance at figuring out who he is. Bring her back to Hawaii. That's an order."

Pid sighed. "Yes, Sir."

"Give the phone back to Mustang," Huttner ordered.

Pid held out the satellite phone to his team leader without another word.

There was so much he wanted to say to Monica, but had no idea where to start. A part of him was glad she'd insisted on listening in on the conversation. The last thing he would've wanted to do was break the news that instead of going back to her life as a nanny for the Laws family, she was being forced to fly back to Hawaii with them.

"I—"

That was as much as he got out before Monica shook her head. "Don't. Will I at least get to say goodbye to August and Remington before we leave?"

Pid looked at Mustang, who had hung up with their commander and looked just as frustrated as the rest of the team. His team leader nodded. "Yes."

The next thirty minutes were some of the most excruciating in Pid's life. They all headed for the building where the American citizens were waiting for their flight back to the States.

It was obvious how much Monica cared for her charges, and they for her. She spent a bit of time reassuring the boys that she was fine and listening to their stories about how they'd gotten to fly in a real-live helicopter.

Mustang explained to the ambassador that they were going to have to find another nanny, as Monica was being taken to Hawaii. Little August cried when he found out she wouldn't be going with them, and Monica didn't look any happier.

She hadn't said a word to him or the rest of the team since they'd been ordered to bring her back to the States. It felt as if all the progress he'd made with her in the last few hours had been wiped out in the blink of an eye.

Pid couldn't stop thinking about what had happened in the field. He'd been desperate to get her into the chopper and away from whoever was shooting at them, getting onto the ladder first to stabilize it before helping her get on and strapped in. Being above her would've also give him a better vantage point to fire back at the mystery shooter, if given the chance.

But she'd frozen when he'd reached down for her. In hindsight, he had a feeling it was because of what had happened with her father; she'd told him and Slate enough for Pid to know better. Though he couldn't have known she had post-traumatic stress disorder related to the incident.

The horror in her eyes had been enough for him to realize what was happening almost immediately, and he'd been able to shift to plan B. But he hated that he'd caused her such angst in the first place. He'd been relieved to see recognition in her eyes in the chopper, and that she'd allowed him to help her with the headphones.

Still, he was certain that any progress he'd made toward helping her trust him even a little bit had been blown out of the water.

She didn't say a word when he told her it was time to go. She didn't make a sound as they led her toward the military plane that would fly them all back to the States, and then on to Hawaii. She kept her lips pressed together as she got settled in a seat, then turned her head away from Pid and the rest of the team.

He sighed and took a seat a few rows away, leaving her alone as she so obviously wanted.

Slate sat on one side of him, Mustang on the other side.

"She's not taking it well," Mustang observed after they'd taken off.

"Ya think?" Pid said sarcastically.

"She doesn't have the best opinion of men in the military," Slate offered.

"Why?" Mustang asked.

"Her dad was a controlling asshole," Pid told his team leader. "I'm guessing he ran his house with an iron fist. Taught his daughter that asking for help was strictly forbidden." He told Mustang the story of how Monica had hurt her hand. By the time he was done, his friend was just as furious as Pid had been when he'd heard the story.

"Well, shit. Being forced to come with us isn't helping her opinion of the military, is it?" he asked.

"No. And speaking of which, have you ever seen

Commander Huttner so worked up about something before?" Pid asked.

"Absolutely not. He's usually very even-keeled. This guy has really gotten under his skin," Mustang said.

"Enough to basically order us to kidnap a woman who likely won't have enough information to ID the asshole," Slate added.

Pid agreed. He hadn't really been looking forward to saying goodbye to Monica, but this *definitely* wasn't the way he wanted to stay in her life, that was for sure.

"Well, hopefully she'll tell Huttner what he needs to hear and she'll be headed off to wherever she wants to go fairly quickly," Mustang said with a shake of his head.

The men fell silent as the plane climbed higher, giving Pid time to think about the situation. It was honestly fucked up. Monica literally had nothing beyond what she was carrying on her person. The fact that she'd had her passport on her made their lives much easier as far as leaving the country and entering the United States, but everything else was completely up in the air. He supposed Huttner would arrange for someplace on base for her to stay. He'd have to. She also needed clothes, food, possibly transportation.

The more Pid thought about it, the angrier at his commander he became.

He totally could've interviewed her via video chat. He also had enough connections that he could've arranged for someone to go to wherever the ambassador and his family ended up. Instead, he'd used his position to force their team to bring her back to Hawaii.

No wonder Monica had a poor opinion of the military.

Sighing, Pid glanced over at the woman he couldn't get off his mind. Her hands were clasped in her lap and she was staring blankly into space. It was going to be a long trip home.

* * *

By the time they landed at the Naval base in Honolulu, it was once again dark outside. They'd been traveling for over twenty hours and Pid was exhausted. All he wanted to do was go home and crash. But first, he wanted to make sure Monica was settled in and had everything she needed.

Mustang, Midas, and Aleck were more than ready to see their women, and even Jag and Slate had been focused on their phones the second the wheels of the plane touched the tarmac. The latter two might not be hooked up, officially, but they may as well have been, considering how eager they were to touch base with Carly and Ashlyn, respectively.

Pid hung back and waited for Monica as his teammates exited the plane.

"You okay?" he asked quietly as she headed his way.

"Fine," she said stiffly.

Pid mentally sighed. He didn't blame her for being in a bad mood. If he'd been caught in the middle of a riot, had to hide from a man intent on doing him harm, run to avoid being trapped in a burning house, hide out, get shot at while dangling from a ladder on a moving helicopter, then be told that he wouldn't be returning to the job and children he loved and instead was forced to fly with people he didn't know or trust, to a state he'd never been to, with no idea of what his future held...Yeah. He'd be in a bad mood too.

"For the record, I'm sorry," he blurted.

Her gaze met his for the first time since they'd gotten on the plane. "For what?"

"For this entire fucked-up situation. But I'm gonna make sure the commander treats you with respect and that you're fairly compensated for all of this."

Monica stared at him for a beat before her shoulders slumped. She shifted her gaze, concentrating on a spot in the middle of his chest. "I don't think it's any surprise that I'm not happy with this. But I do want to help. Whoever that guy was, he was smug and very sure of himself. The look in his eyes scared the shit out of me, and that's why I hid. If he's been taking advantage of volatile situations in countries around the world, and scaring or possibly killing other women...I want to do my part to stop him."

Pid was relieved, even as he heard a "but" coming.

"But that doesn't mean I'm happy being here. I'm uneasy being on a military base, and I'm so far outside my comfort zone it's not even funny," she finished.

Pid made a quick decision. He had no idea if his commander would agree, or if *Monica* would agree, but he had no intention of not voicing his concerns about the entire situation.

"Come on, Pid!" Midas yelled from outside the plane. "Get a move on! I want to get home and see Lexie sometime this century."

Pid knew better than to touch Monica, even though his fingers itched to do just that. He vividly recalled how she felt against him as they rode the ladder up to the chopper. Her skin was warm, he could feel it even through their clothes, and she fit against him perfectly, despite their height difference.

Which was fanciful and ridiculous...but regardless, the memory was burned into his brain.

"Monica? Will you look at me for a second?" He waited until her gaze met his before continuing. "No matter what happens, you aren't alone here. I know you don't trust me, and while I hate that, I understand it and I don't blame you. If you need anything, all you have to do is let me know. If you're hungry, I'll feed you. If you're scared, I'll do what I can to put you at ease. And if anyone pushes you too hard for information, tell them to fuck off, and I'll come get you to give you a break."

Monica swallowed hard and asked in a tone so low, Pid could barely hear it. "Why?"

"Because you didn't ask for this. Because I like you."

Her brows came down. "You like me? You don't even *know* me."

"I know you're tough. You can shoot and field dress a deer. You have more integrity in your little finger than most people have in their entire bodies. You love kids, you're brave even when you're scared, you don't hesitate to do what you think is right, and you don't panic in situations that would overwhelm most people. I don't know the little things, like your favorite color, whether you prefer the beach or the mountains, or what you like to eat...but those are inconsequential compared to the things I consider really important."

Pid had no idea where all this was coming from, all he knew was that he wanted this woman to understand that she had an ally. She wasn't alone.

Then he remembered her story about asking her dad for help—and what had happened as a result.

She wasn't going to ask him for help. Ever.

That fact just made him more determined to keep his eye on her. To keep her best interests in mind. If she wouldn't ask for help, he'd do what he could to anticipate what she needed and give it to her.

"Pid!" It was Aleck calling his name impatiently this time.

"We should go," Monica said.

"Right." Pid turned and walked toward the door of the aircraft, ready to make sure Monica was settled in with everything she needed before he stepped foot off the Naval base.

Commander Huttner was waiting for them when they entered the small terminal attached to the military air base.

"Welcome home," he said to the SEALs. Then he turned to Monica. "And welcome to Hawaii, Miss Collins. I wish it were under better circumstances. But I appreciate your willingness to assist in this very important investigation."

"I don't recall being given a choice," Monica replied. Her tone was perfectly respectful, but she didn't hesitate to make her thoughts on being there loud and clear.

It was all Pid could do not to smile at the surprised look on his commander's face.

"Right, well...if you come with me, we'll get the initial interview out of the way. The sooner you tell us everything you know, the sooner you'll be able to leave," Commander Huttner said.

Pid took a step forward, not quite standing in front of Monica, but almost. "No," he said, a little harsher than he meant to.

"Pardon me?" Huttner said.

"It's late," Pid reasoned, doing his best to remember who he was talking to and temper his tone. "We've been traveling for hours. I'm hungry and tired and need a shower, so I'm sure Monica feels the same way. She's here. She isn't going anywhere. Surely you can talk to her tomorrow? Or better yet, the day after that. The more comfortable and rested she is, the better her memory will be."

The two men stared at each other, their wills clashing even though they didn't speak a word.

Finally, the commander let out a long breath. "Fine," he said. "But I expect her to be at my office at eight o'clock sharp the day after tomorrow."

Pid looked behind him and saw Monica's grateful gaze glued to him. He much preferred that look than the disdain he'd seen so often in her eyes. He raised an eyebrow as if to ask if that was acceptable. She nodded, and Pid turned back to his commander. "Yes, Sir," he told him, a little belatedly.

Huttner ran a hand through his already mussed hair, and Pid realized for the first time that his commander was extremely rattled. The mysterious man claiming to be a SEAL had Huttner acting completely out of character.

It piqued Pid's interest, but at the moment, he had other things on his mind. "Where did you arrange for Monica to stay?" he asked.

"Gabrunas Hall."

Pid stiffened, and he saw Mustang do the same. "The unaccompanied personnel barracks?" he asked in disbelief.

"There was an empty room and it's close to my office," Huttner said.

"Why not the Navy Lodge?" Pid asked. It was more like a hotel than the barracks. The rooms weren't fancy, but many had small kitchens and, more importantly for Monica's sake, most of the people who stayed there were retired military members and their families. They wouldn't be in uniform. She'd be more comfortable around them.

"It's full," Huttner replied. "It's tourist season and all the rooms are booked."

"She can stay with me," Pid blurted.

He'd already made the decision to offer her lodging if necessary, so he could better look after her, but now he was going to insist.

"I can stay at the barracks," Monica said quietly from behind him.

Pid turned to her. "The men and women who live there are mostly single. They'll be coming and going at all hours of the night. While it's frowned upon, there are often loud parties and you'll be surrounded by sailors in uniform, every second of every day. I know you don't trust me, or really even know me, but I swear on my life and that of my teammates that you'll be safe at my place. I've got a guest room, it's quiet, and I live off base."

Pid practically held his breath as he waited to hear Monica's response. He was aware that he should've asked Huttner for permission to take her off base, but having her stay at the rowdy barracks would definitely stress her out and wasn't conducive to her cooperating and giving the commander the information he wanted.

"It won't be any trouble," Pid cajoled. "I'll leave you alone. You won't even have to talk to me if you don't want to. It's not huge, but I swear it'll be more comfortable and relaxing than the barracks."

"Fine," Monica said after another long moment.

Relieved, Pid turned back to his commander. "I'll have her at your office at eight o'clock the day after tomorrow."

"I'm not sure—" Huttner started, but Pid interrupted. He knew he was pushing his luck, and he'd most likely be reprimanded, but he didn't care. This was important.

"She didn't have a choice in coming here," he

reminded his superior officer. "The least we can do is make sure she's as comfortable as possible. And you know as well as I do that Gabrunas Hall isn't a relaxing atmosphere for someone who isn't in the military."

For a moment, Pid thought his commander was going to deny his request to house Monica—as he probably should. But after an uncomfortably long silence, during which he studied Pid carefully, he finally nodded. "I'll approve her staying at your home, but that means you're responsible for her."

"I know," Pid said, ignoring the way Monica shifted uncomfortably at his commander's words.

"And I'll remind you, this is a matter of national security," Huttner pressed.

Once more, Pid wished he knew exactly why their commander was so worked up about the man Monica had seen. But for now, his first concern was getting her settled and comfortable, despite being in a very uncomfortable situation.

"Understood," Pid said.

Huttner nodded at him, then at the rest of the SEAL team, before heading out of the terminal without another word.

The second he was out of earshot, Aleck whistled long and low. "It sounds as if we need to have a conversation with our commander," he said needlessly.

"I'll come in and talk to him tomorrow," Mustang said immediately.

"Appreciate it," Pid said. Then he turned to Monica. "You ready to go?"

"I'll stay in a hotel off base," Monica said stiffly.

"Go with Pid," Jag urged. "You'll be safer with him."

Monica's spine straightened. "I can take care of myself. I don't need a babysitter."

"Of course you don't," Aleck said. "You're a grown-ass woman. But based on how our commander is acting, something's up. Something big. I'm not sure it's the best idea to be on your own right now."

"That asshole saw you," Slate threw in. "He's likely got connections. The last thing you want is him coming after you to make sure you can't ID him."

"Besides, you're in Hawaii," Mustang said. "Maybe against your will, but you're here. You might as well enjoy it as much as you can before you leave. Staying on base or in a hotel without a car means you won't see much of anything. At least if you're with Pid, you'll see some of the island."

"And Pid's place is quiet...even if it *is* messy as fuck," Midas added.

"Shut up," Pid groused. He knew he wasn't the best housekeeper, but he didn't appreciate his friends letting *Monica* know that before she agreed to stay with him.

"I'll talk to Lexie tonight about the situation. I'm sure she, Elodie, and Kenna will be more than happy to pick up some clothes and stuff and drop it by your place tomorrow," Midas said.

"El will probably want to whip up some meals too, so don't be surprised to see her tomorrow with a ton of food," Mustang added.

"If you get a chance, bring her down to Duke's. Kenna will be happy to comp you a meal," Aleck added.

"Thanks, guys, but can we maybe not overwhelm Monica on her first day? Besides, I'm not sure how long she'll be here anyway. The last thing Elodie will want is for her food to go bad in my fridge because she made too much," Pid warned. He was aware that while his friends had been talking, Monica's head was on a swivel, looking from man to man as they spoke.

"I'll try to get El to control herself," Mustang said with a smile.

"Thanks."

"I'm headed home," Aleck said. "See you all later."

"Me too," Jag agreed. "Drive safe, everyone."

Within a minute, Pid was standing alone with Monica in the nearly empty terminal. He stuffed his hands into his pockets to make sure he didn't reach out to touch her. "Come on. It's late, and I know you have to be exhausted."

She didn't agree or disagree, just fell into step next to him as he headed for the exit. Without a word, they walked through the parking lot toward the back, where he'd left his car.

Monica stopped abruptly as he clicked his remote to unlock the doors and the lights blinked on and off. "You drive a minivan?" she asked in disbelief.

Pid was used to getting shit about his choice of vehicle, but he didn't care. The Honda Odyssey was awesome for hauling all sorts of shit around. It could fit all five of his teammates and still have room for gear in the back. As far as he was concerned, a minivan was the perfect vehicle.

He grinned. "Yup," he replied with no embarrassment whatsoever.

"You're constantly surprising me," she admitted quietly.

Pid had never heard such welcome words. "Good." He opened the passenger door for her and saw surprise flash in her eyes once more. She didn't comment, merely climbed up into the seat.

When they were on their way to his house, Pid said, "If

you want, we can stop and grab some stuff for you tonight. Though, I'm beat, and I know you have to be as well. You can borrow a shirt and sweats tonight, although you'll swim in both, and we can do your laundry while you're sleeping. I've got soap, shampoo, conditioner, and an extra toothbrush to tide you over until you can get the brands you like. But if you really want to stop tonight, it's not an issue."

"I can wait," Monica said. Then she surprised him by adding, "You have conditioner?"

Pid chuckled. "I know, it's not exactly manly...just like my minivan. But my hair is thick and conditioner makes it softer." He shrugged.

"I wasn't judging, just curious," Monica said.

They rode the rest of the way to his place in silence. Pid thought about attempting to point out landmarks, but it was dark and she wouldn't really be able to see them anyway, so he remained silent and enjoyed not having any traffic on the roads, since it was so late.

He pulled into his driveway and was relieved the security lights he'd installed were working. They lit up the front of the house, giving them plenty of light to see the small bungalow. He'd lucked out by finding the place to rent. It was a perfect size for him, and he loved the fact that it was tucked back into a corner of the property. On one side, a large field separated the bungalow from his landlord's house, and there were trees all over his backyard, blocking much of the sun.

Elodie complained about his backyard being dark, but that was one of the things Pid loved most. He'd grown up in Alaska, where sunlight in the winter was scarce, maybe only a few hours a day. He liked the dark; it reminded him of home. Having the sun blasting into his windows long into the evening wasn't something he enjoyed.

And it was quiet, like Midas said. The older man who owned both homes never had many visitors himself, and he didn't bother Pid. As long as he paid his rent on time, his landlord left him alone. The highway was far enough away that there was no road noise, only the sounds of the many animals that made the area their home.

He climbed out with the idea of opening Monica's door, but she was already out and walking around the van toward *him*. And all of a sudden...Pid was nervous. He wondered if he'd made a mistake. Monica might've been more comfortable in a hotel after all. Or maybe he should've asked Aleck to put her up in the guest room in his penthouse. She'd probably enjoy the view from his balcony much better than his small, dark house. And she would've had Kenna to keep her company.

But it was too late now. There was no way he'd do anything to make Monica think he didn't want her around. He unlocked his door and gestured for her to enter before him.

She walked into his house and he followed, closing and locking the door. Pid flicked on the lights—and winced at seeing the condition of the main living area. The team knew that he wasn't exactly Mr. Clean. They joked about it all the time. But seeing his home through a stranger's eyes made him realize exactly how long it had been since he'd thoroughly cleaned his space.

The bungalow was small and compact. The main living area was an open space with the kitchen along one wall. A long counter separated it from the rest of the room. He had a leather sofa with an oval coffee table, and a suede recliner with a small side table in the living room. The TV was mounted on the wall, a long skinny table sitting under it that held his video game console, DVD player, and his modem for the internet.

There was a hallway to the right that led to the two bedrooms and the bathroom. He hadn't mentioned the fact that they'd have to share a bathroom, but it was too late now.

It wasn't his furniture or the quaintness of the house that was causing Pid to mentally wince, it was the general messiness of the place. It wasn't dirty, per se, even though there were a few dishes sitting in the sink from before he'd left on the mission to Algeria. It was more that his shit was *everywhere*. He spotted at least two T-shirts—one on the floor and one on the couch—two pairs of boots and a pair of sneakers strewn around the space, and there were too many coffee mugs and plastic cups on the tables to count. Junk mail was sitting on the counter separating the kitchen from the living room, unopened, and the laundry he hadn't bothered to finish folding was piled in a laundry basket next to the couch.

He was embarrassed—and vowed to never leave for deployment again without at least doing a preliminary clean-up of his place.

"Yeah, um...I obviously need to clean a bit," he muttered.

Monica merely shrugged. "I've seen worse," she said.

Pid figured she was just being polite, but was happy to change the topic. "Help yourself to whatever you want in the kitchen. Though I'll warn you, I need to go to the store. There's probably some questionable greens in the drawer in the fridge. Don't touch it," he joked. "But I've got lots of granola bars and stuff to make protein shakes. The laundry room is there," he said, pointing toward a small room to the left. And the rooms are this way." He gestured to the hall.

She walked in that direction, and Pid pushed open the guest room door. "I've got some clean sheets in the closet in the hall. I'll make the bed for you."

"I can do it," Monica told him.

"Okay. Anyway, this will be your room. It's not much, but I promise you'll be more comfortable here than in the barracks."

"It's fine," Monica said.

Pid wished there was more to the room than a double-size bed, a bookcase overflowing with the historical fiction he loved to read, and a small desk piled with computer parts. "The bathroom is out here to the right. There's only one, but I won't go in if the door's shut. There are clean towels and stuff in the cabinet over the toilet. And the extra toothbrush I promised is in the drawer to the right of the sink."

"Thanks."

She certainly wasn't saying much, but Pid didn't push. She had to be out of her element, and he was essentially a stranger. "Do you need anything?"

"No."

"Okay. I'll just go and get you a shirt and sweats. Monica?"

"Yeah?" she asked, finally looking up at him.

"I'm sorry about everything that's happened...but I'm not sorry you're here. I wouldn't have offered my guest room if I didn't want you here." Pid didn't know why he wanted to make sure she understood that, but he did.

Monica nodded, and Pid couldn't read the expression on her face. Knowing he couldn't stand in the guest room and stare at her all night, he backed toward the door. "I'll be right back."

She didn't respond as he turned and headed for his own room. He gathered a shirt and an old pair of sweats and brought them to her. Their hands brushed as he passed them over...and Pid swore he felt a jolt move through his fingers.

"Feel free to use the washer when you're changed," he said, feeling awkward again.

"I will."

"Okay. Then I guess I'll see you in the morning."

Monica nodded once more, then walked toward the door. Getting the hint, Pid left, wincing when the door clicked shut behind him.

"Shit," he mumbled. He didn't know why he wanted the prickly woman to loosen up and talk to him, but he did. It was likely she'd only be there a couple of days, three or four at most, before she'd be headed back overseas to continue her job. It didn't matter if she talked to him or not...except it did.

Sighing, Pid ran a hand through his hair. He was exhausted and needed to get some sleep. He also didn't want to make Monica feel awkward when she came out to put her clothes in the washer. The best thing he could do to help her feel comfortable was make himself scarce. So after checking the back door and the windows to verify they were locked and secure, he headed for his bedroom.

# CHAPTER FIVE

Even though she was exhausted and stressed, Monica couldn't go to bed until her clothes had been washed and were in the dryer. She needed to make sure she had something to wear tomorrow that wasn't the oversized T-shirt and sweats Stuart had given her. Though she appreciated the clothes more than she could say. They were comfortable, even if they were huge on her small frame.

But even after she'd started the dryer and had climbed into the comfortable bed in the guest room, Monica didn't sleep well. It was too quiet. And she was too nervous about her unfamiliar surroundings.

She lay awake for at least an hour before finally dozing fitfully, tossing and turning. Until something woke her.

Sitting up, she looked over at the clock. It was four twenty-one in the morning and still pitch black outside. She tilted her head, trying to figure out what had woken her up, and she heard something out in the living room.

Her heart beating a million miles an hour, wondering if perhaps somehow the man she'd seen in Algeria had found her, Monica threw the covers back and crept out of bed.

She reached for the knife Stuart had given her; he hadn't asked her to return it and she hadn't offered. She unsheathed it and tiptoed toward the door.

She'd noted when she'd gone to bed that the door didn't squeak, which she was grateful for now. She slowly opened it and silently walked down the hall until she could peek into the living area of Stuart's house.

Blinking in surprise, she let her hand with the knife fall back to her side as she stared at the sight in front of her.

Stuart sprayed the coffee table with cleaner, then he wiped it down with a paper towel. She realized the sound she'd heard was the squirting of the bottle as he sprayed surfaces.

"What are you doing?" she asked.

Stuart jerked in surprise and spun to face her. "Shit!" he breathed in reply.

"It doesn't *look* like that's what you're doing," Monica quipped, surprising herself with the joke.

His lips twitched as he straightened and looked everywhere but at her. If she didn't know better, she'd say he was embarrassed. "I woke up and couldn't go back to sleep and figured I'd clean up a bit. I didn't mean to wake you."

"I wasn't sleeping well," she told him.

"You prepared to use that?" Stuart asked, gesturing to the knife in her hand.

Monica nodded. "If I have to, yeah."

"Good."

His reply wasn't what she'd expected. She thought he'd give her a lecture about how sharp and dangerous the knife was. She went back to her room and put the knife in its sheath and left it by the bed, then headed back out into the living room. She was up now, and knew from experience she wouldn't be able to fall asleep again.

Besides, she was increasingly curious about Stuart. She definitely didn't trust him to have her best interests at heart; her father had always taught her to "know thy enemy." While Monica didn't really think of Stuart as her enemy, he wasn't exactly a friend either.

"You didn't have to clean on account of me," she said as he continued to wipe down the coffee table. Though admittedly, the room looked much better, now that he'd picked up the dishes, shoes, and random clothes that had been strewn about the space.

Stuart winced. "Yeah, I did. I hadn't realized how bad this place had gotten until we walked in last night."

Monica had also been surprised by the state of the house. In her experience, military men were meticulous neat freaks. Her dad certainly had been. She'd been required to make her bed every morning, pick up all her toys and put them away, and if she'd left a cup sitting in the sink—or, God forbid, anywhere in the living room—instead of rinsing it and putting it in the dishwasher, she'd have been in big trouble.

She'd done her best over the years to break some of the compulsive habits her dad had taught her, but she was still tidier than most. Seeing how messy Stuart's house had been was a shocker.

"I thought military guys were neatniks," she couldn't help saying. No matter how many times she told herself she didn't want to know anything about Stuart or his friends, he continually surprised her...which made her want to learn more.

He chuckled and walked over to the counter to set down the cleanser, then threw away the paper towels in the kitchen before going to the sink to wash his hands. "I think because I was forced to have everything in its place and not a single wrinkle in my bedding in boot camp, something within me rebelled. I was never this messy growing up."

"But you lived with your parents, right?" Monica asked.

"Yeah. And if you're insinuating that my mom picked up after me, you're right. I played soccer throughout high school, and she was always harping on me to put my shin guards and balls away. It didn't help that my sister was perfect. Her room was always clean and she never left her stuff around the house."

"You have a sister?" Monica asked.

As Stuart dried his hands on a towel hanging from the fridge, he nodded. "Yeah. She's a year younger than me and a pain in my ass." He smiled when he said it, letting Monica know he was teasing.

"Are you close?"

"As close as we *can* be with me being in the Navy and her being a traveling nurse. But growing up, I thought she was a pain, and she thought I was a jerk."

"Were you?" Monica asked without thinking.

Stuart didn't seem offended by her question. "Probably. I think most teenagers are. Hormones and trying to figure out who they are and where they fit in the world," he said easily as he leaned against the counter.

He had on a navy-blue T-shirt that said NAVY across it in big white letters and a pair of gray sweatpants. She hadn't really understood women's fascination with that particular garment before now, but suddenly it was all she could do to keep her gaze away from Stuart's crotch. The soft-looking material hugged his body...and it was more than obvious that Stuart was very well endowed.

"What about you?" he asked.

"Huh?" she asked, mentally kicking herself for not

paying better attention.

Stuart grinned as if he knew her mind was in the gutter, but he didn't call her on it. "Do you have any brothers or sisters?"

"Oh. No, thank God. I'm very thankful no one else had to suffer through a childhood like mine."

Stuart didn't immediately respond to her statement, and Monica regretted her words the second they were out of her mouth. She didn't tell many people about the hell she'd gone through in her father's house, but the few times she had, she'd immediately been treated differently. As if she was a powder keg ready to explode.

But Stuart's facial expression didn't change. He simply said, "That's why you're such a good nanny. You're determined to treat your charges the opposite way you were treated."

Monica was shocked by his insight. He was mostly right. The day she left her father's home, she swore that she'd never make a child feel the way *she* had for so long. Scared. Walking on eggshells, terrified of saying or doing the wrong thing to bring her father's wrath down on her. She tried to anticipate children's needs and wants before they had to ask.

Her throat closed up, and she fought to keep her emotions in check. How in the world did this man seem to know her so well after such a short period of time? It was unnerving, making Monica feel extremely uncomfortable.

And once again, as if he knew how she was feeling, he changed the subject. "You hungry?"

"It's not even five in the morning," Monica told him.

Stuart shrugged. "You're up. I'm up. Might as well start the day."

"I could eat," Monica said cautiously.

"As I said last night, I need to go to the store, so I don't have any eggs. But I've got pancake mix. I can also make some biscuits, and I think there's some bacon in the fridge too. And before you say anything, I realize none of that is super healthy. I'll pick up some fruit, oatmeal, eggs, and more milk today. I do have some canned peaches if you're craving fruit though."

Monica stared at him in confusion. He was being extremely nice, but she didn't want to be in his debt any more than she was already. "I can make something for myself," she said.

"I got it...unless you object to me fixing you breakfast?"

"I don't understand you," Monica blurted, frustration clear in her voice.

Stuart frowned. "I don't know what's going on in your head, but there's nothing to understand. You're a guest in my home, and I'm offering to make you something to eat."

"What do you want in return?" Monica asked.

His face registered his surprise—followed swiftly by irritation. Stuart stood up straight, no longer relaxed against his counter. "Nothing. Absolutely *nothing*. Hasn't anyone done something nice for you before without any strings?"

"No." Her answer was immediate.

"Well, that fucking sucks," Stuart said. "Guess I'll be the first...if you let me. Go shower, take your time. The place might not look like much, but I've got a kick-ass water heater. I'll make a bit of everything I've got and you can choose what you want to eat. If it'll make you feel better, after I get back from the store later, I'll let you make us lunch."

Monica relaxed. "Yeah, okay."

But her response didn't really seem to make Stuart any

happier. The frown stayed on his face until, finally, he sighed. "You're killin' me, Mo," he said softly. So quietly, Monica wasn't sure she heard him correctly. Then he gestured toward the hall with his head. "Go on. The bathroom's all yours."

She hesitated for a beat, wanting to stay and talk to Stuart more, yet relieved she had an out. In the end, old habits kicked in, and she fled.

Stuart made her nervous. She didn't understand him. He didn't act like she was used to people acting toward her. She knew she was standoffish and put off major "stay away" vibes, but Stuart didn't seem to see or feel them. He was treating her as if they were old friends. It was weird.

And at the same time, so incredibly tempting.

For years, Monica had longed to find a man she could trust. Who she could fall in love and have children with... but not someone in the military. Not someone like her father.

Many people who'd grown up like she did would be afraid to have kids of their own, but not her. She'd make them feel as if they were the most important people in her life, because they *would* be. She'd never hurt them, never treat them as if they were expendable, like she'd been.

Looking down at what remained of her left hand, Monica closed her eyes and did her best to block the memories that seeing her mangled flesh always brought back. The pain. The confusion. The fear.

Determined not to let this man past the shields she'd spent a lifetime erecting, Monica took a deep breath after locking herself in the bathroom. If Stuart wanted to make her breakfast, fine. She wouldn't read anything into it. She'd be gone in a day or so. Back to her predictable, somewhat lonely life.

# CHAPTER SIX

The day had gone by surprisingly quickly for Pid. He left Monica at his house while he ran out to get some grocery shopping done early, before the store got crowded. He'd hoped to find her more relaxed when he returned, but that hadn't been the case.

Elodie had stopped by, as he expected, with two casseroles and a bowl of saimin. She was practicing making Hawaiian dishes, and saimin was a soup dish with wheat egg noodles, seafood stock, green onions, thin slices of kamaboko, and Elodie had added shredded nori. Pid hadn't been so sure about the dish at first, but he'd grown to love it after living in Hawaii for a while.

Monica had been polite but distant. Pid could tell Elodie was a little disappointed, though he recognized the spark of determination in her eyes. It was obvious she would do whatever she could to make Monica loosen up.

After lunch, Lexie had stopped by with a stack of clothes for Monica to choose from. She hadn't seemed bothered by the other woman's reticence, babbling on happily about how Kenna was sorry she couldn't stop by, but hoped to meet Monica before she had to leave.

It was now dinnertime. Pid had dished up some of the chicken and rice casserole Elodie had brought over, and he and Monica were eating out on his deck. He had a small table out there he rarely used, but it seemed appropriate to do so now.

Monica hadn't talked much, but Pid tried not to take it personally. He'd never met anyone as quiet as she was. "I'm sorry you haven't gotten to see much of Oahu yet," he said, desperate for some sort of conversation.

Monica's gaze met his, and he watched her swallow carefully before picking up a napkin and daintily wiping her mouth. The woman had impeccable manners. Pid felt like a Neanderthal compared to her.

"It's been one day," she said after a moment.

"Still, this is an amazing place and I'd love to share some of it with you."

Monica shrugged.

Several minutes went by before he tried again. "You don't talk much." It wasn't really a question, so much as an observation.

She sighed and put down her fork. "At my house, it was frowned on to talk at the table."

"Really? I mean, I always thought dinner was a time when families caught up on what everyone had done during the day," Pid said.

"Not my family," Monica said. "Besides, Dad knew what my mother and I had done all day because he'd been right there."

"You didn't go to school?" Pid asked.

"No. I was homeschooled."

"Did you do any sports? Participate in any activities

outside the house?" Pid was fairly certain he knew the answer to that question, but asked anyway.

"No."

That was it. Just "no."

Pid was disappointed by her simple answers. Every minute he spent in her presence, he wanted to know more. He leaned his elbows on the table and said, "As you've seen, I'm not that keen on conventional rules. I'm messy. I argue with my boss. And I'm not overly concerned with always doing the polite thing."

"Like not putting your elbows on the table?" Monica asked.

She didn't smile, but Pid knew she was teasing him.

"Exactly," he said with a grin. "It's obvious you don't like to talk about your family, and that's okay. But in my home, you can do whatever you want. Talk with your mouth open, eat dessert first, lay around and watch TV all day. I don't care. I just want you to relax, Mo. I have a feeling you haven't relaxed much in your life, and while you're here in Hawaii, it's a perfect time for you to do just that. No one here will judge you. Or hurt you. Or make you do anything you don't want to...well, besides be here in the first place," he finished lamely.

Monica stared at him with her big blue eyes. He could see the confusion there, and the longing. For what, he didn't know, but he wanted to give her anything and everything she needed to feel more comfortable. The kicker was that he knew she wouldn't ask for it. Her left hand was a painful reminder of what happened when she asked for assistance with anything.

"Mo?" she asked.

Pid chuckled. Figured that was what she focused on

out of everything he'd said. "Yeah. You seem like a Mo to me."

"What does a Mo seem like?" she asked.

Pid shrugged. "You."

Her lips twitched, but not enough for her dimple to show itself. "You're weird," she said.

Pid laughed outright at that. "Yup. I'm an electronics nerd, as I'm sure you gathered by the amount of computer parts in your room. I'm clumsy as hell. I live in Hawaii, yet prefer rainy, cloudy days to sunny ones. And my house is usually messy as all get out. I'm weird all right. But I am who I am, and I'm all right with that. Life is short," he told her. "I could live my life trying to be perfect, to live up to the expectations of everyone I meet, but that would drive me crazy. I'd be unhappy and an asshole. So I let most of that shit roll off my back."

Monica's gaze was glued to his as if she was soaking in his words, straight to her soul. So Pid continued.

"I had a good childhood. My parents were great, and even when I fucked up by skipping school and smoking pot with some friends, I always knew they loved me, and I was never scared of what they'd do to me if I made a poor decision. I can't pretend to understand anything about your childhood...but I *can* admit that I'm glad your father is dead. I feel sorry for your mom, while at the same time, I'm pissed at her for not protecting you the way she should have.

"But, Mo, somehow, you survived. You got out of there. And look at you. You're successful, your charges love you enough to make sure you were safe from that situation in Algeria, and you've got a backbone of steel."

"I have baggage," she said.

"Who doesn't?" Pid replied. He wasn't sure how they'd

ended up having this intense conversation, but he wasn't sorry about it. "I'm not trying to make light of what happened to you, but honestly, the human race is fucked up. I've seen things I never want to think or talk about ever again. Horrible things. But I've made a conscious decision to not dwell on them. If I did, I'd be curled up in a ball somewhere, my brain a pile of mush.

"What happened to you doesn't define who are you. It says more about the kind of people your parents were than it does you. Your dad was an abusive bully and your mom was weak. You are neither of those things. You're a survivor. You're Monica Collins—and you're pretty damn amazing."

Pid couldn't regret the tears he saw in Monica's eyes. He wanted her to know how much he admired her. He had a feeling no one had ever praised her before.

Eventually, she got control over her emotions—which again, didn't surprise Pid—before saying, "I guess Mo is a better nickname than being called Stupid."

He smirked. "Yup."

"Stuart?"

He loved hearing his given name on her lips. "Yeah, Mo?"

"I'm not good at this."

"At what?"

"This. Idle chitchat. Being...friendly. Other than with kids."

"You don't want to talk, you don't have to talk," Pid told her. "It doesn't bother me. I can babble away. I just don't want you to be *afraid* to talk to me. You want to talk about makeup and nail polish, awesome. You want to talk politics and the state of the world, fine. But if you want to sit there and let me run my mouth, that's completely all right too.

"You're safe with me, Mo. I know right now, you might not believe me, but for as long as you're here, whether that be a day or a week or a month, I give you my word. I'll even go out on a limb and say the same for my teammates. Mustang, Midas, Aleck, Jag, and Slate are also safe zones for you. And their women. Elodie, Lexie, and Kenna. Hell, even Carly and Ashlyn. You don't have to be anyone but who you are around them. Understand?"

"No."

Pid chuckled. "I love your honesty."

"It's just that...I know myself. I'm standoffish. Downright unfriendly at times. People don't like me," Monica said.

Pid's heart nearly broke at her words. "*I* like you," he said quietly.

"But you're weird," she said.

He couldn't help but smile. "True. To be honest, so are you. We're all weird in our own way. Be your own kind of weird, Mo. Own it. Who cares that you're an introvert? Everyone in the world can't be an extrovert. We need people who prefer to stand on the sidelines and watch and observe. To be the voice of reason when we need it the most. Just know that whatever happens while you're here in Hawaii, you've got people who will have your back."

Monica looked down at the food on her plate and took a deep breath before lifting her head and meeting his gaze once more. "This is really good. Elodie is an amazing cook."

And just like that, the heavy emotional talk was done. Pid was all right with that. He'd made his point. "That she is. Her story is pretty amazing too."

"Her story?" Monica asked.

"Eat," Pid said, gesturing to her plate with his head, "and I'll tell you how we met her. We were on a ship near the Middle East, discussing how we were going to get onboard a hijacked cargo ship, when a female voice sounded over the radio..."

For the next twenty minutes, Pid explained Elodie's harrowing story and how she came to be living on Hawaii and married to Mustang. By the time he was finished, Monica had cleaned her plate and was leaning forward, listening with interest.

"It's hard to believe all that happened, considering how open and friendly she is," Monica said.

"I think Mustang has a lot to do with that. Also, she's a naturally friendly person. She had to keep her guard up while on the run, but now that she's safe and happy, she's more herself again. And she's definitely done with working on a fishing charter."

The dimple Pid had longed to see finally made an appearance as Monica laughed. Actually laughed out loud. "I can't blame her."

"She's now working with Lexie at Food For All, a charity organization that helps feed those in need with ready-made lunches. She wasn't happy with the bland and somewhat gross peanut butter and jelly sandwiches and potato chips that were being given out. So now she's on a mission to provide healthy, gourmet lunches to their clients."

"That's cool."

"Yeah," Pid agreed. He hadn't noticed that clouds had moved in until he heard the sound of raindrops hitting the cover of his deck. It had also gotten cooler. "You want to go in?" he asked.

Monica shrugged. "If you do."

"What do *you* want?" Pid asked. "You don't have to do whatever I want."

She bit her lip and sighed. "Sorry. Habit."

"I know," he said gently. And he did. "I personally love rainstorms. And while I'm not sure I miss the extreme cold I grew up with in Alaska, I'd much rather be chilly than hot. But if you're cold, you can go inside. Or you can grab a blanket and come back out. Or if you're comfortable, you can stay right where you are. Or you can go inside and watch TV. Or grab something for dessert. Or read a book. Or go to sleep."

For the second time in minutes, Monica chuckled. "All right, all right. I get it. The world is my oyster."

"Exactly," Pid said with satisfaction. "And for the record, I think I'm going to stay out here for a while and listen to the rain. Feel free to join me or not. It's up to you."

"What about the dishes?" she asked.

"I'll get them later."

"Later as in tonight, or three days from now?" Monica asked.

Pid snorted. "Was that a joke?"

"Maybe," she said with a small grin.

"Smart-ass. I'll bring them in later. And in honor of you being here, I'll even put them straight into the dishwasher."

"I can do it now," she suggested.

"Nope. Leave them. You're my guest. And guests don't do dishes."

He thought she was going to protest for a moment, but then she nodded. "I wouldn't mind sitting out here for a while."

Internally, Pid jumped up and down and cheered. Outwardly, he smiled at her and said, "Cool."

For the next thirty minutes, the two of them sat in silence, lost in their own thoughts as they watched and listened to the rain.

Then Monica said, "I think I'm going to go inside. If that's okay."

Pid didn't like that she was essentially asking permission, but the fact that she was making the first move to go inside was a step in the right direction. "No problem. I'm gonna sit out here for a while longer."

"I can bring the dishes inside when I go," she offered.

"Nope. I'll get them. I'm thinking we need to leave around seven-thirty tomorrow morning to get to the base by eight," he told her.

"Okay. I'll be ready." She scooted her chair back and stood.

When she reached the door to go back inside, Pid said, "Mo?"

Turning, she said, "Yes?"

"I'm sorry for the reason you're here, and about being forced to come here to talk to the commander, but I'm pleased to get to know you better."

She stared at him for a beat before nodding and slipping into the house.

Sighing, Pid closed his eyes and rested his head on the back of his chair. The sound of the steady rain soothed him, but he wished he knew better how to make Monica feel more comfortable. He had no idea how long she'd be in Hawaii; it was entirely possible she'd talk with Huttner tomorrow, then be on a flight back to wherever the ambassador and his family were in the evening.

But it was also possible the commander would want to

keep her close until he found this mystery man he'd apparently been searching for. Monica probably wouldn't like that, but Pid didn't find the prospect unpleasant in the least.

He hadn't lied. He liked Monica. Yes, she was quirky and hard to get to know. But that just made him even more interested in chipping away at the shield she'd put around herself. He also had a feeling the more time she spent around Elodie and the other women, the more she'd win them over too.

Pid stayed outside for another thirty minutes, until the rain tapered off, then he went inside. He rinsed their dishes and put them in the dishwasher just as he promised he would. There wasn't much else to put away around the house, so he headed for his bedroom. He stopped outside Monica's door and didn't hear anything from inside.

As he stood there, an idea formed. He thought about how he'd first met her and some of the things she'd said since then. It was a pretty crazy thought, but the more he considered it, the more he wanted to do it.

He'd need to get permission from the owner of the house, and his plan only made sense if Monica was there for longer than a day or two. He'd have to wait and see what happened in her meeting with the commander tomorrow.

As he continued to his room, Pid felt guilty for actually hoping Huttner would request that she stay in Hawaii. It wasn't fair to her, she deserved to get back to her life, but there was a lot Pid wanted to show her. His mind swam with the places he'd like to take her to, all the special things he wanted to share about Hawaii.

He supposed he should be alarmed at how excited he

was over the prospect of spending more time with the wounded woman, but he wasn't.

Pid fell asleep a couple hours later, thinking about Monica...and when he woke up just three hours after, he had a sudden urge to get up and make sure all was well. He'd never had that feeling before, but with Mo in the house, he wanted to make sure the doors and windows were locked up tight.

Not even questioning the need, Pid rolled out of bed and silently went through the house, double checking the locks. Everything was as it should be and when he climbed into bed once more, he was satisfied that for tonight at least, Monica was safe.

Tomorrow would hopefully bring a lot more answers as to what would happen in the immediate future with his houseguest, and hopefully about whatever was going on with the man their commander was so desperate to identify. While Pid wasn't thrilled about Huttner's actions, he couldn't deny he was glad to have a chance to get to know Monica better.

# CHAPTER SEVEN

Monica sat stiffly in the chair across from Stuart's Naval commander. Dylan Huttner was an imposing man, and it didn't help that he reminded her a lot of her father. He had similar brown hair and eyes, as well as an authoritative presence. He was a man who was used to being obeyed and not questioned.

But in other ways, he was as far from her dad as he could get. The commander was obviously in great shape, unlike her father the last time she'd seen him. He was also doing his best to put her at ease, which was something Darren Collins never worried about.

She still couldn't believe Stuart had spoken to his superior officer the way he had when they'd arrived this morning. When he'd been informed that he wasn't allowed to sit in on the interview, Stuart had pitched a fit. There was no other way to describe it. Monica was sure he was going to get court martialed, or whatever it was called in the Navy, but after a tense moment, the commander finally nodded once.

"It'll be fine," Stuart had told her before steering her

into the conference room they were currently occupying. The chair she was sitting in was surprisingly comfortable. She'd kind of expected a metal folding chair and a spotlight. That was ridiculous, of course, but she hadn't expected the cushioned swivel chairs, the glasses and pitcher of water, and the muted lighting. If she didn't know better, she would've thought she was in some high-end business conference room. Although, wasn't that what the Navy was? A business?

Her gaze flicked to the other man in the room. Mustang, Stuart's team leader, was also sitting in on the interrogation. That's not what the men were calling this, but that's what it felt like. She was there against her will, and it sure felt as if she was being blamed for something.

"Tell me what happened the day of the evacuation. And don't leave anything out," Commander Huttner said without preliminaries.

Monica wanted to roll her eyes, but she refrained. There was no point in antagonizing the man. Even if he'd given her no choice in the matter, he'd let her stay at Stuart's home, and had let him remain in the room.

So she started the retelling of what had happened in Algeria. She explained how she'd been concerned when the Laws family hadn't returned when they said they would, and how she was considering going to the embassy on her own when she heard a sound at the sliding glass door at the back of the house. She described the man she saw, the feeling he'd given her, and how she'd hidden in the secret room in Desmond and Ophelia's bedroom. She told the commander about watching the man on the security monitors as he rifled through the rooms.

She didn't leave anything out in her retelling, including the fact she'd been prepared to shoot Stuart and Slate.

She was describing how they'd escaped the house when the commander interrupted her.

"Can you tell me more about the man who shot out the door?"

"Like what?"

"Go over what he looked like again."

Monica mentally sighed. She'd already given him as good a description as she could. But she didn't let her irritation show. She simply told him again. "He was shorter than Stuart and Slate," she said. "Older too. I'm not great with ages, but if I had to guess, I'd say anywhere between forty-five and fifty-five? He had a piece of cloth pulled up over his mouth and nose, but his hair was visible, and it was black with gray streaks. Not a lot, but they were there. I know that doesn't automatically make him older, but that's the impression I got from the lines around his eyes and from his overall demeanor. He was in shape. His eyes were dark. I'd say they were black, but that's not really possible. So probably a dark brown."

Monica stopped speaking and waited for the commander's next question.

"What else?"

She frowned. "What else *what*?"

"What else can you tell me about him? I need more than that if I'm going to ID him."

"Um...he had a tattoo on his left forearm," Monica said.

The commander leaned forward. "Of what?"

"I don't know."

Monica jumped when the man slammed his palm on the table and barked, "Think!"

"Sir—" Mustang began, but Stuart wasn't as composed as his friend.

He abruptly stood and put a hand on the table as he leaned toward his boss. "Not happening," he said in a tone Monica hadn't heard from him before. It was low and extremely pissed off. "You and I both know forcing Miss Collins to be here wasn't exactly legal. But she still came. She's trying to help, and you scaring the shit out of her isn't going to make her remember anything else. Ease. Off."

Monica held her breath. She was certain Stuart was about to be thrown in the brig any second. She had no idea if the Navy still used such a thing, but she didn't think there was any way the commander would put up with one of his subordinates speaking to him like that. And she was right.

"You know I can put a letter of reprimand in your file for continually talking to me like, right?" the commander asked Stuart in a stern voice.

Monica tensed further. She didn't like being the reason Stuart might get in trouble.

"I'm sorry, Sir," Stuart replied. "But Monica is doing the best she can."

To her surprise, the commander sat back in his chair. "I know." He turned to her. "I appreciate your assistance."

Monica was surprised at the man's sudden acquiescence.

He then stood and began to pace. "This situation is delicate," the commander told them.

"Then explain it to us," Mustang said. "When I tried to discuss it yesterday, you said you'd brief me later. It's later."

"Not in front of a civilian."

"Monica might be a civilian, but in order to work in the ambassador's home, she had to get security clearance," Stuart pointed out. "And she's involved. It's obvious she's one of the best leads you have to catch this guy, whoever he is, and it seems increasingly obvious her life may be in danger because of him. The least you can do after forcing her to upend her existence and come to Hawaii is share why IDing this guy is so important."

The commander released a frustrated sigh. "Because this guy is good. *Really* fucking good. He's got an unending number of aliases and he's able to slip into any country he wants without leaving a trace. His MO is the same everywhere he goes. He picks countries dealing with civil unrest and blends in with the protestors. He incites them to violence, leads the charge in looting, helping himself to whatever he can get his hands on, then he disappears like the wind when things have spiraled out of control."

"How do you know all this?" Mustang asked.

"Because he's been taunting us," the commander answered.

"How?" Stuart asked.

"By sending encrypted emails."

"To who?" Stuart pressed.

"High-ranking Naval commanders. Myself, Storm North, Dag Creasy, Patrick Hurt, and others. *SEAL* commanders," Huttner clarified.

"Shit," Mustang swore.

"He really *was* a SEAL?" Monica asked softly.

"Probably," the commander verified. "I'd bet my career on it."

"Could it be someone from a team that's been assigned to the area?" Stuart asked.

"No. I've already checked. There were two other SEAL teams helping with the extraction of civilians in Algiers, and they were all accounted for when Monica said she saw this guy. He's older, like Monica suggested, and I'm thinking he's retired...or maybe he was kicked out of the Navy and now he's pissed."

"And using his training to 'stick it to the man' so-to-speak," Mustang said.

"Exactly. But he's escalating. There was a particular incident in Hong Kong a while back, and this asshole claimed to have beaten, raped, and killed three women in the midst of the chaos...which was later confirmed. Same thing in Barcelona, Beirut, Santiago...he takes great pride in emailing details about the people he's killed."

The commander paused in his pacing to reach for the tablet he'd been taking notes on while interviewing Monica. He clicked on it a few times, then handed it to Mustang. "While you were traveling back from Algeria, he sent that to me and the other commanders."

Monica itched to see what the email said, but she sat quietly as Mustang read the screen. Without a word, he passed the tablet to Stuart. Monica studied his face as he read, and it was obvious whatever the mystery man had sent, it wasn't good. Stuart's jaw ticked in agitation and his breathing sped up.

"Damn," he said when he was done, handing the tablet back across the table to Huttner.

"This behavior is partly why I insisted Ms. Collins accompany you," the commander said.

"What'd he say?" Monica asked, not able to keep quiet anymore.

"It wasn't what he said, so much as the picture that accompanied his email," Huttner answered.

"Can I see it?" Monica asked.

All three men tensed. "No," Mustang and Stuart said in unison. The same time their commander said, "Yes."

"She doesn't need to see that," Stuart insisted.

"Maybe if she does, she'll understand that I'm not trying to be an asshole," Huttner countered. "She's one of the only people we know of who's seen this guy, who might be able to identify him. If my assumption is right, and he's a former SEAL, maybe she can ID him from pictures."

"You know the chances of that are slim to none," Stuart argued. "He had his face covered, and there's no telling how long it's been since he was active duty."

"She's all we have right now. And the longer he's out there, the more people are in danger," Huttner insisted.

Stuart and his commander glared at each other, neither backing down.

"If you're worried about me seeing something gruesome, don't be. I've seen a dead body before."

At her words, all three men turned to stare at her in disbelief.

"*What?*" Stuart asked.

She couldn't really blame him for being shocked. Her declaration had come out of left field. But she wanted to assure the men that she wasn't going to faint away at whatever picture the former SEAL had emailed.

She addressed the commander. "My father wasn't a good man. He was paranoid and obsessed with security around our property. When I was twelve, a man was hunting and accidentally wandered onto our land. He stepped into one of the traps my dad had set out. His leg was completely mangled, and he was in a lot of pain. My father made me go with him when he confronted the man, and when he didn't believe his story that he'd been hunting and had gotten turned around, my dad shot him in the head. Point blank. Then he made me help him drag the man's body to his truck and go with him up into the mountains, where I had to help dig a hole to bury him."

Monica could've heard a pin drop in the room, it was so silent.

She'd been so eager to assure the men that she could handle whatever was in the picture that she hadn't thought through her confession. She began to shake, wondering if she'd be thrown into the brig herself, now that she'd admitted to not only being a witness to murder, but helping to dispose of a body.

"When I escaped my father, I wrote an anonymous letter to the police," she continued softly, not able to stop her shaking. "I told them what happened and where they could find the man's body. I knew his family had to be suffering during the years he'd been missing. Wondering where he was and what happened to him. All I'm saying is that, if that guy sent a picture of something violent...I'm not going to fall apart by seeing it."

To her surprise, instead of immediately hauling her up and putting her in handcuffs, the commander sighed and sat back down in his chair, studying her.

Stuart reached over and took her left hand in his, holding it tightly. For once, she didn't flinch at someone touching her mangled fingers. His thumb brushed back and forth soothingly over the back of her hand.

"Tell me your father went to jail," Mustang said.

Monica shook her head. "I can't. The police investigated, but I can only assume my dad had moved the body at some point. So there was no evidence against him except my word. But karma got him in the end. He fell out of a deer stand and froze to death one winter."

"Good."

The single word was said with such feeling and satisfaction, Monica couldn't help but blow out a breath in relief.

"Show her," Stuart said.

The commander slid the tablet across the table and Monica picked it up with her right hand, as Stuart hadn't let go of her left.

She inhaled sharply at seeing the picture in the email. A petite blonde woman was lying on a pink comforter. She was nude, her blue eyes staring sightlessly up at the ceiling, her limbs obviously posed in a starfish position. There was a bright red pool of blood around her body, glaringly obscene against the pretty pink flowers of the bedding. A knife was sticking out of her chest, right where her heart would be.

Swallowing hard, realizing the woman kind of looked like her, Monica turned her attention to the words accompanying the picture.

*I'd like you to meat my latest work of art. Isn't she pretty? Pictures are better in the raw, makes the blood stand out more. As always, there will be no fingerprints, no DNA evidence, nothing that will show I was here at all. I'm no bull in a china shop. I was taught by the best. They said I was insane...does this look like the work of an insane man? The answer is no. I'm in control at all times. I know exactly what I'm doing, and you'll never catch me until I want to be caught.*

"Holy shit," Monica breathed. As much as she didn't really want to look at the picture again, she turned her attention to it once more.

"What do you see?" Stuart asked quietly.

"It was quick," Monica said. "She doesn't have any defensive wounds on her hands, unless he cleaned them up. It reminds me of putting an animal out of its misery after being shot. That was my dad's favorite part of hunting. Plunging a knife into the animal's heart."

"She's right," Huttner said.

Ignoring him, Monica continued. "And that knife looks a lot like the one you gave me." She was well aware that Stuart hadn't exactly given her his K-BAR to keep, but it was a moot point at the moment.

"I noticed that too," Mustang said. "It's the kind most SEALs are issued and prefer to use."

Monica took a deep breath and pushed the tablet back across the table toward the commander. She tightened her hold on Stuart's hand with her thumb, needing the connection with another human right now. "I didn't get a good look at his tattoo. I mean, I did, but it's a blur in my mind. It was all black, I know that much. And it took up most of his forearm. It might've had a snake on it? I'm sorry. I was more worried about running and making sure he didn't find me than memorizing identifying marks."

"It's more than we had before," the commander said. "Thank you."

"That email sounds off," Mustang noted.

Stuart nodded. "It's grammatically correct, except for him using m-e-a-t instead of m-e-e-t."

"He claims he left no trace behind," Mustang said, "but that last line makes it sound as if he wants someone to figure out who he is."

"But what's his motivation?" Stuart asked.

"Revenge?" Mustang asked with a shrug.

"If he got kicked out, maybe he's trying to prove that the Navy made a mistake," Stuart said.

"And that part about being insane...maybe records should be searched for anyone who was discharged for a mental condition? Something that maybe wouldn't quality for a disability pension?" Mustang asked, turning to the commander.

"Already on it," the older man reassured him.

Watching Stuart and his team leader brainstorm was fascinating. They bounced ideas off each other seamlessly and were definitely on the same page.

"You can see why it's so important we catch this guy," Commander Huttner told Monica. His chocolate-brown gaze bored into her own, making it hard for her to look away. "He escalated from causing disturbances and inciting riots, to theft, and then murder. He has to be stopped. And you're the only one who's come face-to-face with him and lived to talk about it—that we know of. You're a very lucky woman, Ms. Collins. There's every possibility that it could've been you on that bed with the knife in your heart. I need your help. The country needs your help. Women literally around the world need your help to help prevent them from being his next victim."

He was laying it on thick...but it was working. Monica knew she'd feel extremely guilty if something happened to someone else if she could've prevented it. Still... "I'm not sure what else I can tell you," she said quietly.

"Maybe you can look through dossiers of former SEALs. See if anything about them strikes a chord."

"How many files are you talking about?" Monica asked.

Huttner winced and dropped his gaze. "SEALs make up only about one percent of Navy personnel. But we'll do our best to narrow it down for you. By age and dishonorable or mental discharge."

Monica had a feeling even though he was trying to downplay how many files would still remain. Still, if they were narrowed down, at least that was something. Otherwise, she could probably study files for eight hours a day for a year and still not make it through all the former SEALs that were out there.

Regardless, what other choice did she have? Could she really just leave and tell the commander "good luck" and go about her life? What if this guy decided he wanted to make sure she couldn't pass on any information to the government? She was apparently the one who got away, and it wouldn't be too hard to find her if she continued to work for the ambassador.

She looked over at Stuart, surprised to see his gaze locked on her. She expected him to try to convince her to stay, as his boss was obviously doing, but he shocked her when he said, "Whatever you decide, you've got my support. This isn't an easy decision to make, and I'm sorry you're in the middle of it."

"If you stay, the Navy will make it worth your while," the commander said. "I'm sure a room will open up in the lodge soon, and you can move in there. You'll get a stipend for living expenses. I'll have a word with the ambassador as well. Make sure he knows that you're serving your country and not just quitting for the hell of it."

"He'll hire someone else," Monica said, looking at the man across the table. She felt a pang of remorse at the thought of never seeing August and Remington again. But their dad would find another nanny, and while she hoped they'd always have fond memories of her, they'd adjust soon enough.

"Then the Navy will help you find a job once this is over," the commander countered.

Monica pressed her lips together. She had no idea how long IDing this man would take, but she had a feeling it wasn't going to be a quick thing. The man was obviously very good at staying under the radar. And if the commander and all the other investigators in the Navy hadn't been able to figure out who he was, she didn't have high hopes that she'd come in and ID him just like that. If she decided to stay, she'd probably be here for quite a while.

Could she do it? Could she stomach being around military men all day while she went through files? She honestly wasn't sure.

Then she felt Stuart squeeze her hand once more. Her hand with the missing fingers.

Realization hit her hard and fast. She hadn't known this man even a week, and she felt comfortable enough with him to let him touch her mangled stubs. She didn't feel panicky or the need to rip out of his grasp, as she had just days ago. It was confusing, and once more she felt completely out of her comfort zone.

Despite that, she found herself saying quietly, "I'll stay and do what I can to help."

Huttner let out a relieved breath. "Great. I'll set up a computer you can use to start looking through files. If you're willing, I'll contact an interrogator who's really good at what she does, who might be able to help you to remember something you don't realize you know. And there's a hypnotist that the Navy has used in the past. I'll see about arranging that too."

"Easy, Sir," Stuart said quietly. "Monica's said she'll stay and help, there's no need to do everything in one day. She needs clothes and other essentials. She arrived in Hawaii with nothing. Paperwork needs to be done to set up the allowance as well."

"Right. Of course. But she'll need to come in every weekday and look at files."

"She will."

Monica should've been annoyed that the two men were talking about her life as if she wasn't sitting right there... but it felt too good to have Stuart sticking up for her, despite how nervous he made her. She wouldn't have minded starting on the files right then and there, but admittedly, she was overwhelmed. While there a chance she'd get lucky and be able to quickly pinpoint the man the commander was desperate to find, it wasn't likely.

"I'll keep you updated about an opening at the lodge," Huttner said.

Monica didn't know if he was talking to her or Stuart, but supposed it didn't matter.

"Um...am I in trouble for what I told you?" she asked. She didn't really want to bring it up again, but would rather know now if the commander planned to report the fact that she was an accessory to murder, rather than be surprised by police showing up at her doorstep later.

For the first time since she'd met the commander, she saw kindness in his eyes. "No. You were twelve. It was a long time ago...and I have the feeling you went through hell with the man who called himself your father."

"I did," she whispered, feeling exhausted. She also felt off-kilter. The meeting today hadn't gone anything like she thought it would. In her experience, military men were no-nonsense hardasses who didn't care about anything other than their own agenda. And while it was obvious Stuart's commander was professional and no-nonsense, and his frustration got the best of him for a short moment, it was clear he also had a soft side. Which was bewildering.

While being here hadn't been something she would've agreed to do in a million years, she was kind of surprised to find that she wasn't feeling more antsy to do what she was asked then get the hell out of Hawaii as fast as possible. Maybe that therapist who'd suggested she actually spend time around military people knew what she was talking about after all. She was learning that, while intense, most of the men she'd spent time with since the shit hit the fan in Algeria were nothing like her father.

It was a massive relief.

Huttner stood, and Stuart and Mustang did the same, so Monica followed suit.

"Thank you for being so understanding about the situation," the commander said. "I realize I used my authority to force you to come to Hawaii, but I hope you can maybe now understand the urgency of the situation, and why I did what I did."

"Yes, Sir," Monica said, not sure what else she could say at that point.

"You'll bring her back tomorrow?" the older man asked Stuart.

He sighed. "After lunch. We have our after-action-review then, and she can start to look through profiles while we're in our meeting."

Monica held her breath, waiting to see if the commander would agree.

"That'll be fine." Then he turned and headed out of the conference room.

Monica let out the breath in a long whoosh.

"Ready to go?" Stuart asked, as if nothing about the last hour had been out of the ordinary. She nodded.

"I'll talk to the rest of the team," Mustang said. "Bring them up to speed."

"Good."

"I want to catch this guy," Mustang said.

"Same," Stuart agreed.

"Being a SEAL is one of the most prestigious professions someone can have. And to know that this guy is using what he learned against his country, against *other* countries, and against women...it's repulsive and unacceptable," Mustang said in a heated tone.

"Agreed."

Monica remained still, feeling the angry vibes coming off Stuart's friend and not wanting him to turn his ire her way.

But Mustang took a deep breath and seemed to contain his fury. "Sorry," he told her.

Monica blinked in surprise.

"I'm just pissed way the hell off."

"I bet Elodie can help make you feel better," Stuart said with a small grin.

"Hell yeah, she can. Just being around her makes me relax. Monica, thank you. I know this is a shitty situation and one you don't deserve to be in the middle of. But if there's anything Elodie or I can do to make it easier for you, just let us know."

"Um...okay," Monica said, knowing she would do nothing of the sort.

Stuart reached out and shook Mustang's hand. "Thanks for coming in with us today."

"Anytime. The commander should've let us know about this guy before now. We could've been on the lookout when we were in Algeria. Especially considering it was just the kind of situation the asshole would try to take advantage of."

"Agreed," Stuart said again.

"Oh, by the way, did you happen to talk to Aleck this morning?"

"No, why?"

"Apparently he's not willing to wait any longer to marry

Kenna. They're currently planning a luau wedding," Mustang said.

"No shit?" Stuart asked with a grin.

"No shit. I guess the concierge guy, Robert, has taken it upon himself to give them the best wedding ever, right there on the beach at the Coral Springs condos."

"Awesome! Can't wait to hear the details," Stuart said.

"Same. See you tomorrow," Mustang said as he walked down the hallway.

"Luau?" Monica asked when it was just the two of them.

Stuart grinned. "Oh, yeah. It's the most Hawaiian thing ever. You'll love it."

"Oh, but...why would I be invited?" she asked as Stuart put his hand on the small of her back and encouraged her to precede him down the hall.

"Are you serious?"

"Yes?" she asked, looking up at him.

Stuart waited until they were outside and headed for his minivan in the parking lot to say, "I know this will be difficult for you to understand, but as long as you're here, you're a part of our group. You'll be invited to barbeques and girls' night out, and you're certainly under my team's protection. If Aleck and Kenna get married while you're here, you'll definitely be invited."

Monica was speechless. She'd never met anyone like Stuart and his friends before. They were generous to a fault. They didn't *know* her. Probably wouldn't even like her much, yet Stuart was telling her that they'd act as if she was one of their best friends. It made no sense.

"You'll see," Stuart added, as if he could read her mind and knew how confused she was.

He waited until she was settled in the passenger seat

before closing her door and heading around to the driver's side. "I figured we could swing by the Alana Moana Mall on the way home. While Lexie did a good job in guessing your size and bringing you some things to tide you over, I'm sure you want to pick out your own clothes. And don't worry about the cost. The stipend you'll get will more than cover whatever you need to buy."

"Okay." Monica had never really liked shopping, but she wouldn't mind picking out some things for herself, like he'd said.

"And there's something else I'd like to talk to you about."

Monica braced.

"I know the commander said he'd let us know when a space opened up at the lodge...but I'd like you to consider staying at my place."

Monica was genuinely flabbergasted. She figured Stuart would be more than happy to see her move out of his space sooner than later.

"I honestly think you'll be more comfortable at my house than on the base. I've seen how stiff and uncomfortable you get every time you see men and women in uniform. And since you'll be spending quite a bit of time on base looking over those files, having a place where you don't have to keep your guard up all the time will probably be good for you."

He had a great point, but Monica would never dream of being a burden. Not to anyone. If he was offering his house out of a sense of obligation, she'd decline in a heartbeat.

Stuart went on. "And...I like having you there. I hadn't realized how quiet and lonely my place was until having you there all day yesterday. Even when we weren't talking, it was nice to not be alone. The rest of the guys are busy with their women now, and I have to admit, I miss hanging out with someone else."

"Mustang, Midas, and Aleck are the only ones who have girlfriends or wives, though, right?" Monica asked, not immediately answering his question.

"Good memory. Yes. But while Jag and Slate might not be dating Carly and Ashlyn officially, they're definitely interested. And they're patient. Jag spends a lot of time checking in on Carly, who still hasn't recovered from something her ex did, and Slate spends most of his spare time trying to rein in Ash, without much luck. She's a spit-fire for sure. Slate has his hands full with her."

Stuart chuckled, and Monica could only sit and stare at him as he drove them toward the mall.

"Anyway, if you truly don't want to stay at my place, that's okay. But know that I definitely don't mind you being there and would love the company."

Truthfully, Monica *didn't* want to stay on the base. She was trying not to let her experiences and fear rule her life, but being surrounded by military men all the time might not be the best thing for her psyche. "I'll stay as long as I'm not in the way," she said.

Stuart beamed at her. "Great. If you don't mind, I'd like to stop at the hardware store before we head home too."

"For what?" she asked.

"I want to put a better lock on your door so you really feel safe."

"That's not necessary," Monica said, though she couldn't help feeling a twinge of relief. She liked Stuart, but that didn't mean she completely trusted him. He was still military. And if they got to know each other better, he might get some ideas in his head about their relationship.

No matter how many times she told herself that Stuart wasn't like her father, a niggling of a doubt remained.

"It is. But there's something else I've got planned too, and I need to get some supplies."

"What's that?"

"It's a surprise," he said with a small grin.

Monica couldn't help but be curious. She opened her mouth to ask more questions, but he turned left into a parking garage and said, "We're here."

Mentally shrugging, Monica let it drop. She found herself looking forward to sitting on the back deck of Stuart's house and not thinking about much of anything for a while. Her brain hurt. She'd had to think about too many bad memories that day, not to mention the fact that as hard as she tried, she couldn't picture the tattoo that had been on the SEAL's arm. She had a feeling that would be one of the most important keys to figuring out the man's identity.

And somehow, even though she'd only been there a short time, the cozy house surrounded by trees felt more like home than anywhere else she'd ever lived.

# CHAPTER EIGHT

It was hard to believe an entire week had gone by since Pid had returned from Algeria with Monica. After the AAR, he'd requested a few days off so he could finish the surprise he was making for his houseguest. He drove her to the base each morning, accompanying her to the small office where Commander Huttner had requisitioned a computer for her to go through the files of former SEALs.

It was a daunting project, but Monica didn't seem put off by it. She seemed more...resigned. It was obvious she wasn't super excited about having to look through all the pictures on file, but she hadn't refused either.

While she was at the base, Pid worked as efficiently as he could at his house to finish the surprise he'd planned. She'd been intrigued by the mess he was making as he cut and measured boards, but hadn't complained about sawdust on the floors or all the hand tools he'd left sitting around.

But today was the day he could show Monica what he'd been working on. This morning, his landlord—who was a general contractor—came over and helped him with part of the project.

Pid then asked Aleck to come over in the afternoon to help him finish, and somehow the entire team had shown up. But he was grateful. He hadn't gone into Monica's room before today, except once to measure, because he hadn't wanted to give her a head's up about the surprise. So having the five extra sets of hands was extremely beneficial. The team managed to finish the entire project by the end of the day.

As Pid stood back and studied their work, Midas slapped him on the back. "It looks good, Pid."

"If I didn't know what I was looking for, I wouldn't even know it was there," Jag agreed.

Pid eyed the room critically. It wasn't perfect. He didn't have the time or the knowledge to physically move the window to even out the dimensions of the room, but he thought it would be okay.

"What are the odds Monica's gonna be able to ID this guy?" Slate asked.

Mustang had left five minutes ago to pick up Monica from the base and bring her home. She'd probably be surprised Pid wasn't retrieving her, like he had every other day this week, but he needed to clean up at least a little bit before she got home.

Pid sighed and leaned over to grab some tools from the floor. The rest of the guys followed his lead and began to clean up, so the room would appear just as Monica had last seen it when she'd left that morning. Almost.

"Honestly? Slim to none," he told Slate.

"That's what I thought," his friend replied.

"It's really an impossible task," Midas threw in. "There are thousands of former SEALs out there between the ages of forty-five and fifty-five. And if her guess of his age is off, that adds thousands more. I'm guessing she'll have to look through *all* of them if narrowing the field down based on discharge type doesn't help. *And* the guy's file photo could've been taken when he was much younger."

"I know," Pid said.

"And the tattoo isn't very useful, as he could've gotten it after he left the Navy," Midas said.

"Not to mention the fact that his face was covered," Aleck threw in.

"I *know*," Pid said again.

"So what's the plan?" Jag asked. "She lives here forever in this little fortress you've built for her?"

"No," Pid said in annoyance.

There was no doubt Monica was a prickly little thing, but damned if she hadn't grown on him in the week he'd known her. He didn't want her living in his guest room for the rest of her life. He wouldn't mind eventually seeing if maybe they were compatible as *more* than friends and roommates.

He was well aware it would take time for her to learn to trust him. She didn't trust *anyone*, as far as he could tell, but especially not military members, which ate at him. A woman like her, so strong and brave after everything she'd gone through, shouldn't go through life closed off and afraid because of one man.

He had no idea if he could be the one to help Monica let down her guard and learn to enjoy life, but he wanted to try.

"That's it? Just no?" Slate teased.

"That's it," Pid told his friend.

"Right. So, moving on, clear your schedule for a month

from now. Kenna and I are getting married and if you all aren't there, I'm gonna have to hurt you."

The guys all thumped Aleck on the back and congratulated him.

"How're you managing to plan a wedding in such a short period of time?" Slate asked. "I thought it took women months to work all that shit out."

"It often does, but we have Robert," Aleck said with a grin.

"Ah, the magical concierge. Another perk to being rich," Jag joked.

"Actually, I think the man would've taken on the task of organizing everything for free. It's Kenna. Somehow she just makes people want to bend over backward for them," Aleck said.

A year ago, Pid never imagined he'd be standing around talking about wedding details, but as Aleck told them all how their parents would be there, and about the permits Robert had somehow managed to get in order to bury a pig on the condo property for the luau, he couldn't help but smile. Some men would've resented how much their friendships had changed once girlfriends and wives entered the picture, but not Pid. He loved seeing his friends happy.

"Oh, and Kenna is having a bachelorette party, and she told me to tell you that she really wants Monica to come," Aleck told him.

His smile faded a bit. "I don't know," he hedged. Even though he'd all but told Monica that she was now a part of their tribe, going to a wedding was one thing, attending a bachelorette party with women she didn't know would be a harder sell.

"I tried to tell Kenna that it was odd to invite a woman

she didn't know to her bachelorette party, but she insisted. Said that if she was your friend, that made Monica *her* friend, and she wants her there."

"Monica has a hard time warming up to people," Pid explained. He hated to say anything negative about the woman he was beginning to care about more than he knew he probably should, since she'd eventually be leaving, but he wanted to warn his friends, so they could warn their girlfriends in return.

"I think that's obvious," Midas said. "Lexie's been texting her and trying to get her to open up, without much luck."

"It's just that she struggles with trusting people," he said.

"Because of that asshole father of hers," Slate growled.

Pid nodded.

Everyone now knew about her father forcing her to help bury a man. Not to mention how her hand had been damaged.

"How about we have dinner at Duke's one night before the bachelorette thing? Hanging out in a neutral setting might help them get to know each other better," Aleck suggested.

Pid nodded. He really did want Monica to get along with his friends' women, but if she didn't? It wouldn't be a deal breaker for him. He liked Monica exactly how she was. Quiet. Introspective. She was definitely more apt to watch and listen than join in any revelry. He had no doubt she'd get along with Elodie, Lexie, and Kenna, but being best friends with them wasn't a requirement for being his girlfriend.

Then again...what the hell was he thinking? Monica was in Hawaii for one purpose and one purpose only—to identify the man who'd broken into the ambassador's home. That's it. Once that happened, or if it became obvious it *wouldn't* happen, she'd be gone. Back to her life as a nanny.

"Great, I'll ask Kenna when she thinks the best time will be," Aleck continued.

"And I'll talk to Lexie, who will let Elodie know."

"Any objections to letting Ashlyn come too?" Slate asked.

"Not from me," Aleck told him. "The more the merrier."

"I'd love for Carly to get out of her apartment, but it might be too soon for her to go back to Duke's," Jag said.

"Do you think she'll come to our wedding?" Aleck asked.

Jag shrugged. "Don't know. But I'll do my best to convince her."

"Look at us," Midas joked. "Arranging a playdate for our women."

Everyone laughed, and Pid couldn't help but join in. They certainly didn't sound like a bunch of badass Navy SEALs at the moment, but he knew not one of them cared.

His phone vibrated with a text, and Pid looked down at the screen. Mustang let him know he'd picked up Monica and was on his way back. "All right, time for everyone to go. I appreciate your help more than you know, but Mo's on her way back here."

He'd already explained why he didn't want everyone there when he showed her what he'd done, and his friends were cool with that. Monica wasn't fond of being the center of attention, and having his entire team staring at her, waiting for a reaction, wouldn't be easy for her.

Pid couldn't believe how nervous he was as he paced, waiting for Mustang to arrive with Monica. He wanted his houseguest to feel comfortable. She hadn't wanted to be here and was doing the commander, and her country, a big favor. The least he could do was make sure she felt as safe as possible while in the States.

The sound of tires on the gravel outside his house had Pid heading to his front door. He waved at Mustang, who was behind the wheel of his beat-up pickup truck. It might look like a piece of shit, but Mustang took care of it meticulously. The engine was probably in better shape than nine out of ten cars on the road.

Pid eyed Monica as she walked toward him. She looked tired. He hated how much looking at profiles all day seemed to drain her energy. Making a mental note to talk to both Monica and the commander about shortening the hours she spent at the base each day, even if that meant it took longer to go through the profiles, Pid smiled at his guest.

"Are you all right?" she asked with a frown.

"Me? Of course. Why?"

"Mustang wouldn't really tell me why you weren't there to pick me up today. He just said that you were busy. I didn't know if that was man-speak for being sick...or maybe for being tired of chauffeuring me around all the time."

"I'm not sick, and I'm definitely not tired of driving you where you need to go," Pid said. "You know that thing I've been working on?" He waited until she nodded before continuing. "Well, I finished it today."

Interest lit up her eyes. "You did?"

"Yup. Wanna see?"

"I'm not sure."

Pid's brows drew down. "Not sure?"

"I'm not a huge fan of surprises," she explained.

"Let me guess," Pid said. "Your father?"

Monica gave him a sheepish look. "Yeah. The most memorable being when he told me to go outside, that he had a 'surprise' for me. It was five chickens that had been killed overnight by some predator. A sixth was still alive, but unable to walk. It was squirming on the ground, obviously in pain. He told me to kill it, pluck the feathers from all six, cut off the heads and feet, remove their internal organs, and bring them inside for my mom to wash and bag for later. I was six."

Pid closed his eyes and took a deep breath, trying to retain his composure.

It wasn't until he felt a hand touch his arm that he opened his eyes again. Monica was standing right in front of him, a worried look on her face. "It wasn't so bad," she said.

"Don't," Pid said with a sharp shake of his head. "Don't try to defend what that fucker did. He scarred you, and while you're an amazing woman, someone I admire a hell of a lot, everything he did has stuck with you. And I *hate* that for you."

They stared at each other for a long moment, and Pid longed to hug her. But he didn't want to scare her away or make her think he pitied her. Because he didn't. How could he pity someone who'd done what they needed to in order to survive?

"Maybe if I had more good surprises under my belt, I'll feel differently about them," she said after a moment, gifting him with a small smile.

Damn, that dimple he only got glimpses of now and then was Pid's weakness. All she had to do was smile at him and he'd bend over backward to give her whatever she asked for, if only to see that dimple again.

"All right. I've still got some more cleaning up to do, so ignore the dirt and sawdust."

"You mean like I've been doing all week?" she teased.

Pid chuckled. "Yeah. Like that."

"You know what?" she asked as they headed inside.

"What?"

"I'm getting used to not living in an immaculate house. I hadn't realized that part of my childhood had stuck with me so strongly. Everywhere I've lived, I've kept my room clean. Made sure my bed was always made. Nothing was out of place. I even did my best to clean the homes of my employers. It's kind of freeing to not worry about sawdust on the floor or leaving a dirty dish in the sink."

Pid laughed. "I'm not sure if I should be horrified that I've been such a negative influence on you or proud."

"Proud, definitely," Monica told him as she put her purse on the kitchen counter and looked around.

The living area wasn't too bad. The guys had helped him sweep it up, but the sofa and coffee table were still pushed against the wall and covered in a sheet to try to protect them from the dust and debris.

"Wow, were you breakdancing in here or what?"

Pid burst out laughing. When he had himself under control, he asked, "Can you seriously see me breakdancing?"

She looked at him with a straight face and said, "I think you could probably do anything you set your mind to."

Shit. She was killing him.

"Thanks, Mo. Okay, your surprise is in your room. Go on and take a look."

She gave him a nervous glance, but slowly walked down the hall toward the room she'd been using for the last week.

Pid followed and crossed his fingers she'd like what he'd done.

At first she simply stood in the doorway of her room, looking around in confusion. Everything was exactly how she'd left it that morning. Pid had made sure to put everything back after he and his friends had finished.

Monica looked back at him. "Um...thank you?"

Pid smiled. "Notice anything...off...about the dimensions of the room?" he asked.

She turned back to study the space, and Pid knew the moment she realized what he'd done by her gasp.

"Oh my God, Stuart! Did you..."

"Yup," he said, still grinning. "I didn't get to study the safe room at the ambassador's house in Algiers, but I built the same kind of thing. The wall on the left is false. There's about two and a half feet between it and the original wall. There's not a lot of room in there, but for someone your size, I figured it would be more than enough for you to move around."

Monica hadn't said a word, just turned around and stared at the wall as if she had x-ray vision and could see behind it. So Pid brushed past her and went over to where he'd hidden the switch that would open the door. It was near the floor, and he pressed against a part of the floorboard with his foot.

A small door opened next to him. It was only about four and a half feet tall, far from regular height. He had to bend way over to get inside. But he hadn't built this for himself, he'd done it solely for Monica's peace of mind.

"I wanted you to be able to open the door even if your

hands were full, so that's why I decided to put the switch near the floor," he explained. "Right now, there's a blanket, pillow, an extra cell phone, a radio with earphones, and a small stool in there. The only thing I haven't done is hook up the electricity to the new plug on the wall. I'll do that later. But the plug on the original wall still works, so the radio can be plugged in and the cell phone charged. And there's one more big thing."

"More?" Monica whispered.

Pid nodded. "I started thinking about the room in Algeria, and it occurred to me that if Slate and I hadn't gotten there when we did, you would've been trapped in that room when the rioters set the house on fire." It had been confirmed by satellite surveillance that the entire neighborhood had been destroyed by the mob.

"The very last thing I want is you going into this safe room and then being trapped there. So I had my neighbor come over and help me make an egress point. It's even smaller than this one, so you'll have to get down on your hands and knees to use it, but I tried it, and I was able to get out, so you'll be fine. I planted a bunch of bushes on that side of the house recently, so it should give you enough cover to get out unseen. Then if you need help, you can run to the neighbor's house, or anywhere else for that matter."

Pid knew he was speaking fast, but he couldn't get a good read on how Monica felt about what he'd done.

"I just wanted you to feel safe," he said quietly. "And that room in Algeria kept you hidden from that asshole who definitely would've done you harm. I don't expect any danger to come knocking at my door, but I can't say it'll never happen either. I've made some enemies in my job, and while for the most part my identity is kept secret, there's always a chance it could be leaked. Or maybe some roving asshole might target my house since it's away from the road. Anyway...I just thought having a place to hide might make you feel more comfortable being here."

Pid stood next to the open door to the safe room and shifted uneasily. Monica still hadn't said a word, and he was getting nervous. He kept his eyes on her as she slowly walked toward him. She leaned over and looked into the space between the new false wall he'd built and the original outside wall. He'd plugged in a small lamp so she'd be able to see it clearly.

Then she stood up, and he saw tears in her eyes.

Pid panicked a little, thinking something was wrong, that she hated what he'd done. So he started babbling again, trying to keep those tears from spilling over her cheeks. He had a feeling nothing would gut him more than seeing Monica cry.

"You don't have to use it. It was just a thought I had. I know it made this room a bit smaller overall, but it's not too bad. And if you really hate it, we can switch rooms. I can stay in here and you can stay in the larger room."

Monica reached up and put her hand in the center of Pid's chest and he stopped talking immediately. He barely breathed as he looked down at her and waited for her to speak.

"No one in my entire life has ever done something so amazing for me before," she said after a moment. "No one. Thank you, Stuart."

"You're welcome."

"I can't believe you did this all in one day," she said, leaving her hand on his chest but looking back at the door next to where they stood.

"I built the frame out during the week and kept the

boards in my room. It was just a matter of bringing them out and putting them up."

Monica rolled her eyes. "And drywalling, and painting, and cutting a hole in your house to put that other door in." She looked back up at him. "I'm assuming your friends helped?"

Pid nodded.

"Honestly, I'm speechless," she whispered.

Reaching up and putting his hand over hers on his chest, Pid said, "You don't need to say anything. I'm just glad you don't think I'm some crazy prepper or anything."

He wasn't trying to be funny, but at his words, Monica threw her head back and laughed hysterically. He could only stare at her in wonder as she did her best to get herself under control.

Pid had never seen anything as beautiful as a joyful Monica. He wanted to memorize the moment in case he never got to see it again. Slow time down, bottle her infectious, jubilant laughter.

All too soon, she got herself under control and shook her head at him. "My father was one of those crazy preppers, and you could never be in his league. Not even close. His idea of safety was the concrete bunker at the back of our property. I hated that thing. Every time he made us go down there, it felt like a coffin lid slamming shut when he locked us in. It smelled funky, it leaked, and the only way out was the way we came in. This is nothing like that. *Nothing*. And it's the best present I've ever gotten. Thank you."

Then she blew his mind by leaning in and giving him a hug. It wasn't long, but Pid had never been affected by a woman's touch in the way he was by that brief embrace.

She stepped away from him and asked shyly, "Can I try to open the door?"

"Of course." Pid stepped back and shut the door. It clicked closed with barely any noise, and he had to admit, he'd done a good job. When the door was shut, he almost couldn't see where it was. If someone didn't know it was there, they'd never notice the slight imperfection of the wall.

He watched with a grin as Monica pressed her foot where he had to the floorboard and the door opened. She ducked down and went inside, inspecting the space. "Can I go outside?" she asked.

Pid leaned down to peer inside the space between the two walls. "Of course. There's no hidden mechanism for that door. But it's double bolted shut. Just unlock the deadbolts and press down on the knob."

She did just that and sunlight streamed into the space from outside. She got down on her hands and knees and climbed halfway out. Then she backed up to look at him. "Can I get in from outside?"

Pid shook his head. "No. With the amount of rain we get here, I wasn't convinced I could come up with a lever that was both hidden and strong enough to withstand the humidity and still work. I didn't want to put a knob on the side of the house either, that would be a dead giveaway that it was a door. So for now, it's only an egress point. Not an entrance."

Monica scooted back inside and pulled the outer door shut. She secured the locks once more then headed his way. Pid stood back as she exited the small room. She closed the door and stood there for a moment, staring at the wall with a pensive look on her face.

"You good?" Pid asked.

She turned to look at him. "I'm great," she said with a grin, gifting him with a peek of her dimple.

"Good. You hungry?"

"Starved."

Pid frowned. "Did you eat lunch?"

"Yeah. But that was hours ago."

He chuckled. "Right. How does steak sound for dinner?"

"Delicious. What can I do to help?"

"Want to make a salad?"

"Sure."

They walked back out into the living area, toward the tiny kitchen. It really wasn't large enough for both of them to work comfortably, but Pid didn't complain. He liked having her near. Liked bumping into her when he moved too quickly. And he couldn't help but notice Monica didn't exactly jerk away from him anytime he accidentally brushed against her.

As he prepped the steaks, he asked, "Any luck today?"

She knew exactly what he was talking about. "No."

"But it's going okay? You're comfortable enough in the room the commander put you in?"

"It's fine," Monica said. "But honestly, I don't think this is going to work."

"Why not?" Pid asked. He wasn't exactly surprised by her statement, but wanted to hear why she wasn't very confident in her ability to pick out the man who she'd seen.

"Because everyone looks so different from the guy I saw. They're younger in the pictures. And way more formal. And their eyes are different."

"In what way?"

"I don't know that I can explain it. The man at the

door had his lower face covered, but I knew he was smiling. I could see wrinkles around his eyes. But I imagined it wasn't a friendly kind of smile, so much as one of...anticipation. His eyes were cold," she said in a whisper. "I could tell he wanted to hurt me. To get inside and do something awful."

"Mo," Pid said gently, turning and gently pulling her into his chest, as he'd wanted to do earlier. He didn't think about what he was doing, just reacted to the fear and pain in her tone.

To his surprise, she didn't yank away from him. Instead she seemed to snuggle closer. Her arms were trapped between them and he felt her fingers press against his chest, her forehead resting against him as well.

"The men in the pictures all seem...proud. Happy to be having their picture taken for their official record. And why wouldn't they be? They were SEALs. They'd worked very hard to get where they were. Maybe if I could see pictures of the men in camouflage, all dirtied up, I might be able to recognize someone, but in their pressed uniforms with excitement and pride in their eyes...I just don't think it's going to be possible for me to pick anyone out with any kind of certainty."

Pid was frustrated for her. For his commander. The situation sucked. There was a man out there somewhere who wouldn't hesitate to stay his course. Encouraging violence against others, killing women, stealing what wasn't his. Generally causing as much suffering as he could.

With one hand at her upper back and one resting on her lower, Pid held Monica against him, giving her all the support he could muster without making her feel trapped.

He felt her take a deep breath and knew she was going

to pull back before she moved. He immediately dropped his hands, letting her step away from him.

"Guess that means you'll have a houseguest for longer than you thought, huh? How long do you think your commander will keep me here looking at pictures even when it's obvious I'm not going to recognize anyone?"

"Honestly? I have no idea," Pid told her.

"He's pretty worked up about this guy, isn't he?" she asked.

"Yeah."

"Can I tell you something?" she asked.

"You can tell me anything," Pid said with feeling.

"I don't hate being here. I thought I would. I mean, being surrounded by military guys all the time isn't exactly my idea of a good time. But so far the people I've met on base have been nice. Or at least, not *not* nice, if that makes sense."

"It does."

"Being around you and your friends has made me realize that I was partly only going through the motions with the therapists I've seen over the years."

"What do you mean?" Pid asked.

"Just that...they've all told me my hatred of everyone who has anything to do with the military is irrational. That my father was one person, not representative of everyone who wears a uniform. But while I nodded and said I understood...I don't think I did. Not really. Until now. I *hate* that all these years later, he's still controlling me."

"Cut yourself some slack, Mo."

"I'm trying," she said, looking up at him. "And you're helping. A lot. You've been so nice, even when I haven't given you a reason to be."

He smiled down at her. "I don't mind your prickliness."

She rolled her eyes. "Then again, maybe I don't mind being here because the weather's so nice."

He chuckled.

"I miss being around kids, but it's also been a nice break."

Pid nodded. "You think you'd like to see some more of the island? Get out more?"

"With you?"

"No, I thought I'd just give you the keys to my precious minivan and give you a map and shove you out the door," Pid teased.

She grinned up at him. "Your precious minivan?" she asked.

"Yup."

Monica rolled her eyes. "I wouldn't mind seeing something other than your house. Not that I think your place is bad; it's actually very comfortable and I love the yard. But yeah, I guess since I'm in Hawaii, I might as well see some of the sights. I never know when it'll come in handy when I'm trying to entertain kids under my care in the future."

Pid didn't want to think about her leaving, even if it was inevitable. "Great. Oh, and one more thing."

"Yeah?" she asked suspiciously.

"Kenna would like to invite you to her bachelorette party. I know that's weird, considering she doesn't know you, or you her, but that's just the kind of person she is. She's super friendly."

"I don't know," Monica hedged.

"The guys and I talked about it and thought maybe we could all meet up at Duke's for dinner one night. It'll be super laid-back, with no pressure. I thought it might be a good idea to let you get to know her and the other women before you say yes or no to the bachelorette thing." He held his breath as he waited for Monica's reply

"And if I say no?" she asked.

Pid couldn't help the pang of disappointment that hit, but he made sure not to let any of that show on his face. "Then we won't go."

"I'm not good at making friends, Stuart. It's not that I think Kenna or the other women aren't good people, I just never know what to talk about, and people tend to think I'm stuck up or something when I don't participate in conversations."

"They won't think that," Pid told her.

Monica looked skeptical.

"I promise. They won't."

She sighed. "I'll go. But you have to let me say 'I told you so' when we don't hit it off."

Pid's hands itched to hug Monica again, but he managed to refrain. "Okay. Deal."

Just then, her stomach growled, and Pid chuckled. "Right. Enough talk. I need to feed you." He turned to the steaks he had on the counter once more.

"Stuart?"

"Yeah, Mo?"

"Thanks."

"For what?"

"Everything. The safe room. Being patient with me. For letting me stay here. All of it."

"Being with you isn't a hardship, Mo," Pid said, then forced himself to concentrate on fixing dinner. If he didn't, he'd probably say more than she was ready to hear. Mainly that he might just give her the world if she let him.

It was crazy how infatuated with this woman he was becoming, but Pid didn't care. He had no idea if she'd be in his life for another day, week, or month. But he planned to do whatever he could to show her she was safe here with his friends, his team, and with him. She could let down her guard and be herself, and she'd still be liked...and loved.

Not that Pid was in love with Monica. Not yet. But he had a feeling if he continued spending time around her, he'd fall. Hard.

And that didn't even freak him out. Not at all.

*One day at a time*, he told himself. Anything could happen. She could ID the man the commander was looking for and be gone...or maybe, just maybe, with a whole lot of luck on his side, she'd decide to stay, whether or not she ever figured out who she'd seen in Algeria.

Either way, Pid was determined to not let even one day go by without making Monica smile. His goal was to see that dimple as much as possible until she left.

"What are you smiling about over there?" Monica asked, eyeing him suspiciously.

"Just thinking about dinner," Pid told her.

"Well, get a move on, my belly's yelling at me."

"Yes, ma'am," he said with another smile.

Yeah, he was definitely okay with having this woman in his space.

# CHAPTER NINE

The next week went by much as the previous one had, except when Stuart dropped her off each day, she spent hours looking through official Navy files, while he went to a different building on the base to do his own work.

Monica wasn't sure what he did all day, but apparently he was always busy. He also left the house early each morning to work out with his team. Sometimes they went for an "easy" five-mile swim in the ocean, other times they ran a half marathon, still other times they went to the Naval base and worked out with others.

At first, Monica had been leery to be left alone in his house, but eventually she relaxed. How could she not? Sitting on his back deck, surrounded by fruit trees, and seeing the occasional wild chicken rooting around for food made her feel at home in a way she'd never felt anywhere before.

It actually worried Monica how comfortable she felt in Stuart's house. And she hadn't gone this long without a job since fleeing her childhood home. Though she couldn't help but admit that it felt good to have some time to herself and not have to worry about what to make her small charges for breakfast, or to get them up and dressed, or the million other things that went along with taking care of children.

Here she could just be...Monica.

The problem with that was, without a job to focus on, without someone dictating her every move...she wasn't entirely sure who Monica Collins really was.

Sighing, she took another sip of her coffee, enjoying the quiet weekend morning. She hadn't been much of a coffee drinker in the past, but once she'd tried Kona coffee, and the stuff made with peaberry—whatever that was—she was a convert.

Her mind wandered back to Stuart...where it often wandered to these days. He'd been more than generous, and she knew it. She wasn't a normal houseguest. She'd been a stranger, one who hadn't been all that thankful for his and Slate's help in Algeria. Actually, Monica knew she'd been downright belligerent. But he'd still invited her to stay with him, knowing how uncomfortable she'd be on the military base.

Not only that, he'd gone out of his way to build that amazing safe room. She still had a hard time wrapping her mind around the fact that he'd done so. She'd sat inside the small space that first night, after she'd gone to bed, and simply cried.

Cried because Stuart had been so damn nice to her. As had his friends. Cried because for the first time in her life, someone seemed to understand her. Truly understand her fears. It was scary as hell, because Stuart didn't even really know her. Didn't know all the things she'd suffered through while growing up. And yet he instinctively knew what she needed; still went out of his way to make sure she felt safe in his home.

With every day that had passed since, Monica relaxed a little more. But now she had a different problem than she had when she'd first arrived on the island.

Before, she couldn't wait to talk to the SEAL commander and get the hell back to her life. Now, after just two weeks, she'd settled in. She liked waking up without an agenda. She was beginning to get used to the men and women she saw on a regular basis in the building where she spent her days.

And more than anything, there was Stuart.

Monica was tremendously conflicted. She liked the man. A lot. But she still wasn't sure she completely trusted him. And she hated her father all over again for doing that to her. He'd been very successful in making her question everyone's motives. In teaching her to look for signs of deceit in every person she met. It was part of the reason she began to work with children. They hadn't learned how to be deceptive yet, especially the younger kids.

Monica took another sip of her coffee and closed her eyes. Trust or not, she had to admit—to herself, at least—that the urge to know more about the man she was essentially living with was growing stronger by the day. Because she hadn't wanted to talk about her family, Stuart had followed her lead. She knew he grew up in Alaska, and had a sister, but that was about it.

Turning when she heard a noise behind her in the house, Monica saw Stuart in the kitchen. That was just another little thing he did to try to put her at ease. He always made noise when he was coming and going, so as not to surprise her. She had no doubt he could move as silently as a ghost if he wanted to, he was a special forces operative after all, but the man clomped around his house as if he was one of the children she'd looked after over the years.

Smiling, she took another sip as Stuart opened the door and joined her on the deck.

"Wow, now that's a sight to come home to," he said quietly as he pulled a chair closer to hers and sat.

"What?" she asked, scanning the yard for whatever had pleased him so much.

"You," he said—blowing her mind. "Smiling. You don't do it often."

"Yes, I do," Monica countered, even though she knew he was right.

Stuart shrugged. "Just sayin'. I like it."

Feeling uncomfortable with his praise, Monica asked, "How was your workout?"

"Tough, but good. Mustang decided it was time to do another session on the obstacle course with our packs."

"I can't believe you guys went in to work out on a Sunday," Monica said.

Stuart took a sip of his coffee and relaxed into his chair. He crossed his long legs at the ankles and sighed, resting his cup on his belly and closing his eyes. "Days don't mean much to us," he said easily. "It's important we stay in shape, and many times the weekends are easier for us to use the equipment on base, since not as many people are there."

Monica could understand that.

They were quiet for a while, enjoying the balmy morning temperature. From experience, Monica knew it could get quite warm during the day, especially when the sun was out.

"If you want, I thought I might give you a small tour

of the island today. I figured I'd take you to the Moanalua Gardens and show you the huge monkeypod tree they have there. It's interesting because its canopy is as wide as the tree is tall. It's a sight to see for sure. There aren't many flowers there though, even though it's called Moanalua Gardens. After, I thought we could go downtown. It's not a trip to Oahu without seeing the National Memorial Cemetery of the Pacific, and the punchbowl."

"Punchbowl?" Monica asked.

"The punchbowl crater's an extinct volcanic tuff cone. The Hawaiian name is Puowaina, which is most commonly translated as "hill of sacrifice." Appropriate, since the cemetery is there. There's also a kick-ass scenic lookout too."

Monica couldn't help but feel excited about the day. She hadn't been out much since she'd been here, and seeing a bit of the island sounded fun.

"If lookouts are your thing, we could go to the Tantalus Lookout at Puu Ualakaa State Park. It's got a great view of Diamond Head, Waikiki, downtown Honolulu, and the ocean in the distance. Wait—you don't get car sick, do you?"

Monica shook her head. "Seasick, yes. Car sick, no."

"Whew, because the roads to get up there are pretty curvy. We could end the afternoon in Waikiki, where you can get some souvenirs if you want, and where we'll meet up with the gang at Duke's."

Monica sighed and stared out into the yard. She knew today was the get-together at the popular Waikiki restaurant. She still wasn't jazzed about it, but if Kenna was determined to invite her to her bachelorette party the next weekend, and to her wedding, she figured it was a good idea to at least try to get to know her, and the other women as well.

"It'll be fine," Stuart said, putting his hand on her arm and squeezing.

Monica felt horrible about being reticent to meet them. But she hadn't lied when she'd told Stuart that she had a hard time making friends. She never seemed to have anything in common with most people, and she always felt awkward trying to make small talk. So she usually just sat and listened, which sometimes weirded people out. "I know," she said.

"I wouldn't expose you to anyone who I thought wouldn't like you," Stuart said quietly.

Monica nodded.

He sighed. "I won't ask you to trust me, because I know trust is a hard thing for you, but you'll see. It'll be fine. Besides, if nothing else, you'll get to try Duke's hula pie. It's to die for. Do you drink?"

Monica shook her head. "Why? Is that a problem?"

"Not at all."

"It's weird," she mumbled, looking down at her coffee. "Another reason why I don't get along with people, especially in a social setting."

"It's fine. I only asked because Duke's has some popular cocktails. They also make them without alcohol. No one's going to care if you drink or not, Mo."

"Sometimes I ask for water in a martini glass," she admitted. "It keeps people off my back about not drinking."

"Smart. But you won't have to resort to tricks when you're with Elodie and the others. They really aren't going to care."

The more Monica heard about his friends' women, the

more she hoped they liked her. But that was a dangerous road for her to go down. First, because she wasn't sure how likely that was, and second, because she'd probably be leaving soon. The commander was getting frustrated with her inability to recognize anyone. Stuart kept telling her to be patient, but it was hard when his boss was so obviously *impatient*. And when she herself was getting more and more anxious to figure out who the mystery guy was.

"Mo, look at me."

Monica swallowed hard and looked over at Stuart. It was ridiculous that he could be so damn good-looking after working out for an hour and a half or more. He had white salt lines on his T-shirt where he'd sweated and the cotton had dried. His hair was sticking up all over his head and his face was scruffy from the overnight growth of his beard. She could even smell him from where she was sitting...and it wasn't exactly a fresh, clean scent either.

But all of that didn't do a damn thing to diminish her attraction to the man.

Monica should've been freaking out about the revelation. Instead, all she could do was stare into his dark brown eyes...and wonder if they'd be the same color when he was aroused.

Shit.

She had to get her mind out of the gutter and concentrate on what he was saying.

"—will be fun. And if for any reason you aren't having a good time, you just need to let me know and we'll leave."

Monica blinked. "What?"

"If you're miserable, let me know somehow. We can even come up with some sort of cue so no one else will notice, and I'll bring you back here. There's a new book that came out this week that you haven't had a chance to read yet, right? You can snuggle up in your room and read."

Monica could only stare at him. She had, in fact, told Stuart about a book that had just been published that she wanted to read, but hadn't realized he was paying such close attention. And the fact that he would be willing to leave an outing with his friends for *her*, someone he'd just met and who would probably be leaving his life soon, floored her.

Wait...what was she saying? Probably? There was no probably about it. She *would* be leaving.

"Mo?" Stuart asked, the concern easy to hear in his tone.

"Sorry, I'm listening. And I'll be fine."

"I don't want you to be *fine*," he said. "I want you to genuinely have a good time. And you don't have to talk or drink in order to do that. Elodie, Lexie, and Kenna are pretty damn funny. And if Ashlyn shows up, it'll be even crazier. Wait until you see Slate and her go at each other. They both like each other but don't want to admit it. It's pretty hilarious."

A pang Monica had never felt before gripped her. She didn't have a close group of friends. And listening to Stuart talk about the others made her long for what she'd never had.

"How about this, if you tug on your right earlobe, I'll know you want to leave," Stuart suggested.

Monica stared at him for a beat, before her lips quirked upward. Then she was laughing so hard, she almost spilled her coffee.

"What?" Stuart asked, smiling at her.

"Tug on my earlobe?" Monica asked. "For a SEAL,

someone who's supposed to be some sort of super-soldier-spy type person, that's really lame."

Stuart's smile didn't wane. "Okay, what do *you* suggest?"

She was glad she didn't offend him. "I don't know, but jeez, that's like out of some cheesy spy movie for sure."

"I like you like this," Stuart said.

Monica wrinkled her nose. "Like what?"

"Happy."

She had to admit that she liked herself like this too. But she didn't say that out loud. "How about if I want to leave, I just tell you?" she suggested.

"Okay, Mo. That'll work."

Stuart settled back against his chair again and inhaled deeply.

"So...you grew up in Alaska?" Monica asked. She had no idea why he got a huge smile on his face at her question, but he nodded.

"Yup. In Palmer, which is a small town north of Anchorage. There were only around seven thousand people who lived there, which gave it quite an intimate feel. And by that, I mean everyone knew everyone else's business." He chuckled.

"Was it cold?" Monica asked.

"It was Alaska, so yeah," he teased. "But I didn't think much about it, because I was so used to it. The thing people always complained about was how short the days were in the winter, but I loved—and still love—the dark. We didn't live north enough to get darkness for twenty-four hours, but in the middle of winter, there's only about four hours of sunlight a day. And of course in the summer, it's the opposite. It was hell on my mom to try to get my sister and me in bed when it was still so light outside.

Everyone has blackout curtains on their windows for the summer."

"It's hard for me to imagine."

"I'll..." Stuart's voice trailed off.

"You'll what?" Monica asked.

"Nothing. It's a unique place to live for sure. My parents love it there and will never leave."

She wondered what he didn't say. Had he been about to say he'd show it to her? No, that would be crazy, considering she was only a temporary housemate. "So they're still there?" she asked.

"Yup. Both are healthy and happy. Mom volunteers at one of the homeless shelters and my dad is a doctor at the Alaska Heart and Vascular Institute."

"Wow. Impressive."

Stuart shrugged. "He's just dad to me. One day he's annoying me, and the next I'm so proud of him I can't stand it."

Monica couldn't imagine what that was like.

"I'm sorry."

She looked over at Stuart. "For what?"

"For talking about my family too much."

"I asked," Monica said. "And you have nothing to be sorry for. Just because you had a great upbringing and family, and I didn't, doesn't mean you need to apologize for that."

"I just hate that you didn't have the same," Stuart said.

"Me too. But I think I'm doing all right," Monica said. And for the first time in a long time, she actually believed it. She'd been told so many times that she'd never amount to anything. That she was only good for being a breeder. That her worth in life was tied to making sure a man was able to slake his needs on a regular basis and keeping a clean house. But in the last few weeks, having more time to actually think about herself and her life, Monica realized that Stuart may be right...she was pretty damn strong. She'd lived through shit people wouldn't believe if she told them.

Flexing her left hand, Monica stared down at her mangled fingers. Yeah, it was safe to say she'd survived pretty well, despite her fucked-up childhood.

"You good?" Stuart asked.

The concern in his tone had her turning away from the sight of her stubs. "Yeah, I am," she told him, meaning it.

"Good. You showered yet?"

"Nope."

"You want to go first, or me?"

Monica wrinkled her nose comically and said, "You. Definitely."

"Hey," he protested. "Are you trying to tell me I smell?"

"Not trying, I *am* telling you that," she told him.

She could only stare at Stuart as he threw his head back and laughed. God, she could sit and stare at him all day. It wasn't a hardship, that was for sure.

"Fine. I'll go. You had breakfast?"

"No. But I can make something while you're in the shower," she told him.

"Nope. I got it. How about scrambled eggs, bacon, and biscuits with gravy?"

"I'm not sure I need to eat that much."

"We'll be walking around a lot today. You'll burn it off." Stuart stood, then shocked the hell out of Monica by leaning over and kissing the top of her head.

It was a spontaneous gesture. Even *he* looked taken aback by what he'd done.

"Sorry...I didn't mean to cross a line there."

"It's okay," Monica said, glancing up at him.

Stuart stared for a beat, as if to make sure she meant it, then nodded. "Okay, I'm headed in." He mock-glared at her. "No going into the kitchen, woman, I mean it. I've got breakfast."

"All right. I won't. I'll sit right here and count chickens until you're done," Monica said.

"Good. I have a feeling you haven't gotten to relax enough in your life." Then he turned and headed inside.

Monica could feel her heart beating hard—and for the first time, she worried that the longer she stayed with Stuart, the more feelings she'd develop for him.

Her dad would be thrilled she was falling for a military guy, but less than pleased that Stuart was so honorable. He'd definitely think his teammates were pussies for showing so much affection for their women. He'd hate Stuart for being gentle with her.

She couldn't remember one time when her dad had made a meal for her and her mother. He'd expected them to do all of the "womanly" things around the house. Cooking, cleaning, mending their clothes...all of it. He sat around and complained about anything and everything while they did it too.

The fact that Stuart frequently insisted on cooking was so far outside what she was used to, it wasn't even funny. But Monica liked it. A lot. Not being waited on, but the fact that Stuart was willing to do his share of the domestic work around the house.

Monica had never lived with a man since moving out of her father's house. Being the hired help didn't count. She wasn't a guest in the houses she lived in, but an employee. She was expected to care for the children, doing whatever was necessary to keep them fed, happy, and entertained.

Living with Stuart was unlike anything she could've imagined. In a good way.

Drinking the last of the coffee in her cup, Monica stood and headed inside. Stuart never took very long in the shower, and suddenly she was excited to get the day started. She wanted to see all of the sights he'd mentioned...and there was even a spark, a small one, of anticipation for dinner with his friends later that evening.

# CHAPTER TEN

Pid was becoming increasingly worried. Monica had warned him that she wasn't great in social situations, and she hadn't lied.

Everyone had gathered at Duke's, and things had started out well enough. Kenna had the night off, and she was able to sit at the table with them and enjoy the meal instead of waiting on their group. Elodie and Lexie were there, as was Ashlyn. Carly hadn't shown up, which Jag was visibly upset about, but generally, everyone was in a good mood.

Except for Monica.

She was sitting next to him in the middle of the rectangular table, sipping ice tea, and mainly concentrating on the food in front of her. She'd greeted everyone, but otherwise hadn't said a word since.

Elodie had tried to include her in the conversation, but since talk had centered around the plans for the luau wedding in a few weeks, Monica didn't have much to offer. Pid had caught the concerned glances his friends threw his way, but he'd given them a small shake of his head, and they'd turned their attention back to the conversation.

The day itself, before arriving at Duke's, had gone extremely well. Monica had smiled more than he'd ever seen so far, and she'd even agreed to let him take a selfie of the two of them at the lookout at Puu Ualakaa State Park. It was a picture Pid knew he'd treasure forever. Her eyes were closed and she was laughing, the dimple that did him in on full display. Her blonde hair was blowing around her head in the wind and a few strands were entangled with his own. She looked like a woman with no cares in the world, and it was how he always wanted to remember her.

They'd had an amazing day, and she'd even insisted on buying him a hula girl for the dashboard of his minivan. He had no intention of defiling his precious vehicle with the obnoxious toy, instead planning on putting it on the windowsill over his kitchen sink, where he'd still see it every day and think of her.

He liked Monica more than he ever thought he would. He hadn't spent as much time getting to know a woman as a friend as he had her. And for his part, that friendship was slowly morphing into more. He looked forward to seeing her when he got up, and delayed saying good night each evening for as long as he could before going to his bedroom alone.

But the woman he'd gotten to know over the last couple of weeks, and during the last several hours, wasn't the same one sitting next to him right now. She was grim faced and didn't seem interested in engaging with anyone.

"Want to see the beach?" he asked after their dishes had been taken away and they were waiting on dessert to be served.

"Sure," she said quietly.

"We'll be right back," Pid told the group.

"We'll be here," Elodie joked.

Pid held Monica's chair as she stood and put his hand on the small of her back as they headed through the restaurant, toward the stairs that would lead them to the stretch of sandy beach.

Once they were away from the bright lights and noise of the restaurant, he asked, "You okay?"

She sighed. "I told you I'm not good with people."

"You're fine with *me*," he countered. "And when you've been around the guys, you've been relaxed."

"I don't fit in," she said softly. "I've *never* fit in. I don't know what to say to add to the conversation, and the last thing I want to do is say something awkward that will make everyone think I'm a freak."

"Mo," Pid said, stopping and turning her to face him. He put his hands on her shoulders. "All you have to do is be yourself."

She shook her head. "That's what I'm afraid of. Monica Collins isn't very interesting."

"Bullshit," Pid said. "You have a great sense of humor and you have more compassion in your little finger than most people have in their entire bodies. You just need to relax. Stop worrying about what you say before you say it. The women in that restaurant aren't going to judge you. About *anything*."

"I'll try."

Without asking permission, Pid pulled her close. He wrapped his arms around her and squeezed her in a long heartfelt hug. He felt her relax against him and couldn't help but sigh in contentment with the way they fit. Her cheek rested against his chest, over his heart, and she grasped his shirt at his sides as she stood quietly in his embrace.

"Feel better?"

She nodded. "My meal was delicious."

"You're gonna love the hula pie too. Promise."

After another moment, they walked back toward the restaurant. The pies had been served while they were gone. Pid didn't hesitate to fork a huge bite into his mouth as soon as he and Monica were settled again.

Everyone laughed at his over-the-top enjoyment.

"I don't know what they put in this thing, but it's got to be some sort of illegal substance," he said with his mouth full.

In contrast, Monica took a dainty bite, but he heard her moan in appreciation as she experienced Duke's hula pie for the first time.

"Told you," he said as he nudged her arm with his shoulder.

"You did," she agreed.

Pid watched as she took a breath and turned to Elodie, saying quietly, "Stuart mentioned you're an amazing chef, and he wasn't wrong. Those dishes you brought over were delicious. What's your favorite thing to make?"

It was the right thing to ask. Elodie beamed and immediately launched into a discussion of some of her favorite dishes. And while Monica didn't exactly participate much in the conversation that followed, she was paying more attention and nodding at some of the things the others said.

Pid was proud of her. It was obvious she was still uncomfortable, but she was trying. It was all he could ask for.

When Ashlyn asked what he and Monica had done

that day, he told them all about their leisurely drive and how glad he was that the weather had cooperated for pictures at the scenic overlooks.

"You should bring her up to the North Shore so she can meet Baker," Elodie said with a grin.

"Baker?" Monica asked.

"He's a retired SEAL. He's *hot*. And he surfs!" Elodie explained.

"Hey, watch it. I'm gonna think you like him more than you do me," Mustang grumbled.

Elodie leaned over and kissed her husband on the cheek, patting his chest. "Never." Then she turned back to Monica. "He's mysterious and a little scary, but my God, the man isn't hard on the eyes."

"Jesus, El," Mustang said with a roll of his own.

Pid saw Monica's lips quirk into a small smile. He'd never been so glad to see that in all his life.

"Elodie's right," Kenna added. "I thought I was gonna pee my pants when he leaned in and said in a deadly tone, 'No one fucks with the SEALs,'" she mimicked, shivering dramatically. "He's like James Bond without the accent, and way more good-looking."

"Which one?" Ashlyn asked. "Because there have been a lot of men who've played James Bond, and they're all pretty damn good-looking."

"Nope. None of them beats Baker," Lexie threw in.

"All right, can we stop talking about how hot Baker Rawlins is," Jag whined.

All the women giggled.

"El's suggestion isn't a horrible one," Mustang said when the ladies had gotten themselves under control. "With Baker's connections, and since he still has his hand in the pie, so-to-speak, he might have some insight into the guy Monica's been looking for."

Pid nodded. He should've already thought about that. "You're right. I'll see if I can make the arrangements, and I'll talk to Huttner about it as well. He may already have spoken with Baker about everything that's been going on."

"True," Mustang agreed.

"Um, if this guy is as scary as he sounds...maybe we can just call him?" Monica said.

It was Kenna who leaned on the table with her elbows and pierced Monica with a look. "Baker *is* scary, there's no doubt about that. But the man is good at what he does. He met with a freaking *mobster* to make sure Elodie was safe from anyone else coming after her. And he vowed to do whatever it took to find Shawn's son to make sure *I'm* safe. He's got a core of integrity that's shocking in its intensity. He's one of the good guys, no matter how he might come across."

Lexie's phone rang before anyone could say anything else. She didn't bother getting up from the table, just apologized and said, "It's Natalie. She wouldn't be calling me this late on a Sunday if something wasn't up."

Everyone quieted as they listened to Lexie's side of the conversation with her boss at Food For All.

"Hey, Nat, what's up? Oh my God, seriously? All right, I can head out there right now. I'm down in Waikiki, so it'll take me twenty minutes or so to get there, is that all right? Good. The cops are there now though? Okay, I'm glad. I will, thanks. No, enjoy your vacation, I'll call once I talk to the police and find out what the damage was. Right. Okay, talk to you later. Bye."

"What's going on?" Aleck asked as soon as she hung up.

"Natalie said the alarm was tripped at Food For All down at Barbers Point. She asked if I could go check things out and let the police know if anything's missing. She said no one was hurt, obviously, since we're closed. The front window is smashed to pieces though, which most likely set the alarm off."

"Right. We're going," Midas said.

"I'm coming," Ashlyn said. "I want to make sure they didn't mess up my organization of all our supplies."

"I'll take you," Slate told her.

"I want to go too," Elodie threw in. "I want to check on my kitchen."

"If you guys are going, so am I," Kenna insisted.

"Fuck. Looks like we're all headed to Barbers Point," Jag said, standing.

"I'll take care of the bill tomorrow when I come in to work," Kenna told them.

"Wrong. I'll take care of the bill when I drop you off at work tomorrow," Aleck insisted.

"Whatever," Kenna said with a roll of her eyes.

Pid took hold of Monica's elbow as they stood. "You okay with heading down to the food pantry and seeing what's what?"

"Sure," she said. "I'm interested to see the place after hearing Lexie and Ashlyn talk about it."

The confirmation that she *had* been listening to the conversation swirling around them over dinner was reassuring. Pid had a feeling it would take her a few times of hanging out with all of them to get comfortable, but he suspected it would happen.

The entire group headed for the exit. Pid wasn't sure what they'd find down at the food pantry, but he couldn't help but hope it was a completely random break-in and nothing connected to the trouble any of the women had been through. The last thing any of the SEALs wanted was for Elodie, Lexie, or Kenna to suffer anything they'd already survived, all over again.

# CHAPTER ELEVEN

Monica hadn't expected the night to end up like this. With her hanging out two blocks from the Food For All pantry in a parking lot with Elodie, Lexie, Kenna, Ashlyn, and Slate, while the rest of the guys went down the street to talk to the police on scene and make sure it was safe for them to approach.

She'd watched the easygoing men morph into deadly soldiers as they insisted the women stay where they were while they did their thing. It was a surprise to realize that she wasn't that nervous about being around them. Even Slate, who was extremely imposing as he stood guard over the five of them in the parking lot.

It was a revelation, one that Monica knew she'd be thinking about later, but for now, she was just as anxious to make sure everything was all right inside the food pantry. She didn't work there, had never even laid eyes on the building, but listening to the other women talk passionately about the people they were helping, and hearing their worry about what the break-in meant in regard to the essential service they provided, made Monica equally keen to see what the damage was.

Slate's phone pinged with a text and he looked down at it. "Okay, it's safe," he informed them all.

Lexie and Elodie were on the move almost before he'd finished speaking, obviously eager to get inside the building and see firsthand what had happened.

But before they'd gone a dozen steps, a man stepped out of the shadows in front of them.

Slate moved faster than Monica had seen him move before. He was in front of the two women before she could blink.

"It's okay, Slate, it's Theo," Lexie told him, putting a hand on the SEAL's arm.

Monica didn't know who Theo was, but obviously Slate did, because he nodded and she could see his muscles visibly relax.

"Hi, Theo. There's a bit of excitement around here tonight, huh?" Lexie asked him.

Monica realized almost immediately that the man wasn't in his right mind. He kept his gaze on the concrete at his feet and he rocked back and forth slightly.

"Theo, are you all right?" Lexie asked.

Monica guessed the man was in his mid-forties or so, but when he spoke he sounded much younger. "Bad things happened," he said.

"Did you see them?" she asked gently.

"Kevin McCallister," Theo said, still not looking up from where he was studying the ground as if it was the most interesting thing he'd ever encountered.

"Who's that?"

"Tonight. Kevin McCallister," Theo repeated.

Lexie looked up at Slate and shrugged. "I don't know anyone with that name."

"Me either," Elodie agreed. "But maybe he's a homeless person he knows from the streets."

"Come on, do you want to come with us to Food For All? I can get you a snack if you want. Did you eat tonight?" Lexie asked.

"No, no snack," Theo said in agitation.

Monica wasn't sure it was her place to step in, but she felt the need to help. Along with children, the other people she seemed to easily click with were the mentally handicapped. Maybe because in many ways, they were like kids stuck in adult bodies. She stepped closer to where Lexie and Elodie were talking with the man and said, "Hi, Theo. I'm Monica. It's good to meet you."

He glanced upward, then returned his gaze to the sidewalk, shifting in distress.

"Theo's one of my friends," Lexie told her. "He was there for me when a bad man tried to hurt me. He got injured in the process. He lives near here in a studio apartment," she explained.

Monica definitely wanted to hear the story Lexie was referencing, but she was more interested in calming Theo down at the moment.

Slate's phone pinged again. "The guys are getting worried," he said. "We should get going."

"Come on, Theo, come with us," Lexie urged.

He shook his head almost violently. "Kevin McCallister," he repeated.

"You guys go. I'll see if I can get him to talk to me," Monica volunteered.

"You sure?" Lexie asked.

"I'm sure. I can see the front of the building from here, so I'll be fine."

"I'll send Pid as soon as I get to Food For All," Slate said.

"That's not necessary—" Monica began to protest, but at the look on the man's face, she pressed her lips together, cutting off anything else she was going to say.

"Thanks for talking to him," Lexie said in a low voice after she turned away from the agitated man. "He's been much more mellow after moving down here. I haven't seen him like this in a long time."

Monica nodded, and once the group had left to head toward Food For All, she tried to talk to Theo once more. "Can you tell me about Kevin McCallister?" she asked.

"He's me. I'm him," Theo said.

Monica frowned. She knew Theo was trying to tell her something, but she wasn't sure what it was. It had to be frustrating for him. "Did you see whoever it was who broke into Food For All?" she asked.

Theo nodded and rocked back and forth.

"Did you talk to him?"

He shook his head.

"Have you seen him before?"

He nodded once more.

Monica knew she needed to get this info to the police officers. If Theo knew the man, it was likely Lexie and Elodie did as well. "Are you scared to go back to Food For All?"

Theo nodded.

"The man who broke in is gone. The police officers are there. They'll keep you safe."

Monica watched as Theo's face lost all its color. "No, they'll take me to jail."

"Theo? Can you look at me?" It took a full minute, but she was so proud of him when he finally looked up and met her gaze. "No one will take you to jail. You didn't do anything wrong," Monica said.

"Kevin McCallister," Theo said once more.

Monica frowned. What was he trying to tell her?

Out of the corner of her eye, she saw Stuart coming her way. She needed to warn Theo so he wasn't startled. "Here comes Stuart...you probably know him as Pid."

Theo glanced behind him, then nodded again.

There had to be a reason why the man was still standing there. If he was as scared as he seemed to be, the likely thing for him to do was to go back to his apartment, where things were familiar and safe. But instead, he'd sought out Lexie. And he wasn't leaving now, even though Monica was a stranger to him. Whatever he was trying to tell them had to be important.

"Hey," Stuart said as he neared.

Suddenly, something popped into Monica's head. She wasn't sure if she was on the right track, but it was worth a shot. She held up a hand to Stuart, who paused several feet from where she and Theo were standing. She didn't have time to explain what was going on to Stuart, but hopefully he'd give her and Theo some space so her new friend didn't get distracted or spooked.

"Kevin McCallister was the boy who was left home alone, right?" she asked, remembering how much past charges had loved those movies.

Theo's head flew up and he met her gaze as he nodded. "Uh-huh."

"And you said you're him and he's you?" she asked.

Theo nodded more enthusiastically. "From New York, not Chicago."

"Right, the second movie when he got on the wrong plane and ended up in New York by himself," Monica prodded.

"Yeah. Toy store. Turtle doves," Theo agreed.

"Why are you Kevin?" she asked.

Theo's brows came down and his lip began to quiver.

Monica hated seeing him so distressed. "Can I touch you?" she asked, knowing better than to touch someone like Theo without his permission.

Theo reached out so quickly, Monica was startled. He grabbed her left hand and held on as if she was his lifeline. Normally, she would've recoiled from anyone holding her damaged hand, but she was too concerned about what Theo was trying to tell her.

"Toy store. Robbers hiding in the dollhouse," he said urgently.

"That's right. They hid inside the store until it was closed, then came out to rob it. Was that what happened at Food For All?" she asked.

Theo shook his head. "After."

Monica racked her mind trying to remember the movie and what happened next. Then it came to her. Without turning her head, she raised her voice and asked, "What was the damage to the building, Stuart?"

He kept his voice low, and Monica had never appreciated someone being as astute as Stuart seemed to be. "It doesn't look like the lock was jimmied or the door was busted in. But the front window was shattered by a cinderblock."

Monica nodded and squeezed Theo's hand. "You saw the man inside and broke the window, didn't you?"

Theo's eyes filled with tears. "He ran away. The policeman will take me to jail."

Monica shook her head. "No, he won't. You did that to get help, to set off the alarm, right?"

Theo nodded once more and looked back down at the pavement.

"You did so good, Theo. It's so lucky you were there to see the man go inside. How did you know he was a bad guy? That you needed to break the window to get the police to come?"

"He had on black. And he didn't turn on the lights. It's dark. He had a bag and I saw him put things inside. Lexie wouldn't like that."

"No, she wouldn't. Thank you for telling me what happened. If I promise nothing bad will happen to you, will you come with me to Food For All? I'll stay right by your side and I won't let the police put you in jail."

"Promise?"

The frightened sound of his voice touched a chord within Monica. "I promise."

"Okay. If you stay with me."

"I will. Lexie and Elodie are going to be so proud of you. Just like Mr. Duncan was proud of Kevin."

At that, Monica saw a small smile cross Theo's face. "I trust you," he said.

His words made Monica jolt slightly. This man-child, someone she'd literally just met, trusted her...and she couldn't manage to trust anyone, even after knowing them for weeks. It was somewhat depressing.

Pushing that aside, and without letting go of Theo's hand, Monica turned to look at Stuart for the first time. The look of admiration on his face nearly made her trip over her feet. She couldn't remember a time when anyone over the age of ten had looked at her like that.

"Hey, Theo, you're gonna give me and the rest of the

guys a complex. We came all ready to be a hero, only to find out that, once again, you're the hero of the night," Stuart said.

Monica felt the man next to her stand up a little straighter. "Theo's a hero," he declared.

"Yes, you are, bud," Stuart agreed. He approached Monica's right side and reached for her other hand.

They walked like that, her in the middle, Theo and Stuart holding her hands, down the sidewalk toward Food For All, which was now lit up, every light in the building shining bright.

They paused before going inside and Monica asked Theo, "You ready?"

"Ready," he agreed.

She felt a tug on her right hand and looked up at Stuart. "You're amazing," he said quietly, then kissed her temple quickly, before squeezing her hand and letting it go.

Feeling warm and gooey inside, Monica led Theo into the building, careful to avoid the broken glass that was all over the floor just inside the door.

\* \* \*

Twenty minutes later, after Theo had admitted to breaking the window and telling the police officers what he'd seen, he and Monica were seated at one of the tables. Someone had gotten Theo a piece of paper and a pencil and he was bent over it, drawing.

Pid stood off to the side and kept his eye on Monica. The way she'd patiently talked with Theo and gotten to the bottom of what he was trying to relay was impressive. It was no wonder she was as good at her job as she was. He wasn't surprised the ambassador's son had been so worried about her back in Algeria.

He felt someone come up beside him and turned to see Elodie. She looped her arm in his and leaned her head against his biceps.

"I like her," Elodie said softly.

Pid couldn't help but smile. "Good."

"I mean, at first, I wasn't sure about her. You and her seem so different. And she didn't seem interested in getting to know any of us."

"She was nervous."

"I get that. It's not easy to come into a close-knit group of people. Mustang told me a little bit about her, but not a lot. I wasn't sure what to expect, and when she didn't even try to join in our conversation at dinner, I was a little upset. But after you guys went out to the beach and came back, she was better."

Pid nodded.

"So, I figured she was probably just trying to figure out the dynamics of the group. I know us women can be a bit overwhelming at times. But hearing how she was with Theo? And how she figured out what he was saying with that Kevin McCallister thing? And how she is now? I get it."

"What do you get?" Pid asked, genuinely curious.

"She's quiet. Introspective. She doesn't like to bring any attention to herself. She's never going to be super outgoing, especially in public. But get her around someone like Theo, and she blossoms as if she's a flower seeing sunshine for the first time."

He nodded. "It just takes her a while to warm up to people," he said. "It's taken her two weeks to really be herself with *me*."

Elodie nodded and dropped her arm from his. "If you don't keep her, you're crazy, Pid."

"She's got a career, Elodie," he warned. "The chance of her staying is pretty damn low."

"Then change her mind," Elodie argued.

"It's not that easy."

"Why not? I stayed. As did Lexie. Give her a *reason* to stay, Pid."

"Hey, El, can you come here a sec?" Lexie called from across the room where she was still talking to the officers.

"Coming!" she yelled to her friend. Then she turned back to him. "You look...content. I haven't seen you so laid-back in all the time I've known you. If you let her leave, you'll regret it." Then she turned and walked across the room to see what Lexie needed.

"Sorry, man," Mustang said as he approached.

"You heard?" Pid asked his friend.

"Most of it. Elodie's on a mission to see everyone on the team as happy as we are."

Pid nodded, but didn't comment.

"For the record, Monica does seem to have a calming effect on you. Lately, you've seemed more settled. If that makes sense," Mustang said.

It made perfect sense to Pid. Because that was exactly how he felt. He looked forward to spending his evenings with Monica. She was easy to be with, and instead of obsessively watching the news, trying to figure out where their next mission might be, he spent his time talking with Mo and seeing if he could get her to smile.

His friend slapped him on the back and headed across the room to his wife.

Slate had left a while ago to take Ashlyn home, and Jag had already left after making sure everything was more than adequately handled. Lexie and Elodie had insisted Kenna head home with Aleck, as well. They were meeting with Robert in the morning to go over some wedding details and it was getting late.

Pid was lost in his head, thinking about what Elodie had said, when he saw Monica walking toward him. She had a piece of paper in her hand.

"What's up?" he asked in concern.

"Theo drew this. I think it's the guy he saw in here tonight."

Looking down at the paper, Pid saw a perfect rendering of a man. "Holy shit, Theo can draw!" he exclaimed.

"I know. I mean, I knew he could; look at the beautiful mural on the wall in here. But many times people are good at one kind of art and not another. I wasn't sure he'd be good at drawing portraits, but when we sat down, I kind of encouraged him to try...and this was the result."

"Why don't you bring that over to Lexie and the others and see if they recognize him? If nothing else, the cops need it to help them figure out who he is."

Monica hesitated. "I thought *you* could bring it over there."

Pid reached out and put his finger under her chin, urging her to meet his gaze. "What are you afraid of?" he asked in a low tone.

Monica shrugged. "Tonight didn't go that great. I know it, you know it, they know it. I figured it would be more comfortable if I just hung out with Theo until you wanted to leave."

"Cut yourself some slack, Mo. It took us a while to get comfortable with each other. Why did you think it would be any different with my friends?"

The look in her eyes slayed Pid. It was obvious she wanted to be friends with the other women, but wasn't sure how to do that.

"I'll go with you. Come on," he said, not giving her a chance to argue. He reached for her hand once more and counted it as a win when she didn't yank it away. They walked over to where Elodie and Lexie were talking to two police officers. They all turned to face them as they approached.

"I asked Theo to draw a picture of the man he saw in the building tonight," Monica said without preamble, as she held out the paper.

Lexie took one look and gasped. "Holy crap, that's Cash!"

Elodie looked over her shoulder and nodded. "Yeah, that's definitely him."

"Who's Cash?" one of the officers asked.

"He was hired recently to take my place at the downtown Food For All," Lexie explained.

"Could he have a key to this building?" the officer asked.

"He shouldn't. But it's possible he was able to make a copy at some point. And it's probably not a stretch that he was able to find out the alarm code, so he wouldn't set it off when he came inside."

"We'll look into it," the other officer said. "That drawing looks pretty damn accurate."

"Thank you," Lexie told Monica.

She shrugged. "I didn't do anything."

"Yes, you did. You figured out that it was Theo who broke the window, purposely setting off the alarm, and you got him to relax enough to draw this. You practically solved the case for the detectives," Lexie told her.

Monica's cheeks turned a rosy pink. "I'm glad I could help," she said. "But really, it was all Theo."

"Whatever. Consider yourself a part of our tribe," Lexie said firmly. "I know you aren't comfortable with us yet, but you'll get there."

Monica looked at her in surprise, her cheeks getting redder. "Oh, um...Okay."

"And I know you aren't sure how long you're staying, but if you could maybe slow down the process of looking at those pictures the commander has you going over, so you can be here for both Kenna's bachelorette party and her wedding, we'd really like that."

Pid and Mustang burst out laughing.

"What?" Lexie asked. "I just want her to be around for as long as possible."

"I'm not sure asking her to interfere in a federal investigation while you're standing in front of two military members and two officers is the smartest idea," Midas said as he walked up and put an arm around Lexie.

"I'm not interfering!" Lexie insisted innocently. "Just making sure Monica knows we want her to be here for the wedding in a couple weeks."

Pid saw Monica give her new friends a small smile. "I'll see what I can do," she promised.

"Great!" Lexie exclaimed.

"Awesome!" Elodie echoed.

"I'll let you guys continue with what you were doing. I'll just be over there with Theo," Monica said, gesturing to the table across the room, where Theo was bent over another piece of paper.

After she walked away, Lexie turned to Pid and said, "She's amazing."

He couldn't keep the smile from his face. "Yup."

"We're almost done here," one of the officers said to Lexie.

She turned back to him, and Pid wandered back across the room to a spot against the wall, closer to Theo and Monica. He could now hear their conversation, and Monica looked up and caught his eye. He gave her a reassuring smile, and she returned it.

The sight of that adorable dimple once more made his heart beat faster. He absently listened in as Monica reassured Theo that the policemen liked his drawing. They spoke about how Theo didn't like crusts on his sandwiches and how he hated waffles.

Monica asked him how he liked his apartment nearby, and Theo said he liked it a lot. He could sleep without worrying about someone stealing his stuff.

"You feel safe there?" Monica asked.

"Yeah, safe."

"It's important, feeling safe," Monica said gently.

Theo looked up at her and asked, "Do *you* feel safe?" he asked.

Pid's muscles tightened as he waited for her answer. Monica answered Theo's question, but her gaze was locked on Pid as she said, "You know what? I do."

"Good," Theo told her, patting her left hand.

Pid knew she wasn't comfortable with people touching her damaged fingers, but she didn't seem to mind Theo doing so.

"Pid is a good man," Theo told her. "Now that he found you, he'll keep you safe."

Monica's gaze returned to his. "He will?" she asked.

Theo nodded as if he could see into the future and knew what would happen. "Yeah. Pid's big and strong."

"He is *that*," Monica agreed with a small chuckle.

Their conversation turned back to his favorite foods, but Pid didn't move from his spot against the wall. He didn't miss the way Monica's gaze strayed to him again and again as she kept Theo company, while Lexie and Elodie finished up their conversation with the police officers.

Pid helped Mustang and Midas board up the front window and, after another thirty minutes, everyone was ready to go. Midas contacted a window company to come the next day and replace the missing pane and the officers had everything they needed for the moment.

Theo gave Monica a hug goodbye, then proceeded to hug everyone else as well. He headed down the sidewalk in the direction of his apartment as the rest of them all walked toward the parking lot where they'd left their cars.

After Lexie promised to keep Monica up-to-date on the investigation, they were all finally on their way.

Pid looked over at Monica and saw her head back, resting against the seat behind her, her eyes were closed. "You all right?" he asked.

"Yup," she said without hesitation.

"That wasn't exactly the ending of the evening I envisioned," he commented dryly.

"It was certainly exciting," she said, opening her eyes and turning her head without lifting it. "I'm sorry I didn't make a better impression."

"Mo, stop. You were fine. Besides, those women love Theo. And not only because he literally dragged himself across the floor, bleeding like a stuck pig, trying to get to Lexie when he knew she was in trouble. Many people don't treat him very well. There's no denying that he doesn't smell all that great. He's odd. He's hard to understand sometimes. And yet without hesitation, you befriended

166

him. Got him to open up to you. That alone has earned you a special place in all our hearts."

"Kids and mentally challenged people like me," she said. "And I like them. I know things weren't going so well at the restaurant. I was trying...but I don't feel comfortable around most adults."

"It's okay," Pid reassured her. "It just takes you longer to warm up to people. There's nothing wrong with that. And after Lexie's declaration tonight, I think it's obvious that you have nothing to worry about."

Monica chuckled. "I thought Mustang was going to die when she told me to slow down looking at the profiles."

"Right?" Pid agreed. "Lord, Lexie's awesome, but that wasn't the best time or place for that conversation, that's for sure."

"Can I tell you something?"

"You can tell me anything," Pid said.

"For the first time in my life, I'm looking forward to hanging out with a bunch of women."

"I'm glad. They're a friendly bunch, and I know you'll have a good time. Although I think I'm jealous."

"Jealous?" Monica asked.

"Yeah. You going out with them for Kenna's bachelorette party means one less evening I get to spend with you."

When she didn't respond, Pid mentally kicked himself. He'd shown his cards too soon and freaked her out—yet again.

"We hang out every night," she said eventually.

"Yup," he agreed.

"It's...nice," Monica whispered.

The hair on the back of Pid's neck stood up. For some women, those two words would be tepid at best. Would make a man think she wasn't happy spending time with him. But coming from Monica, it was high praise indeed.

"Yeah, it is."

They were quiet the rest of the way back to his house. Pid parked and waited for her at the front of the minivan, resting his hand on the small of her back as they walked to the front door. He unlocked it and turned on the light after they entered.

As she headed for the hallway to her room, Pid called out, "Mo?"

She stopped and turned to face him. "Yeah?"

He walked slowly toward her, his gaze fixed on hers. If he'd seen the slightest sign that she was uneasy or nervous about him coming toward her, he would've stopped and merely said good night.

But all he saw in her eyes was a longing that echoed deep in his soul.

Monica licked her lips as she stared up at him.

"I'm going to kiss you," he blurted, waiting for her reaction.

Her eyes widened—and miracle of all miracles, she nodded.

Moving slowly, Pid leaned closer. His lips covered hers gently, and immediately he felt sparks shoot from where they were touching straight down to his toes. He'd never been affected by a woman so viscerally. He wasn't sure what to think...except that he didn't ever want to stop touching her.

He didn't reach for her though. Didn't haul her against his chest like he longed to do. He simply turned his head and gradually deepened their kiss. Her tongue shyly reached out and twined with his, and just like that, Pid was as hard as he'd ever been in his life.

That small token of trust sealed his fate. He wanted this woman with every fiber of his being, but he knew he had to move slowly. Gaining her trust was more important than anything else had ever been in his life thus far.

Even though he could've kissed her all night, Pid forced himself to pull his lips from hers. Her pupils were dilated now, and it was all he could do to keep his hands from grabbing her when she licked her lips after he pulled away.

"Um...wow," she said softly.

Pid grinned. "Yeah." He leaned down once more and kissed her forehead reverently. "Sleep well, Mo."

She looked confused for a second, then nodded. "You too."

Pid had a feeling she thought he was gonna ask for more. He found that he liked surprising her. He didn't want to be like any other man in her life. But that kiss was letting her know that he was interested in more than a platonic friendship. He'd go at her pace, but the change in their relationship felt good. He prayed she'd feel the same way about moving their relationship forward in the morning.

It was almost physically painful to turn away from her and walk toward his room, but he did it. Monica needed to know she could trust him. She'd told Theo earlier that she felt safe in his house, and he'd rather cut off a limb than do anything to put a dent in that progress.

Monica had gotten under his skin, and there was no getting her out. Nothing had changed, she would still probably be leaving soon, but there was no going back now for him. Pid was all in. He just hoped she felt the same way.

# CHAPTER TWELVE

Monica spent every day the following week at the base, looking at more profiles, without finding anyone who even remotely resembled the man she'd seen. Her evenings were spent with Stuart, as always, but after that kiss, things between them had changed. Stuart was more touchy-feely. He never overstepped his bounds, never did anything that made her feel unsafe, but he touched her back as he passed her in the kitchen. He kissed the top of her head all the time. He even held her hand as they sat on the back deck in the evenings.

He told her more stories about growing up in Alaska, and about some of the places he'd been courtesy of the Navy. When she asked about what happened to Lexie, he shared without hesitation. Going on to tell her about Kenna's awful experience, and more about Elodie's as well.

Hearing what the three women had been through somehow made Monica feel closer to them. She hadn't seen them since the other evening, when they'd had dinner and Food For All had gotten broken into, but they'd all texted her. She was slowly beginning to feel as if she could relate to them, and them to her, just a little better.

All those women knew what it was like to suffer. They'd been through their own awful times, and they'd survived, just like she had. Although, Monica had a feeling they had a lot fewer hang-ups than she did. But she was working on them. Being around Stuart and his friends, seeing how they all treated their women, made her desperate to shed the legacy her dad had left her. She wanted to be strong, and funny, and carefree. She wanted to judge people on their actions, and not because of their job or the uniform they wore.

The bachelorette party was all set for the following weekend. Saturday night, they planned on going to a few bars in Waikiki, then heading back to Kenna and Aleck's penthouse to spend the night. Monica hadn't been sure about the sleepover, but when Kenna had called to tell her about the plans for the evening, Monica had found herself responding to the woman's excitement.

Aleck would stay the night at Slate's place, giving the women space to do what they wanted without worrying about the guys hanging around.

Yesterday, when Stuart had picked her up from the base, he'd scowled when he'd seen her bloodshot eyes. Staring at a computer all day was beginning to get to her, even though she'd done her best to not let Stuart know.

Yeah. Right. He'd marched into his commander's office and told him that Monica was taking the day off on Friday. That she needed a break. Luckily, the commander had no problem with that. It wasn't as if he was her boss. Yes, she was there at his demand, but still.

Not only that, the commander had apologized again... and pretty much told Monica that she could leave when she wanted. That he was still desperate to find the rogue SEAL, but he'd had no right to force her to come to Hawaii against her will.

She'd been shocked, to say the least. And assured Huttner that, now that she was there, and since she'd been replaced as the ambassador's nanny by the agency she worked for, she wanted to see this through. To stay and continue trying to identify the man she'd seen.

Her response had surprised both Commander Huttner *and* Stuart, but they'd done their best to hide their reactions. The commander had thanked her...and Monica couldn't begin to interpret the look on Stuart's face. But she wanted to guess he was pleased with her decision.

Today, on her unexpected day off, Stuart was taking her to possibly meet the infamous Baker she'd heard so much about. When she'd told the other women what Stuart had planned via text, there'd been a flurry of responses from them about the man. Elodie had asked her to sneak a picture if she could, and Lexie and Kenna had both been all for it.

Monica had found herself giggling at the thought of pretending to take a picture of the scenery or something, secretly getting this Baker guy in the shot. After hearing about how intense and somewhat scary he was, there was no chance in hell she was going to risk getting caught taking his photo. Besides, she wouldn't like it if someone did that to her...but she couldn't help being curious as to whether the man was as good-looking as the others thought he was.

"You seem different today," Stuart said as he drove toward the popular beaches of the North Shore. "More relaxed or something."

"I am," Monica said. "I think knowing I can leave if I want has taken a lot of pressure off me."

"Have you heard back from the agency you work for about another placement?"

Monica tried to read Stuart's expression, without luck. Did he *want* her to go? Was he asking to be polite or did he have an ulterior motive?

As if he could read her mind, Stuart said, "For the record, I'm one hundred percent all right with you staying here for as long as you want. I think I made it clear the other night that I like you, Mo."

His words made a warm glow spread within her. Had anyone come right out and made it that clear they didn't want her to leave? No. Even with as many nanny jobs as she'd had over the years, none of her bosses had ever asked her to stay past her contract. "I sent an email updating them on my situation, but I asked them to hold off putting me on the placement list just yet."

The smile Stuart shot her way made the warmth morph into something much hotter.

"Good."

One word. That was all it took to make Monica feel like a pile of mush.

Her feelings toward Stuart were quickly changing from being grateful he'd given her a place to stay so she didn't have to be on the Naval base, to something more...intimate...personal. The kiss they'd shared a week ago had been different from any kiss she'd ever received. More satisfying. Definitely hotter.

She genuinely liked Stuart. Liked being around him, liked who he was as a person, and could even admit that the longer she stayed, the more her "like" was deepening into something else. Which should've scared her to death. Instead, when she thought about actually having a relationship with Stuart, the idea made her feel almost giddy.

"You know," he continued. "There are lots of people on Oahu who need nannies."

Monica stilled as his words sank in. It was unbelievable that the thought hadn't even crossed her mind.

"I'm not trying to tell you how to live your life. You're an adult who's made decisions on your own for a long while now. But the good thing about what you do is that there are children with working parents everywhere."

He wasn't wrong.

Monica nodded as her mind spun. She wasn't sure her employment agency would be able to help her with placement here, as they dealt more with dignitaries in foreign countries, but with her experience, she didn't think she'd have any issues finding employment with someone who needed a nanny to look after their kids. Though maybe not a live-in nanny.

"I like that look on your face," Stuart said.

She glanced over and found him smiling as he drove.

There was so much Monica wanted to say, but her mind was spinning with the possibilities for her future. Was she insane for actually thinking about staying here? Probably. But for the first time in ages—maybe ever—she was excited about her future.

She didn't have the words to tell Stuart what she was thinking, but she didn't want him to assume she was dismissing his suggestion. So she reached out and touched his hand, resting on the console between them.

It wasn't until his fingers closed around her hand that she realized she'd used her left. That alone was enough to make her freeze in shock. She never, *ever* forgot about her mangled fingers. But all she'd been thinking when she'd reached for Stuart was connecting with him.

The smile on his face had grown so big when she touched him, Monica didn't have the heart to let go now. So they drove northward just like that, holding hands, Stuart with a goofy grin on his face, and Monica thinking much too hard about what the next steps in her life should be, while also marveling over the fact that a man as amazing as Stuart seemed to be interested in her.

An hour later, Stuart pulled into a large beach parking lot that was almost full. They found a space toward the back of the lot and when he turned off the engine, and Monica started to get out, he squeezed her hand. "Mo?"

She turned back to him. "Yeah?" she asked, feeling shy for some reason.

"I know you were thinking pretty hard on the way up here. I'm sorry Huttner basically forced you to come to Hawaii, but I'm glad I got the chance to know you better. For the record...I'd love it if you decided to stay. But if you don't, I still want to stay in touch. Because I think you're pretty amazing."

Monica swallowed hard. She wasn't ready to lay everything she was thinking and feeling on the table yet. She liked Stuart...but did she trust him? He could hurt her, *bad*, and she'd been protecting her feelings for too long to stop now.

But she also wanted him to know how much she appreciated everything he'd done for her. He didn't have to let her live with him. He didn't have to stand up to his commander for her. He didn't have to do what he could to integrate her with his friends. But he did.

"I don't know what I'm going to do yet, but for now, I want to keep looking through the profiles for the man I saw. He can't continue to do what he's doing, and if I'm the only one who can ID him, I *need* to keep looking. But...I wouldn't mind keeping in touch with you as well."

She could tell her words weren't exactly what Stuart wanted to hear, but she gave him credit for not pushing for more. She knew he'd never pressure her for something she didn't want, or wasn't ready, to give freely.

"Come on, let's go watch some surfers kill it in the waves." Then he raised her mangled hand to his lips and kissed the back.

Monica held her breath as she watched his expression. She saw no disgust, no pity. If she wasn't mistaken, she saw admiration and affection. Then he let go and turned to climb out of the minivan.

Without thought, she did the same, meeting Stuart at the back of the vehicle. As if it was the most natural thing in the world, he took her hand in his once more—her left one—and began walking toward the beach.

The wind was blowing steadily, making Monica wish she'd thought to tie her hair back before they'd left. The blonde strands blew across her face and she wrinkled her nose as she brushed them away.

"Here."

Looking down at the hand Stuart was holding out, she was shocked to see one of her hair ties lying on his palm.

"What...? How...?" she stammered.

He shrugged. "I've seen how often you forget these things, so I stuffed one in my pocket before we left, just in case."

If he hadn't been holding her hand, Monica would've probably keeled over in shock and surprise. He was a *guy*. A freaking Navy SEAL! And he had one of her hair ties in his pocket? *Just in case?*

Holy shit.

She reached for it and stopped so she could put her hair up. Aware of Stuart's eyes on her as she gathered the wayward strands and quickly and efficiently tied them up into a messy bun.

"You make that look so easy," he commented when she was done and they'd started walking once more.

"It's not rocket science," she replied seriously.

Stuart only grinned down at her. With the smile still on his face, they walked hand in hand toward the beach with huge waves crashing on the shore.

"Wow," Monica said as she caught a glimpse of the largest waves she'd ever seen in her life. "I can't believe people are out there voluntarily."

Stuart chuckled. "Not my thing either, but surfers crave this kind of surf."

"Hi!" a feminine voice said from their right.

Turning, Monica saw a woman in her forties or fifties sitting at a picnic table in the shade. She had a large cooler beside her and a pair of binoculars sat on the table. Her dark brown hair was blowing in the breeze coming off the ocean and her brown eyes were friendly and welcoming.

"If I had to guess, I'd say you were one of Baker's friends," the woman said with a knowing smile.

Stuart nodded and walked over to where the woman was sitting. "You'd guess right. I'm Pid and this is Monica."

"I'm Jodelle, but everyone calls me Jody."

"Good to meet you," Monica said as Stuart nodded at her.

"You hungry?" she asked. "I've got some sandwiches if you are."

"I'm good. Mo?"

Monica shook her head. Then blurted, "You offer food to every stranger you meet on the beach?"

Jody laughed. It was a free and easy sound. "Pretty much, yeah. But I bring snacks mostly for my guys. I come here in the mornings before school and make sure my boys don't surf through the start of classes. Most go straight from here to school, and I know they wouldn't eat anything for breakfast if I didn't hand them a tortilla before they jumped in their cars and zoomed away. Then after school, I want to make sure they have enough energy to do their thing out on the waves safely. So I make sandwiches and hand them out."

"Wow," Monica said.

Jody chuckled again. "I know, most people think I'm crazy, but I don't care. The surfing community looked after me when I needed it most, and I'm happy to show my appreciation the only way I can."

Monica studied her closely. Beneath the woman's open and welcoming expression, she saw...pain. Something bad had happened to this woman, and it was still haunting her today.

Monica knew a thing or two about that.

"How'd you know I'm a friend of Baker's?" Stuart asked.

Jody rolled her eyes. "Have you seen yourself?" she asked rhetorically.

Monica couldn't keep the giggle back when she saw the confused look on Stuart's face.

"What?" he asked, his brows furrowed.

That only made Monica laugh harder. Soon, Jody had joined in.

In response, Stuart rolled *his* eyes at them.

Obviously taking pity on him, Jody explained, "It's just

a look you have. You definitely don't look like a surfer here to catch some waves. You have the same kind of air about you as Baker does."

"An air, huh?" Stuart said.

"Like if someone even breathes wrong, you'll be there to take care of it," Monica blurted.

Stuart's gaze met hers.

"Exactly," Jody said emphatically.

"And that's a good thing?" he asked. But his question was aimed at Monica, not the woman sitting at the table next to them.

"Oh, yeah," she said softly. The same time Jody said, "Of course."

Monica stared into Stuart's eyes, unable to look away. He finally made the first move to break the intimate spell that had weaved its way around them by turning toward Jody. "Is he here?"

"Yes. He's out there keeping an eye on my boys." Jody gestured to the ocean with her chin.

Monica looked out at the water and could make out some dark heads between the rise and fall of the waves, but that was about it. Then she saw someone stand up as if they were walking on water and ride one of the monster waves as it rolled toward the shore.

It was poetic, and beautiful, and scary as hell. There was no way she wanted to be anywhere near the power of the ocean like that, and definitely not riding on top of a wave that eventually would have to crash back to earth.

But somehow, the person on the surfboard dropped at the last second, paddling back out to sea as the wave he or she had been riding broke apart in a flurry of foam and angry splashes.

"It's beautiful, isn't it?" Jody asked.

It was, though Monica thought the intensity of the waves kind of overwhelmed the beauty. But she nodded anyway.

"I'm guessing that when he sees you here, he'll head in," Jody told them.

"Because he'll see someone here talking to *you*," Stuart said. It wasn't a question.

Jody shrugged. "He's protective of everyone he knows," she replied, clearly going for nonchalant but not quite succeeding.

Monica had a feeling there was more than just friendship between Jody and the mysterious Baker, but she didn't know either well enough to truly speculate.

Ten minutes passed before they saw a man emerge from the frenzied ocean. He reminded Monica a little bit of Aquaman, how he rose from the waves as if immune to their fury and power. He had a surfboard under his arm and his strides were long and purposeful as he headed in their direction.

Unease swirled in Monica's gut. She remembered all the stories the other women had said about Baker, and she had a feeling he was unlike Stuart or his other teammates.

As the man got closer, Monica saw he was wearing a wet suit with long sleeves. The material clung to him like a second skin, outlining his muscular chest and thighs. The bottom of the suit stopped just above his knees, and his calves flexed as he hiked over the sand.

Monica couldn't help but stare as he got closer. Elodie and the others were right—the man was drop-dead gorgeous. Even though he was probably in his fifties, he obviously kept himself in great shape. The silver streaks in his hair and well-trimmed beard only enhanced his masculinity, rather than making him look old. He was definitely a silver fox, a term she'd seen recently online when someone was describing a Hollywood heartthrob.

But he was also intimidating as hell. Monica found herself taking a step backward as he stalked toward the picnic table.

He took a moment to lean his surfboard against a nearby tree before approaching them. "Pid," he said with a nod.

"Hey, Baker."

"What brings you to my neck of the woods? The women all good? Carly heard from her ex's son?"

"They're all fine. And I don't know about Carly, but I don't think so. Jag would've said something," Stuart told him.

Baker nodded.

"I'm sure you've heard about Aleck and Kenna's wedding in a couple weeks, right?"

"The luau on the beach? Yeah."

Monica watched Stuart and Baker talk, noting the obvious respect the two men had for each other. Then Baker's jade-green eyes turned to her.

"Monica Collins, I'm assuming?" he asked.

She could only nod.

"Nice to meet you. Thank you for not filing an abuse report with the Inspector General against Commander Huttner. He was out of line, forcing Pid and the team to bring you back to Hawaii, but his intentions were good."

"Um...you're welcome."

"No luck with the pictures yet, huh?" Baker asked, then went on. "But you're only up to the H's in the alphabet, so it's to be expected."

Monica had no idea how he knew so much about what she was doing. She'd just finished looking through profiles of men whose last names started with H the day before. "Yeah," she said lamely.

"Well, it's appreciated," he told her. "No one gets away with defiling the SEAL name."

Monica swallowed hard, not wanting to know what exactly he meant and what the consequences were in his mind for being a rogue SEAL.

"See you met Jodelle."

"How're conditions out there, Baker?" Jody asked.

If Monica hadn't been looking at the older man, she would've missed the gentleness that softened his expression when Jody spoke.

"Not bad. The guys are all good. Told them it was getting late, so they should start coming in soon to head home and do their homework."

Jody gave him a satisfied smile. "Good."

Baker turned back to Stuart. "So? What brings you up here, if it's not because of the girls?"

Monica mentally chuckled at Baker calling Elodie, Lexie, and Kenna "girls." But she made sure her thoughts didn't reflect outwardly.

"Mo needed a break from the office. And I wanted you to meet her. And maybe stop and introduce her to the best shave ice on the island at Matsumoto's. Also wanted to see if you had any insight as to who this asshole might be who's got the commander's knickers all twisted."

Monica snorted at that.

"What?" Stuart asked with a smile. "They are definitely twisted. But I can't blame him."

"I wish I did," Baker said. "I've been in contact with Huttner, and we've discussed a few possibilities, but without more info we're kind of in a holding pattern."

"Meaning, without me being able to give you more info on him," Monica said softly.

Baker shrugged, which Monica interpreted as a yes.

She hated not being able to describe the man clearly enough for someone to draw a picture of him. She'd considered asking Theo to give it a shot after seeing the likeness he'd drawn of the man who'd broken into Food For All, but she truly felt she didn't see enough for anyone to draw a composite of the man. She felt as if she'd failed, when she hadn't asked for the responsibility to figure out who he was in the first place.

"Towel?" Jody asked Baker, holding a fluffy dark blue towel toward him.

"Thanks," Baker said as he took it.

There was no mistaking the look of longing on Jody's face. And the second she looked away, the same look was reflected on Baker's.

For a second, Monica had visions of playing matchmaker. Of telling Kenna and the others what she'd observed and seeing if they could somehow set something up at the wedding, get Jody and Baker tipsy and see if they'd act on the sparks flying between them.

But then she thought better of it. She had a feeling *no one* interfered with Baker's life. He wouldn't allow it. She also figured that if he truly wanted Jody, then he wouldn't hesitate to do something about it. So there had to be a reason he wasn't acting on his attraction, and the last thing Monica wanted to do was piss him off by interfering, or spreading gossip and getting Elodie and the others to meddle in his life.

Baker and Stuart chitchatted about people she didn't know, and Monica tuned them out. When Baker began to strip the wet suit off his chest and over his arms, she turned away to stare out at the ocean. It wasn't as if he was getting naked right there on the beach, he was only peeling the wet suit down to dry off, but she still felt awkward about watching.

She heard Stuart telling Baker about one of their recent training exercises and couldn't help but peek over at the older man. She rationalized her eyeballing him by telling herself Lexie and the others would want a full report of her meeting with Baker when she saw them the next weekend at the bachelorette part. Once they heard she'd seen him in a wet suit, they'd want all the juicy details.

But the second she caught a glimpse of Baker bare-chested with the wet suit hanging around his waist, all thoughts of the other women—and even where she was—flew out of her mind. She was abruptly and violently thrown back to the house in Algiers, standing in the middle of the ambassador's living room, staring at the man with evil eyes as he ordered her to open the door. Promising that he was a Navy SEAL...that she could trust him.

Suddenly unable to think about anything other than getting away, Monica stepped backward and immediately tripped over a rock behind her. She went down hard on her ass, but she didn't take her eyes off the threat in front of her.

"Shit...Mo? Are you okay?" Stuart asked, but she didn't register the words. Her only goal was to put as much distance between herself and the man with the black tattoo on his forearm.

She crab-walked backward, scrambling to get away from him.

"What the fuck?" the man asked, taking a step toward her with his hand outstretched.

Monica whimpered and shot to her feet. She started to run, no destination in mind; she just knew that she had to get away. *Now!*

Two strong arms caught her around the waist and pulled her against a hard chest.

She fought. Desperately. But it was no use—

"Monica! It's me, Stuart. Calm down!"

His words barely touched her. She was lost in another time and place. Flashes of watching the man with the tattoo on the security monitors inside the safe room ran through her brain. The thought of what he'd do if he got his hands on her tangled with her father's angry words over the years. Her hand throbbed as she heard him saying, *"You do things by yourself. Asking for help will only screw you in the long run."*

"Monica!" a harsh voice said once more.

The man behind her eased them down to the sand and forced her onto his lap. He kept his arms around her, but she also felt his warm breath at her ear. It took a long moment for his litany of words to register...but when they did, she froze, not fighting him any longer.

"It's me, Stuart. You're safe. I promise. Whatever happened, we'll deal with it together. Come back to me. That's it, good girl. I've got you. Breathe, Mo. Take a deep breath...Good. Another. That'a girl. I can feel your heart pounding a million miles an hour. Just relax."

"Stuart?" she whispered.

"Yup. Right here."

Monica realized where she was...at the North Shore with Stuart. And Jody and Baker—and she'd just embarrassed the hell out of herself. But at the moment, that was the least of her worries. She squeezed her eyes closed and took a deep breath, smelling the salty air and feeling the breeze against her cheeks.

"You scared the hell out of me," Stuart said softly. "Wanna share what that panic attack was about?"

She didn't, but Monica knew she had to. "The tattoo," she told him in a whisper, her entire body shaking.

"What tattoo?" he asked.

"Mine," a deep voice said from above them.

Monica didn't open her eyes as Baker spoke. She simply nodded.

"You've seen it before?" he asked.

She nodded again. "On the man who shot out the window. I knew he had one, but I couldn't picture it in my mind. It was just a black blur. But the second I saw yours, it came back to me."

"*Fuck*," Baker said in a voice so terrifying, it made Monica flinch. She clutched at Stuart's arms around her.

"Easy, Mo. You're safe."

Was she? The fact that the scary man standing above them had the same tattoo as the guy who'd been accused of raping and killing women, as well as pillaging and inciting mobs to violence, wasn't exactly reassuring.

Was Baker in on it? Was he feeding the other guy info? Stuart had said Baker was extremely good at electronic stuff, even better than he was. That he could find information no one else could. If he was a part of the other man's schemes...she was in big trouble.

She felt more than heard someone moving, then Baker's voice came from right in front of her. "Open your eyes," he ordered. "Look at me."

"Baker," Stuart said, the single word a low, menacing growl.

It was the protectiveness in Stuart's tone that gave Monica the strength she needed to open her eyes. Baker was squatting in front of her on the balls of his feet. The anger in his eyes made her want to shrink away, but she swallowed hard and stood her ground...so to speak.

"I need you to be sure," he said gruffly. He held out his arm, displaying the tattoo for her.

The sight of the ink on his skin made goose bumps break out on the back of her neck, but Monica didn't look away.

Another memory from her childhood popped into her head. Of when she'd found a litter of kittens from a stray cat who lived on their property. She'd been cuddling them when her father had found her. He'd forced her to watch as he picked up those one-week-old kittens and killed them. When she tried to look away, he'd hit her. Hard. Told her if she didn't watch, he'd go beat the hell out of her mother instead.

Monica had been five or six. Even then, she knew better than to disobey her father. That he'd absolutely do what he threatened.

She didn't think Baker would beat her if she refused to look at his arm, but she wasn't willing to take any chances.

"Breathe, Mo," Stuart told her. She felt his chin on her shoulder. Could feel his hair against her cheek. She felt surrounded by him...and amazingly, it made her relax a fraction.

She looked again at Baker's arm, at the tattoo inked into his skin. It was a dragon. The tail stretched up to wrap around his bicep and the mouth was open, its many teeth showing in a snarl. She remembered telling the commander that maybe the design had a snake in it, and now she realized what she'd seen was the tail curling around the man's upper arm.

"It's the same," Monica said.

"You're sure?"

"Yes."

"How sure?" Baker asked.

She looked into his eyes then, trying not to flinch at the stark fury she saw there. Somehow, she knew it wasn't directed at her. "As sure as I am that if I didn't get out of my father's house when I did, I would've been dead in a month."

She had no idea if the man in front of her knew what that meant, but when he nodded once and stood, she figured he did. Stuart had told her that Baker had the ability to find out anything about anyone. She'd kind of shrugged it off at the time. Now she was certain he'd done his research on her. Probably the second he'd heard the commander had forced her come to Hawaii to help ID the rogue SEAL.

"You know who he is?" Stuart asked.

"I have a good idea," Baker said.

Monica felt more than heard Stuart growl in frustration. Then he asked her in a gentle tone, "You think you can stand up?"

She wasn't sure. But she nodded anyway. And she shouldn't have worried; Stuart didn't let go of her for one second as he helped her off his lap and to her feet. He led her over to the table where Jody was still sitting, looking extremely concerned now, and gestured for her to sit on the bench.

Monica did so gratefully. She'd fallen on her ass once in front of these people, she didn't want to do it a second time.

"Who is he?" Stuart asked.

"Shane 'Bull' Beyer. He was on my SEAL team. Everyone on the team got the same tattoo one night after an especially gnarly mission. We were as close as a team could get...but as the years went by, something happened in Bull's head. He became reckless, then out of control... then dangerous. It got to the point where I had to write him up and report him to my commander. After a psych eval, he was kicked off the team and ordered to go to therapy. He refused and was given a ODPMC discharge."

Stuart whistled low.

Monica frowned. "What's that?"

"Other designated physical and mental conditions discharge," Baker said. "It's used when someone doesn't qualify for a disability discharge, but still has a condition that interferes with the performance of his duties."

"He wasn't happy about that," Stuart said. It wasn't a question.

Baker chuckled, but it wasn't a happy sound. "No, he definitely wasn't happy. I tried to get him help once he was out, but he told me to fuck off. That I'd already *helped* him enough. I kept tabs on him for a while, but eventually he dropped off my radar. I'm assuming that's when he started using false identities."

"So now what?" Stuart asked.

"Now I go on the hunt," Baker said.

Monica shivered at the threat in his tone.

"If I'd known he was capable of stooping as low as he has, this would've been taken care of before now. I'll call Huttner and have a chat with him, tell him about my suspicions."

"Don't you need proof?" Monica got up the nerve to ask. "I mean, how do you know it's him and not any of the other guys on your team? Or someone who just happens to like dragons and got a tattoo?"

"I've read your description of the man you saw," Baker said. He didn't pace. He didn't look agitated. His stillness as he stood in front of her and explained himself somehow made him even *more* scary. "It fits Bull to a tee. So much so, I should've guessed it was him before now. But it's been years since I've heard from him. A decade at least."

"What's his end goal?" Stuart asked.

"Who knows? To cause as much disorder as he can? To stick it to the United States? He probably gets off telling women he's a SEAL, then terrorizing them. Maybe his way of 'getting back' at the organization he feels sold him out."

"I want in," Stuart said.

Baker shook his head immediately. "No fucking way."

"I have a stake in this," he argued.

"I realize that," Baker said, his gaze flicking to Monica's before looking back at Stuart. "But you're also still active duty. I'm not going to let you do anything that might get you in trouble. Besides...this is between me and Bull."

"Baker?" Jody asked.

And just like that, Baker instantly got control of his anger. His shoulders visibly relaxed and he took a deep breath before turning to the woman sitting at the table. "I'm sorry, Jodelle," he said.

She shook her head. "I don't know what's going on, but I'm guessing you're going to be gone again for a while?"

"It's possible," Baker told her.

"Just be careful," she said softly. "I can't lose someone else I care about."

"You aren't going to lose me," Baker reassured her.

Monica almost felt as if she was intruding on a very

intimate conversation. There was definitely more between these two people than what either of them would probably admit.

"I want to be informed about everything you find out," Stuart told Baker. "And now I'm thinking since Mo is the only one who can ID this guy, she could be in serious danger if he figures out you're on his trail."

Baker shook his head. "No offense to Monica, but I doubt he's going to care about her. He'll be overjoyed to know he's gotten under the Navy's skin. And mine. He'll be positively *gleeful* when he realizes I'm on his trail. It's a game to him. Probably is pissed he hasn't been identified yet and has purposely let himself get sloppy."

"He let Monica see him?" Stuart asked.

"Yup. And I wouldn't be surprised if there are other clues that will seem obvious now. I don't think your woman is in any danger," Baker said.

Monica didn't have time to process the "your woman" thing when Stuart countered with, "Is yours?"

The two men stared at each other for a long moment, before Baker sighed and said, "I'll keep you in the loop."

"Good. You ready to go, Mo?"

She glanced at Stuart. He did *not* look happy. The relaxed vibe he'd had when they arrived was gone. *She'd* done that—and she hated it.

She simply nodded in response.

Stuart put a hand under her elbow and as soon as she was upright, he wrapped his arm around her waist. It felt good. Comforting. Monica knew she should pull away but felt the need to absorb as much of his support as she could for just a while longer.

"It was nice to meet you," Monica told Jody.

"You too."

"I'm sorry about how all this turned out," she couldn't help but add.

"Why? From what I understand, it seems to me that the entire reason why you're here on our beautiful island to begin with was solved in the last ten minutes or so."

She was right. Monica had no reason to stay any longer. She could call up her employment agency and tell them to get her a new placement immediately.

Two weeks ago, she would've jumped at the opportunity. Now, she wasn't sure *what* she wanted anymore.

"Later," Stuart told Baker with a lift of his chin.

"Later," Baker returned.

Monica looked back as they walked toward the parking lot and Stuart's minivan, and saw Baker sitting on the bench next to Jody. He lifted a hand and smoothed back a lock of her hair, an intimate gesture that proved there was more to their association than simple friendship.

And despite everything that had just happened, Monica had to admit that Elodie, Lexie, and Kenna were right. Baker was a fine specimen of a man...even if he did scare the hell out of her.

# CHAPTER THIRTEEN

Pid was having a hard time shaking off his frustration and anger. He was pissed as hell at this Bull guy—but he was more frustrated that he didn't know where Monica's head was at. She'd scared him to death when all the color had leached from her face and she'd had that panic attack. If he hadn't caught her before she could run off, she really could've gotten hurt.

Now he had no idea what she was thinking. Was she going to demand he take her home so she could pack and get the hell out of Hawaii? Back to her nanny job?

He hadn't known her that long, but the thought of never seeing her again made Pid want to throw up. He'd gotten attached. He hadn't meant to, had told himself he was just doing her a favor by letting her stay at his house, even as he enjoyed her company more and more. But he should've known just two days in...when he'd first gotten the idea to build the false wall in her room. He wouldn't have done that for someone he didn't care about. Deeply.

The Monday after the weekend she'd met Baker and things had sort of imploded, he went in with her to talk to

Huttner. The commander hadn't said much. Just listened to Monica explain why she thought the tattoo on Baker was the same as the one she'd seen on the mystery man, then he'd thanked her and said she could go home for the day. So Pid had brought her back to his house, where she'd insisted she was fine, that she was just going to relax the rest of the day.

He pretty much had no choice but to return to work, even though he'd worried about her the entire time.

On Tuesday, he called his commander to find out if Monica was needed on base, rather than driving all the way out, only to possibly turn around and bring her back to his house. Huttner said he'd been talking to Baker and things were progressing, and that he might want Monica to come in at some point to answer questions and look at pictures, but wasn't needed until further notice. So she'd spent another day at home while he was at the base.

Their evenings had been subdued. Monica hadn't really felt like talking, so Pid had given her some space. But he was done with that. He was worried about her, needed her to talk to him.

So after PT with the team and a few meetings in the morning, he headed home early Wednesday afternoon. He had an idea to try to make Monica feel more relaxed. He prayed it would work, and that she wouldn't think he was overstepping.

He'd texted her before leaving work, letting her know he was headed back to the house. The last thing he wanted was to scare her by showing up announced. When he walked through the front door, she was waiting anxiously, standing in the living room practically wringing her hands.

"What's wrong?" she asked the moment he stepped through the door.

"Nothing."

"Then why did you leave work early? Did they find him? That Bull guy?"

"I'm here because I'm worried about you. And no, as far as I know, they haven't found Bull yet, but they will, especially with Baker so pissed off about him."

She frowned. "You're worried about me? Why?"

"Are you serious?"

Monica looked even more confused. "Yes."

Pid walked toward her, not stopping until he was right in front of her. He took her face in his hands and tilted her head back so he could see her eyes. "I'm trying not to be offended that you had to ask that. I've obviously not done a good job in making sure you know how much I care about you. How much I like having you here in my house. Talking with you every night. Sharing how our days went, and just hanging out with you in general. I've also tried to go slow...to not freak you out with my interest in you. But maybe I've gone *too* slow. Ever since I kissed you, my feelings have only gotten deeper, Monica. And now that you're almost free to go, all I can think of is convincing you to stay."

He took a deep breath and continued. "I'm worried about you because you've been stuck inside your head since we got back from the North Shore. You've been quiet, even more than usual...and I'm afraid you're going to tell me that you talked to your boss and you're leaving."

Monica stared up at him, her blue eyes wide, but she didn't say anything.

Pid didn't know if that was a good sign or not, so he kept talking. "I took the rest of the day off today to give you a break from these four walls. To hopefully take your mind off everything that's happened. I made us an appointment somewhere I'm hoping will do just that."

"Where?" she asked softly.

"It's a surprise."

Monica wrinkled her nose. "Another surprise?"

Pid chuckled. "You liked the last one I had for you."

"True," she said.

"In case I wasn't clear enough...I don't want you to go. I'm scared the feelings I have for you are one-sided, and you'll go on with your life without a backward glance."

She licked her lips, and he held his breath as she took one of her own and began to speak. "They aren't one-sided."

Pid let out his breath in a long whoosh.

"But I'm not the best bet for a relationship, Stuart. I don't know if I'll *ever* be able to trust a man again, not after everything my dad did. I've enjoyed living here, but I'm used to taking care of myself. To paying my own way. It seemed okay to stay with you while I was being forced to remain here. But now that they know who that guy is... now that staying or going is *my* choice...I'm uncomfortable mooching off you while I make the decision."

"You aren't mooching," Pid told her. "And as much as this goes against everything within me, if it would make you feel better, I'll let you pay rent."

She looked surprised. "Really?"

"Yup. How does a hundred bucks a month sound?" he asked with a smile.

Monica rolled her eyes. "Like you're not hearing what I'm saying."

The humor fled from his face. "I'm hearing you, Mo. I hate that you feel that way, but I do understand. We can work something out that feels comfortable for both of us.

The last thing I ever want is to take away your independence. But don't mistake my concern for you or my reluctance to take your money as me being overbearing or controlling. I've just learned the hard way that money means next to nothing. Yes, it makes life easier in many ways, but when the grim reaper comes, he doesn't give a shit how much money someone has in the bank or how many doodads and trinkets they've compiled over the years."

Monica nodded.

Pid knew he should let go of her face, but he was enjoying touching her too much. He stroked a thumb on her cheek, marveling at how smooth her skin was...how soft. "So? You'll stay here?" he asked.

He could see the fear in her eyes. He hated it. *Hated* it. Wanted to tell her that she could absolutely trust him not to hurt her or do anything that would emotionally damage her further. That he was on the cusp of falling in love with her, which he knew probably wouldn't take away her anxiety, since it was happening so fast. All he could do was show her by his actions that she was safe with him. Physically, mentally, and emotionally.

"I'll stay for now. If you promise to let me know when I've overstayed my welcome and things aren't working out."

Pid noted she'd said *when*, not if. But he didn't mention it. "Deal," he agreed immediately, knowing that day would never come. It was much more likely that Monica would decide she couldn't be a Navy spouse, or his deployments were too frequent and the uncertainty about where he was going and when he'd be back were too much for her to handle.

"I'm not ready for..." Her voice trailed off.

"No pressure, Mo. Yes, I want a relationship with you, but I'm not some out-of-control teen or an asshole who would ever expect sex if you weren't ready or interested. I *would* like to touch you, like I am now. And hold your hand. And maybe exchange a few kisses now and then. Would that be all right?"

He loved the blush that crossed her cheeks as she nodded.

"I can be a pain in the ass," he warned her. "But I promise never to take a bad day out on you or push you further than you're comfortable. Sexually, or with my friends, or even if we're just talking. I want to know everything about you, everything your asshole parents did to you...but I can wait until you're ready to share."

"I don't like to talk about that stuff," Monica said.

"Because you haven't found someone you trust enough to open up to. I know. My goal is to be your safe place, Mo. The one person you know you can tell *anything* to and I won't judge you, or get mad, or blame you."

"Stuart, I'm not sure—"

Pid cut off her words with a gentle finger over her lips. "I can be sure for both of us," he whispered, then slowly leaned toward her, giving her time to pull away.

But she didn't. Instead, she went up on her tiptoes and put a hand behind his neck and pulled him closer.

When their lips met, Pid was smiling, loving that she was as eager for his touch as he was for hers. Their kiss was long and deep and just as intense as it had been the first time.

Knowing he had to break it off before things went further than she was ready for, and not wanting her to change her mind about staying in his home, Pid forced himself to lift his head. Monica's lips were swollen from their kiss and her eyes were at half-mast. She looked thoroughly pleasured...and he couldn't help but picture her in his bed looking just like this after he'd finished making slow, passionate love to her.

"I'm gonna change, then we need to get on the road if we're going to be on time," he said.

"On time for what?" she asked.

"You'll see."

She frowned at him. "Can't you at least give me a hint?" she asked with a pout.

"Nope." Pid leaned down and kissed her forehead. "I know deciding whether or not to stay in Hawaii is a big deal, and I'm going to do everything in my power to make sure you don't regret it if you do." Then he let his hands drop from her and turned for the hallway to the bedrooms before he did something crazy—like throw all his plans for the afternoon out the window to stay home and make out with Monica.

* * *

Two hours later, Pid watched as Monica sat on the floor of the Head Start Child Care Center and played with two little girls. The dimple in her cheek he always had to work so hard to coax out had been on full display since they'd pulled into the parking lot.

He'd explained that he'd called to see if the center needed any volunteers, and the manager had happily agreed to meet them. She'd been even more thrilled when she'd learned about Monica's experience with children.

Pid had spent part of his time helping to build some shelves in one of the rooms—then he'd been handed a baby, probably around seven months old, who hadn't stopped crying since he and Monica had arrived. He wasn't completely sure what he was doing, but after a few minutes of bouncing the infant and holding him against his chest, the exhausted child had finally fallen asleep in his arms.

Monica hadn't even noticed him standing against the wall, and Pid didn't bother her. It looked like she was in deep conversation with the little girls about the adventures their dollies had been on recently.

This was one of the best ideas he'd ever had. Monica looked a hundred times less stressed than she'd been that morning. It was obvious that being around children fed her soul in a way that nothing else could. She clicked with them on a level he'd never seen. She truly cared about their well-being, and her ease with them shone like a beacon.

As he observed her, still with the sleeping infant in his arms, she looked up and their gazes met. She stared at him for a long moment before mouthing *thank you*.

Pid nodded before one of the little girls tugged on Monica's shirt, and she turned back to pay attention to whatever she was being told.

And just like that, Pid knew this was what he wanted. Monica playing with their two daughters while he held their son. It was a visceral yearning in his belly that he suddenly suspected he'd do anything to obtain.

This was his future—and he'd be damned if he let it slip through his fingers. He had no idea how to make it happen, except to continue trying to gain Mo's trust so he could give her exactly this. Family. Love.

"She's great with them," Sylvia, the manager, said quietly as she approached.

"She is," Pid agreed.

"And you're not so bad yourself," she replied with a grin, motioning to the boy in his arms.

Pid shrugged. "He was exhausted from crying. It's not me."

Sylvia shook her head. "You'd be surprised. He doesn't take to many people. Trust me, I've shoved him in so many people's arms, only to be crushed when he continued to scream no matter what they tried. You took him and it was...what, two minutes before he settled?"

Pid looked down at the child in his arms. His warm brown skin shone with health, his black hair standing out against the baby-blue blanket he was wrapped in. The child's lips were pursed, and Pid imagined he was dreaming baby dreams. He was perhaps the prettiest baby he'd ever seen.

"I don't suppose she's looking for a job?" Sylvia asked.

Pid couldn't stop the smile from curling his lips. "Maybe."

Sylvia beamed. "Awesome. And if you want to quit your Navy job, we could probably find a slot for you too."

It was obvious she was teasing. "I'll keep that in mind," Pid told her.

"You do that." Sylvia got serious then. "I've been in this profession a long time. I've worked with children almost my entire life. And I've seldom seen someone connect with little ones as fast as your girlfriend. She's got that something special that children are just drawn to. I can't explain it, and I know some people would call me crazy for even thinking that's a thing. But I've seen it happen just a handful of times. Monica definitely has that something special."

Pid had to agree. He'd seen it with the ambassador's son back in Algeria and he was seeing it now. The world was a better place because Monica was in it. He didn't know if it was *because of* what she'd been through as a child, or *despite* it. But in the end, it didn't matter. She needed children to thrive, just as they needed her.

Their conversation was interrupted when a woman entered the building, obviously to pick up her child.

Pid hadn't planned on staying as long as they had, but he didn't have the heart to take Monica away from the children. So it was six-thirty before they left the Head Start building. Monica had given Sylvia her email address when she'd expressed interest in sending her more information about volunteering or working at the center. The contented look on Monica's face was an expression Pid wanted to see more often.

"Hungry?" he asked as he held open the passenger door to his minivan.

She situated herself on the seat and nodded. "Starved."

Pid didn't move away from the door. He couldn't. The smile on her face was so big, so different from what he was used to seeing, it blew him away.

"Stuart? Is something wrong?"

In response, he stepped closer, reaching up and palming the back of her neck. He rested his forehead against hers in an intimate embrace. "I should've seen how much you needed this before now."

Monica pushed lightly against his shoulders, and he immediately moved back. She surprised him by cradling his cheeks in her hands. Pid thought it was maybe the second time she'd voluntarily touched him with her bad hand. "*I* didn't know I needed it," she countered. "How could you?"

Pid put a hand on her thigh, careful to keep it close to her knee, and the other he placed over her hand on his cheek. "I'm not so bad at this surprise thing, huh?" he teased.

Monica chuckled. "You're two for two so far."

Just then, he heard her stomach growl loudly.

He smiled, lifted her hand from his cheek, kissed the palm, and said, "Let's get you fed. How do you feel about Vietnamese food?"

"I haven't had it. But I can usually find something I like anywhere."

"Good. There's an amazing restaurant called The Pig and The Lady on the way home that we can get takeout from."

"Sounds interesting," she told him.

Pid closed her door and jogged around to the driver's side. He couldn't stop himself from reaching out and smoothing back a lock of her disheveled hair once he got situated.

Monica wrinkled her nose. "I probably look awful," she said self-consciously.

"You're beautiful," he told her honestly.

She blushed, and Pid vowed to compliment her more often. He had a feeling she hadn't gotten enough compliments in her life.

As he pulled out of the parking lot, she reached over and took his hand in hers.

His woman might be a little gun-shy, and they might be taking things slow, but he couldn't deny that her touch made everything feel just right.

# CHAPTER FOURTEEN

Monica wasn't so sure about this bachelorette party thing.

First of all, she'd never attended one, so she wasn't sure what to expect. Strippers? Silly costumes? Everyone getting so drunk they couldn't walk?

And secondly, she definitely wasn't thrilled about the sleepover part of the festivities. In all her thirty years, she'd never had a sleepover...and she didn't think staying with Stuart counted. There was no way she would ever have invited anyone over to her house when she was growing up. She couldn't be sure what her father would've done, and it wouldn't have been allowed in the first place. Besides that, she didn't have any friends in her youth, anyway.

It was kind of sad that she was thirty years old and was going to have her first sleepover. Stuart had told her if she felt uncomfortable at any time, she could text him and he'd come and get her.

She actually liked Kenna, Lexie, and Elodie. She didn't know Ashlyn quite as well, and Kenna had said she hoped her friend Carly would show up, but wasn't certain she would. Regardless, with so many questions about Luke Keyes—not to mention this Bull guy—Kenna had vetoed going out to the bars on Waikiki, so now they were just going to hang out at the penthouse she lived in with Aleck.

That was perfectly all right with Monica. Since she didn't drink, bars didn't exactly appeal to her.

Stuart pulled up in front of the Coral Springs condo complex and turned to her. "Breathe, Mo. This is supposed to be fun."

"I know," she told him.

"Just be yourself. Everyone already knows you aren't super talkative, and they aren't going to suddenly expect you to be just because you're hanging out with them."

Monica nodded. She knew that. Heck, Elodie, Lexie, *and* Kenna had all reassured her several times via text that they were looking forward to spending more time with her. And admittedly, if she decided to stay in Hawaii, she wanted to get along with these women.

It was difficult for her to believe she was considering staying because of a man. It was very unlike her. Then again, Stuart was unlike any guy she'd ever met. Did she trust him? Not quite...and she felt terrible about that. But she liked him. A lot. Felt safe—as safe as she could around *any* man—when she was with him. But one-hundred-percent, put-her-life-in-his-hands trust him? She just didn't know.

Monica *did* know she was likely completely broken when it came to trust. Her father had successfully beaten it out of her over time. If she had to choose one thing she hated him for the most, it was that.

But she was trying. Baby steps. She loved sitting on Stuart's back deck and chatting about nothing in particular. She liked cooking with him. She *really* liked kissing him. It would have to be enough...for now.

"Mo?" Stuart said in concern.

She realized she'd been sitting in the car, lost in her head for a beat too long. She turned and gave him a brave smile. "It'll be fine."

He reached out and brushed his thumb against her cheek where she knew her dimple was probably showing. He'd admitted the other night how much he loved it. She'd always thought it made her look a bit juvenile, but considering the obvious enjoyment he got when he saw it, she was beginning to think it wasn't so bad.

"Of course it will be. You're underestimating yourself, and the others. But if at *any* time you feel uncomfortable, let me know and I'll come pick you up. Even if it's two in the morning. I'm serious. Okay?"

"Why do I feel as if I'm eight years old and you're dropping me off at a party or something?" Monica mumbled.

"I definitely don't see you as eight years old," Stuart replied. The passion was easy to hear in his voice, and her body heated in response.

That was another thing that surprised Monica. How much Stuart turned her on. She'd had sex before. It hadn't been great, and she never understood women in romance novels and movies when they talked about sparks and tingles and wanting someone more than they wanted to breathe.

She was beginning to get it now.

She leaned over the console toward Stuart and he promptly met her halfway. The kiss they shared curled Monica's toes. Yet another thing she'd never experienced before this man.

He pulled back and caressed her cheek one more time before saying, "Go. Before I kidnap you and take you back to my lair."

Monica couldn't help but laugh. "Um...I'm living in that lair," she told him.

Stuart's eyebrows went up and down as he drawled, "You live in my house, not in my lair."

Monica knew she was blushing, so she pushed open her door to try to hide it. She was becoming comfortable with Stuart's touches to the point of longing. He was definitely a touchy-feely kind of man, which thrilled her. He was constantly reaching for her face, putting his hand on her back, or wanting to hold her hand. Last night, he'd snuggled behind her on the couch when they were watching TV. Monica had stiffened at first, but eventually relaxed against him.

She'd only been inside his bedroom once, when she'd gotten a tour of the house. The thought of him spooning her from behind while in his bed made her cheeks feel even hotter. Did she want that? Yes. And no. She'd enjoyed his embrace last night more than she'd thought possible... and suspected the closer she got to this man, the more it would destroy her if things didn't work out.

She opened the sliding side door to the minivan and grabbed her overnight bag. She stood by the open front passenger window and gave Stuart a small wave. "See you tomorrow."

"Have fun," he said. "As you know, I'm headed to Slate's house with the rest of the guys. We're gonna have a bonfire on the beach and hang out."

Monica nodded. Stuart had mentioned his friend had a small house with beach access not too far from Coral Springs. The house was a street over from actually being *on* the beach, but close enough, and plenty big enough for all the guys to chill comfortably.

She waved one more time and bravely headed toward the doors to the condo complex. Stuart waited until she was actually inside to drive away; it was one more way he always seemed to be watching out for her.

"Hi, you must be Monica," said an older man sitting behind a security desk inside the large lobby.

"That's me," she agreed.

"I'm Robert, and the rest of the ladies are already upstairs. But don't worry, Ms. Greene just got here, so you aren't too far behind. If I can have your ID, and if you'll sign this, we'll get you on your way."

Monica was impressed with how efficient the man was, and with the security at the condo complex itself, but she wasn't really surprised. Kenna had talked a lot about the place, and about Robert and how much he was helping with her upcoming wedding.

In a few minutes, she was on her way up to the penthouse floor in the elevator. Trying not to hyperventilate and telling herself everything would be fine, Monica stepped out of the elevator and headed down the hall toward Kenna and Aleck's condo.

The door opened before she even got to it.

"Welcome!" Kenna exclaimed. "And before you freak out and think I can see through doors, Robert called and said you were on your way up." Her smile was large and welcoming, and Monica didn't see a hint of fakeness.

"Thanks," she told her.

"I'm so glad you came. I know you might still be a bit uncomfortable with all of us, since you haven't known us long, but I promise we're harmless," Kenna said. Not giving her a chance to say anything, which was probably good, since Monica didn't know what to say to that, Kenna reached for her bag. "I'll put this here by the door for now and later we can figure out where everyone is sleeping." She lowered her voice as if telling Monica a secret. "But if you want a spot on the balcony, be sure to claim it early, because it's one of the best places to crash."

Monica couldn't help but smile. "Okay."

"Okay," Kenna agreed, beaming. "Come on. Elodie's in the kitchen trying to figure out the right ratio of margarita mix to tequila, and I have a feeling she's gonna have us all drunk after one drink if someone doesn't hold her back. She'd a bit heavy-handed on the alcohol."

Already feeling a little more comfortable than she thought she would, Monica followed Kenna into the other room. The condo was gorgeous and the view from the balcony was just as amazing as she'd been told it was.

"Monica!" Lexie and Elodie exclaimed when they saw her.

"Hi!" Ashlyn threw in. "Good to see you again."

"Carly's not here," Kenna told her, continuing through the kitchen toward Elodie. "I begged, but she said it was safer for us if she didn't come. Which is bullshit, but she wouldn't budge."

"It was her ex who came to Duke's with a bomb strapped to him," Lexie explained to Monica. "He blew up into a million pieces—which is super gross, though you'd never know it looking at the beach now—but because his son has gone underground and no one can find him, not even Baker—which he's really pissed about—Carly quit her job and stays locked inside her apartment now, much to Jag's disappointment."

"Wow, was *that* a long run-on sentence," Ashlyn teased.

"Hey, you followed along without a problem, right?" Lexie asked. "What does it matter?"

"How much margarita have you already sampled?" Kenna asked with a raised eyebrow.

Lexie giggled. "A bit."

"Oh, Lord, it's gonna be a long night," Kenna said, looking up at the ceiling. "No puking on the carpets. Hear me?" she ordered.

Everyone laughed. "No puking whatsoever," Elodie countered. "We're all respectful, mature adults. We don't need to get shitfaced."

"Just tipsy," Lexie said.

"Maybe drunk," Ashlyn countered.

"Monica's in charge of the drinks," Kenna declared.

Monica looked over at her in surprise.

"Since she doesn't drink, she can make sure we control ourselves. If she thinks someone's getting too drunk, she'll hand you a water. And we all have to agree to drink it no matter what. Okay?"

Monica wanted to protest. She wasn't sure she wanted to be the alcohol police, but when everyone immediately agreed, she supposed she didn't have a choice.

"Don't use all the margarita mix, Elodie," Kenna added. "Make sure there's enough so we can make Monica some virgin drinks."

Once again, Monica was surprised. She assumed she'd just be drinking water all night. If anything, she figured the others might be a little annoyed that she wasn't drinking with them. Instead, they were taking care to include her as much as possible. It felt good.

An hour later, there was a knock at the door. Kenna leaped up and shouted, "Food's here!" before heading for the front foyer.

She returned to the room followed by four men, all carrying bags that looked like they were stuffed to the gills. Robert had arranged to have anything and everything a group of women might want to eat sent up. It was a smorgasbord of appetizers. Things they could snack on all evening whenever they got hungry. There were eggrolls, wings, hummus and veggies, potato chips, deviled eggs, Hawaiian meatballs, pineapple salsa, fruit kabobs, luau Thai chicken, Japanese beef rolls, and, of course, malasadas for dessert.

After everyone had loaded up a plate, they all gathered on the balcony to watch the sun set and talk.

Monica had mostly been listening to the chatter between the women, but no one seemed to mind that she hadn't joined in. And somehow her silence felt more comfortable now than it had at Duke's.

Eventually, Elodie turned to her and asked, "So, were we right about Baker?"

Monica carefully chewed the bite she'd just taken, then swallowed before asking, "What about him?"

"About how hot he is."

Everyone laughed, looking at Monica expectantly.

"Um...yes?"

"More, girl. We need more details," Lexie cajoled.

"Wait. First...are you okay talking about him?" Kenna asked. "I mean, Aleck told me how you reacted when you saw his tattoo. The one that made you remember the guy you saw, who tried to hurt you."

It was actually very kind of her to want to make sure she was okay talking about what had happened. Once again, that warm feeling came over Monica. "I'm okay. And yeah, I kind of had a panic attack when I realized the tattoo on his forearm was the same as the other guy's. If

Stuart hadn't been there, I probably would've run right into the ocean or something. I wasn't thinking about anything but getting away."

"I love how you call him Stuart," Elodie sighed.

Ashlyn rolled her eyes. "That's just because you call Mustang by his given name."

Elodie shrugged. "Probably."

"Hush, let Monica talk," Kenna said.

Everyone turned to her once more, and Monica did her best not to feel uncomfortable about being in the spotlight. "I did trip over myself and fall on my ass before I tried to run," she joked.

"I bet Pid was pissed," Lexie said. "Not at you, but that you might have been hurt."

Monica realized that while he'd been concerned, he *had* also been kind of mad too. She hadn't realized it at the time, since she was focused on Baker's tattoo...but Lexie was right. "He wasn't happy," she said after a moment.

"With our guys, that's the understatement of the century," Kenna said.

"So? Baker? He's amazingly good-looking, right? And super intense at the same time?" Elodie asked.

Monica felt the urge to tease the woman, which wasn't like her at all. "He was okay," she said, as nonchalantly as she could.

"Are you kidding me? Only okay?" Lexie asked in disbelief. "With that silver in his hair? And that beard?"

"That was alright," Monica said. "I was surprised to see he had some gray mixed in with his chest hair too."

Four pairs of eyes nearly bulged out of their sockets as the women stared at her.

Elodie found her voice first. "You saw his naked chest?" she asked.

"Yeah, he was surfing when we got there. He strode out of the water with his board under his arm and wearing nothing but a wet suit. Long sleeves, skin-tight, came down to right above his knees..." Monica drawled.

"Sweet Jesus," Elodie breathed.

"Seriously?" Kenna asked.

"I really want to meet this man," Ashlyn grumbled.

"Seriously," Monica said. "Then he ever so slowly stripped it off. Peeling it down his arms and chest...which is when I got a good look at his tattoo."

"He's coming to your wedding, right?" Ashlyn asked Kenna.

She shrugged absently. "I hope so. He was invited."

"Wow, so you almost saw him naked," Lexie said.

Monica laughed and rolled her eyes. "Not really. I wasn't actually paying attention after seeing that tattoo. Besides, I think Jody would've had something to say about it if I'd ogled him too much."

"Who's Jody?" Ashlyn asked.

"Her name is actually Jodelle, which is what Baker calls her. It's almost swoon-worthy if you ask me, because she said everyone else calls her Jody. I guess she hangs out at the beach and brings sandwiches and stuff to the younger surfers. She kind of looks after them. And it was pretty obvious she and Baker like each other."

"Wait, is she super petite, in her forties or fifties, dark hair, and drives a brightly colored VW van?" Lexie asked.

Monica shrugged. "I didn't see what kind of car she had, but yeah, the other stuff fits."

"I saw her when we went up there," Lexie explained. "I didn't meet her, but Baker definitely made a beeline for her van when he saw her pull in."

"So he's into her?" Elodie asked.

"I would say so," Monica confirmed.

"That's so cool. I mean, he kinda strikes me as a loner," Kenna said. "I can't imagine him actually being in a relationship."

"Yeah, he was an asshole to me at first," Lexie said. "But he was looking out for Midas, so I understood after a while. But still."

"But he's nice to look at," Elodie said. "Did you get a picture?"

Monica couldn't help but laugh. "Sorry, no. I was too busy having a panic attack to try to snap a pic without him knowing."

Elodie sighed. "That's okay. But I bet he was pretty amazing in that wet suit."

"He might be in his fifties, but he definitely takes care of himself," Monica agreed.

"I'm guessing all of the guys will probably look like that in twenty years," Kenna said. "I can't imagine any of them will just stop working out when they retire from the Navy."

As talk turned to their men and what they might look like when they were in their fifties, and how it wasn't fair that some men aged so much better than women, Monica stood and gathered up the plates. She headed inside to the kitchen and decided, with the food everyone had eaten, it was safe to pour another round of drinks.

She brought the pitcher out to the balcony and was greeted by loud, happy whoops from the others.

Hours later, long after the sun had set, and after two more rounds of drinks, they were all inside sitting on the floor in the living room, playing Truth or Dare. Monica forgot who'd first suggested it, but she felt awkward not participating, so she'd joined in.

Elodie, Lexie, Kenna, and Ashlyn were definitely feeling no pain from the margaritas they'd been consuming all night. They were giggly and in happy moods. Monica didn't add to their talk about past boyfriends, and she listened with interest as Kenna babbled on about the plans that had been made for her wedding.

"Truth or dare?" Kenna asked Elodie.

"Truth," she responded.

"How many orgasms did you have on your wedding night?" Kenna asked.

"You going to try to beat me?" Elodie asked.

"Maybe," Kenna said with a smirk.

"Three," Elodie said.

"Three?" Ashlyn said in obvious disbelief. "I call bullshit."

"I'm serious," Elodie said. "And that was only because we were tired."

Everyone laughed.

"Your turn," Kenna told Lexie.

Lexie looked around the room and finally pinned her gaze on Ashlyn. "Truth or dare?"

"Dare," Ashlyn said firmly. "I have an idea what you guys will ask if I say truth."

"You mean like what the hell is going on with you and Slate?" Elodie blurted.

Ashlyn blushed. "Yup. But since I picked dare, you can't ask that."

Monica wanted to laugh, but instead merely smiled.

"Fine. Dare, dare, dare..." Lexie muttered. "I dare you to send a picture of yourself to Slate right this second."

"Juvenile," Ashlyn said, but her cheeks got even more rosy than they'd been before.

"So you're refusing?" Lexie asked. "You'll lose."

"Lose what?" Ashlyn asked.

"I don't know. The game?" Lexie said.

"Oooh, that would be a tragedy," Ashlyn said sarcastically.

"Come on," Lexie whined.

"Fine. I'll do it. Monica, you take the picture though since you're the only one not drunk. And make me look good," Ashlyn ordered.

Monica took her phone and nodded to say she was ready.

Ashlyn tilted her head, stuck her tongue out, rolled her eyes, and held up her hands in peace signs next to her face. Monica clicked the button, even though she was laughing so hard she could barely see. Everyone else had joined in as well.

"Oh, that'll reel him in for sure," Kenna joked.

Ashlyn merely smiled and took her phone back from Monica. She hit a few buttons and said, "There. Done."

"Wait, I want to see what he says when he gets that," Elodie said.

Everyone waited around in anticipation to see what Slate would send in response. Looking at her watch, Monica was surprised to see it was almost one in the morning. "Um, guys, he might not be awake. It's late."

"Holy crap, I had no idea it was past midnight," Elodie said.

"What, do you usually turn into a pumpkin or something at twelve?" Kenna asked.

"No, I'm usually asleep by nine," Elodie returned.

"You're so lame," Lexie teased.

"You aren't any better, and you know it," Elodie told her friend.

Monica loved how everyone could banter back and

forth and not get their feelings hurt. And she had to admit that she liked Elodie and Lexie even better now, just knowing they went to bed early like her. It made her feel as if they had something in common, however small.

"Oh! He's typing!" Ashlyn said. "Damn, I hate those three dots...he needs to learn to type faster." Then she stared down at the phone and started giggling.

"What? What'd he say?" In her drunken happiness, Ashlyn was laughing too hard to respond, so she just handed her phone to Monica. She read what Slate sent out loud. "'Looks like you guys are having a good time.' Oh, wait...he just sent another one," she said, then read that one out loud too. "'If you were trying to turn me off, it didn't work. I think you're sexy no matter what kind of face you're making.'"

Everyone was quiet for a long beat, then they burst out laughing as Ashlyn quickly grabbed for her phone.

"I knew it!" Lexie exclaimed. "I knew there was something between you guys!"

"There's not," Ashlyn insisted. "He's a player. And he just wants me because I told him I wasn't interested."

Elodie abruptly stopped laughing. "Slate's *not* a player," she said seriously. "None of the guys are."

"Right," Ashlyn said. "He's tall, dark, handsome, *and* he's a Navy SEAL. He's totally getting pussy whenever he wants."

"No, he's not," Elodie insisted. "I mean, I don't have any inside knowledge, but from what Scott says, the guys are all well past that time in their lives. Sure, when they were in their early twenties they all dated a lot, but now? No."

"I'm not interested in dating anyone," Ashlyn said.

Monica thought she heard a touch of desperation in

her words. Almost as if she was begging them to believe her.

"After following Franklin to Hawaii, I'm done with men. Carly and I are gonna stay single for a very long time," Ashlyn declared.

"Good luck with that," Lexie muttered.

"My turn," Ashlyn said, turning to Monica. "Truth or dare?"

Monica froze. She was essentially a chicken, and she definitely didn't want to have to send a picture of herself to Stuart or something equally as embarrassing. But she was also scared to death about what the other woman might ask if she decided on truth.

After a long pause, she finally blurted, "Truth."

"You can ask for a different question if you want, but I've been wondering...what happened to your hand? Were you born that way?"

Monica swallowed hard. She had a choice. She could do the cowardly thing and refuse to answer, requesting a new question. Or she could be honest. Open herself up to these women. If she decided to stay, and if she really *did* want to earn their friendship, she needed to open up.

So she told them. And she didn't hold anything back. She explained why and how her dad had done it. Talked about how much it had hurt, and when the infection had set in, how she'd suffered in silence, knowing better than to ask her dad to take her to the doctor. She told the women how she'd woken up after the surgery, alone and scared to death. How her fingers still hurt to this day, even though they weren't there anymore.

When she was done, the room was dead silent—and Monica regretted bringing the mood of the night down so low.

Just when she was about to apologize, Kenna exclaimed, "What a fucking *asshole*!"

"Yeah! Who the hell did he think he was? Hurting a little kid? And his daughter at that!" Lexie agreed.

"I hope his penis shriveled up and fell off!" Elodie added.

Monica couldn't help but chuckle at that.

"How can you laugh right now?" Ashlyn asked softly.

"It's just that...I'm guessing his penis *did* shrivel up," Monica said, before explaining how her dad had frozen to death.

"Good."

"Got what he deserved."

"Fucker!"

"Have you told Pid that story?" The question came from Elodie.

"Yes."

"I bet he was *pissed*."

"Yeah, he was," Monica admitted.

Elodie nodded, as if that settled something she'd been thinking about. "Your turn," she told Monica.

"What?"

"Your turn to pick someone for Truth or Dare."

It was hard for Monica to switch her brain away from her memories. She'd kinda expected the party to break up after her story, but instead her new friends had expressed their disgust with her dad and moved on. She liked that a hell of a lot. "Lexie, truth or dare."

"Dare."

Monica racked her brain for a good dare. Then she remembered something she'd seen on the Internet a few days ago. She picked up her phone and did a quick search for an appropriate picture to use and texted it to Lexie.

"You're scaring me, Monica," Lexie said with a laugh.

"Sorry. I just texted you a picture. Your dare is to send that to Midas and ask him what size he wants, because you're ordering matching ones for you and him."

"Oh my God, this is hilarious!" Lexie said after looking at her phone. "We *all* need to do this and compare responses."

"What? What's the picture?" Kenna asked.

Lexie turned her phone around and showed the others what Monica had sent her. It was a picture of a man standing in front of a white background, wearing a long T-shirt that went down to his knees. Essentially what looked like a nightgown. It was light blue with navy-blue piping at the hem and around the arms and neck. There was even a small pocket on the upper left chest.

"Oh, hell yeah, I want to see what Scott says," Elodie said.

"Marshall is gonna say 'hell no,'" Kenna mumbled.

"You too, Monica," Lexie insisted as she texted the picture to the others.

"Only if Ashlyn does," Monica surprised herself by saying.

"Fine, but since Slate and I aren't dating, it's not going to work on him," Ashlyn said.

They were quiet as they all typed a text.

"Ready?" Lexie asked. "On the count of three, hit the send button. One, two, *three*!"

Everyone giggled as they waited to see what their men would say when they saw the text. One by one, the responses came in.

*Marshall*: Love you, babe, but no.

*Scott*: How much have you had to drink?

*Midas*: I'll wear it if you wear what I buy for *you*.

*Slate*: I saw this trick on the internet the other day. Not playing.

"What'd Pid say?" Lexie asked Monica.

She stared down at his text in disbelief. She looked up at the others and read his response out loud. "I like the blue."

Everyone lost it then, laughing so hard, tears streamed down their faces.

"Oh my God, he has it *so bad* for you," Kenna told her.

Monica couldn't stop the small smile that formed on her lips. No man would agree to wear a nightgown like the one in the picture unless, one, he was completely secure in his manhood—which Stuart definitely was—or two, he really, *really* wanted to please the woman who wanted to buy it for him.

As the game continued, Monica did her best to put Stuart's response out of her mind, but it was impossible. She couldn't believe he would actually wear something like that just because she asked him to.

After another few rounds of Truth or Dare, it was obvious the party was winding down. Lexie was the first to call it quits, and she headed into the guest room she was sharing with Ashlyn. Elodie fell asleep on the couch not too much later, and after helping clean up a bit, Ashlyn headed down the hall to bed.

Kenna gestured for Monica to join her out on the balcony. Even though Monica was tired, she wasn't quite ready to sleep yet. Her mind was too busy replaying the night, and how well she'd gotten along with everyone.

She and Kenna settled into lounge chairs, each with a bottle of water, and stared out at the moon hovering over the ocean in the distance.

"This was the best bachelorette party ever," Kenna said.

"Even though there were no strippers and no tiaras or sashes proclaiming you the bride-to-be?" Monica teased.

"Especially because of that," Kenna said. "I'm sorry, but strippers are kind of gross. Why would I want some stranger grinding up on me with his junk in my face? Yuck. I don't mind admiring a good-looking man from a distance, but someone all oiled up and rubbing himself on me? No."

"Like Baker?" Monica asked.

"Exactly," Kenna said with a smile. "You okay?" she asked.

Monica looked over at her. "What do you mean?"

"I know you probably didn't expect to spill some of your past with us tonight, and I hope you didn't feel pressured."

"I *wasn't* expecting it," Monica said. "But you know what? I feel pretty okay about it."

"Good. I was going to say that story says more about your asshole of a father than it does about you...but that's not true. The fact that you're still as sweet and nice as you are, after all that you've gone through and experienced, says *everything* about who you are. You're a hell of a strong woman, Monica, and I'm proud to call you my friend."

Monica knew Kenna was still tipsy, but her words meant the world to her regardless. "Same," she replied. It felt too pathetic to admit that Kenna and the others were basically the only true friends she'd had in her life, so she kept that part to herself. "Are you excited about your wedding?" she asked.

"So excited I can't stand it," Kenna admitted. "I don't care about the traditional Hawaiian dancers, or the food, or even having a ceremony on the beach. I only care about Marshall. I love him so much. He accepts me exactly how I am. An extrovert who finds it her mission in life to make friends with everyone I meet, who's completely happy being a waitress for the rest of my life, and who doesn't care even a tiny bit about how much money is in my man's bank account."

"He's rich, huh?"

Kenna laughed and gestured to the condo behind them. "Yup."

"Right. You're lucky."

"I am," Kenna agreed immediately. "I'm happy our parents will be here, but honestly, I'd have been just as happy going down to the courthouse and having a civil ceremony. It's more about being able to spend the rest of my life with the man I love and trust more than anyone I've ever met than about a big shindig."

Monica nodded and sipped her water. Then surprised herself by asking, "How did you realize you trusted him?"

"Do you mean when?"

She didn't, but Monica nodded anyway. She really wanted to know *how* to trust someone. She had no idea how to do that.

"I'm not sure I can answer that. It was a gradual thing. But when I was on that beach with Shawn, who wanted to kidnap and torture me, the only thing I knew for certain was that Marshall wasn't going to let that happen. I knew without a shadow of a doubt that if the worst happened, and Shawn was able to get me off that beach, the man I loved wouldn't stop until he'd found me...and killed *anyone* who'd laid a finger on me."

Monica sighed. She loved that for her new friend. But it still didn't really answer her question.

As if she knew she needed to say more, Kenna said, "I think trust is something that's there or it isn't. You don't think much about it day to day, but when you need it the most, you just know down to your soul that someone will have your back when the shit hits the fan."

And that was what Monica was afraid of. That she'd believe someone would be there for her, like her dad should've been, only to be let down once more.

"Thanks for inviting me tonight," she said, changing the subject.

"Thanks for coming. And taking care of us. I know we were pretty obnoxious at times," Kenna said.

"Not really." And they weren't. Yes, the others had gotten tipsy and acted silly, but they weren't mean or obnoxious drunks, and the night had actually been a lot of fun.

"You want to sleep out here with me?" Kenna asked.

"Yeah."

"Good. Because I'm too tired to go back inside."

Monica stood up and grabbed two blankets that were hanging on the back of a nearby chair and gently covered Kenna.

"Thanks," she mumbled sleepily.

Monica settled on the lounge chair under her own blanket and pulled out her phone. It was two forty-five in the morning, but she couldn't help typing out a text.

. . .

*Monica*: Just letting you know that all is well. I'm okay and going to sleep now.

She didn't know why she felt the urge to text Stuart. He was probably asleep already. But she wanted to connect with him, even if it was one-sided.

Surprisingly, three dots blinked at the bottom of the screen, letting her know he was typing a response.

*Stuart*: I knew you would be. And, Mo?

He had more confidence in her than she did.

*Monica*: Yeah?

*Stuart*: If you buy me that god-awful nightgown, I'll find a way to retaliate. :)

She laughed. Clearly he'd known they were all playing a prank and had gone along with it. She texted a smiley face emoji back, then put her phone on the small table next to her. She closed her eyes and fell asleep almost immediately, feeling content and happy.

* * *

Shane "Bull" Beyer sat on the dark, sandy beach, not far from the Coral Springs condominiums, a pair of high-powered binoculars hanging around his neck. He smoked a cigarette and stared out at the ocean waves with a small smirk on his face.

It had taken years to find the right moment to get back at the man he'd vowed revenge against. And now it was time.

When he'd first been kicked out of the Navy, he'd been lost. The Navy had been his life. Being a SEAL was what he'd lived for. It was who he was. And after all he'd done, after all he'd sacrificed, he'd been discarded as if he was nothing but a psycho killer.

He was who the Navy had *made* him.

He'd had a lot of time to think about everything that had happened. The bottom line? There was only one person to blame for his humiliation.

Baker "Meat" Rawlins.

It was *his* performance evaluation that had ultimately gotten Bull kicked out. And he'd vowed to make Baker pay.

The Navy thought Baker was the epitome of a perfect sailor. A perfect SEAL. He was given accolade after accolade, when in reality he was *half* the SEAL Bull was. And jealous of Bull's kill record.

For years, Bull had done as much as possible to discredit the institution that had let him down. He'd sent hints to several SEAL commanders, and not one had picked up on his clues. Idiots. All of them. The teams were obviously nothing like they used to be back in his day. He would've deciphered his emails in two seconds flat.

He'd even let that bitch back in Algeria see his face. He hadn't planned to kill her, just play with her a little, then let her escape to tell the tale to those charged with evacuating the ambassador's household. But she'd gotten away from him.

He'd been so frustrated, so pissed that his plan was derailed and he didn't get to have his fun, he'd lost control with the *other* bitch.

With the ambassador's employee as an eyewitness, he figured the government would ID him within days, especially after the email he'd sent with the dead bitch's picture.

But they hadn't. And the broad who'd eluded him must be stupid or something, because she hadn't been able to figure out who he was.

Now he was in Hawaii. Right under everyone's noses, and they *still* hadn't guessed who he was.

Whatever. He was tired of the subtle hints. He *wanted* the Navy assholes to know who he was...know the continued frustration of never catching him. But there was only one man he wanted to confront in person. His former team leader, Meat.

And he knew just how to do it.

Smiling, Bull looked up in the direction of the balcony he'd been scoping out for a while. Apparently some of Baker's SEAL friends were married, or at least seriously dating. And their women were all friends. It wouldn't be hard to cull one from the herd and use her as bait. The perfect person for his plan was conveniently right here, a world away from where he'd last seen her.

The bitch from Algeria.

He couldn't believe his luck when he'd discovered she was here. In Hawaii. He'd been searching for a way to get to Meat, and she was it. He'd considered using the old broad who was always at the beach in the mornings, but dismissed her when his recon revealed Baker didn't spend any time with the woman away from the beach.

No, the Algeria bitch was a better target. He'd seen her

and another SEAL up at the North Shore the other day, watched their meeting with his former team leader, thrilled when she'd seen his tattoo and had a panic attack. Knew instantly she'd recognized the dragon.

He'd also seen how concerned Meat was over her reaction.

It had taken the bitch long enough to figure things out. He'd deliberately rolled his sleeves up before approaching the house in Algeria, and the stupid fucking government *still* hadn't made the connection.

When she'd seen Meat's tattoo, things had clicked. And now the Navy finally knew who he was...but it was too late. Way too damn late. Now they would lose their golden boy. Baker fucking Rawlins.

Using the bitch from Algeria would wound the other SEAL too, the one she was shacking up with. A sweet side benefit. The more government slaves he could hurt, the better.

Plans swirled in his brain, plans that had been in the works for weeks, once he'd discovered Meat was living in Hawaii.

"Enjoy your girl time," Bull said under his breath before standing. "Because life's about to get very interesting." Then he headed for his vehicle parked a few blocks down, smiling all the way.

# CHAPTER FIFTEEN

Pid glanced over at Monica, standing in his kitchen. She was looking down at her phone with a small grin on her face. Since Kenna's bachelorette sleepover two night ago, her phone had pinged nonstop with text messages. Kenna had apparently made a group text and put everyone in it, and they messaged each other constantly.

Monica didn't join in very often, as far as he could tell, but the happy look on her face made it clear that she liked being included.

"What are they talking about now?" he asked.

Monica looked at him, and her smile grew. Pid was drawn to her like a plant to the sun. He approached her, reaching up and tucking a lock of hair behind her ear. He couldn't keep his hands off her these days, and thankfully she didn't seem to mind.

"Kenna said she wanted to make custom hula dolls that looked like her and Aleck to hand out as party favors," Monica said.

Pid rolled his eyes. The ubiquitous hula dolls that were so popular with tourists were ridiculous. Despite that, he'd put the one Monica had bought for him on his dash, even though he'd planned to put it in his kitchen, swearing it wouldn't get within twenty feet of his minivan.

He chuckled. "I bet Aleck vetoed that idea," he said.

Monica cocked her head in question. "He did. How did you know?"

"Because the last thing I'd want is anyone putting a half-naked hula doll, wearing your face, on their dash to stare at all day."

Monica laughed.

That was another thing that thrilled him. Mo laughed more often these days. When he'd first met her, she barely ever cracked a smile. Now she smiled and chuckled all the time. It was a thing of beauty.

"What?" she asked. "Why are you looking at me like that?"

"Because you're so damn beautiful."

She blushed. "Whatever."

"You are," he insisted. "And I'm so very glad you're still here." He wanted to ask if she'd heard anything else from her employer about a new position, but honestly, he didn't want to know. "You about ready to go?"

He was dropping her off at the Head Start Child Care Center on his way into work, and they needed to get going if he wanted to get to the base on time. She'd agreed to volunteer for the time being, and Pid knew being with the children would relax her even more. She was like a flower finally getting the nourishment she needed to blossom.

"I'm ready. Stuart?"

"Yeah?"

She looked over his shoulder, down at her phone, then at the center of his chest before she took a deep breath and said, "I like it here."

Pid reached out and put a finger under her chin, tilting her head up until she met his gaze. "I'm glad."

"I didn't think I would. I mean, I enjoyed visiting other countries and experiencing new cultures. But Hawaii is fascinating, even though I haven't really even begun to dig into the culture and explore the island. I also didn't think I'd find friends like I have. I realize it hasn't been all that long, and anything could happen...but you were right. Elodie and the others don't seem to mind that I'm not as outgoing as they are. They don't care when I sit and listen rather than join in their discussions."

"That's good, Mo," Pid said, sliding his hand back to wrap it around the side of her neck.

"And I like living here with you."

Pid's smile grew. "I like you living here with me too."

She stepped closer and tentatively rested her hands on his sides. Even that innocent touch made his heart race and his desire for her ramp up. She swallowed hard and inched closer, relaxing against him.

It was the first time she'd initiated any touch more intimate than handholding. And like a smitten teen, his cock immediately got rock hard. There was no way to hide his reaction from her. Not with the way she'd plastered herself against him.

Tilting her head up so they could maintain eye contact, she whispered, "I want you."

This was definitely an abrupt change in behavior—and hard as he was, Pid wasn't sure where it was coming from. Yes, they'd kissed plenty recently, but going from kissing to saying she wanted to make love was quite a leap for someone like Monica. He studied her, trying to figure out what had prompted this.

"No comment?" she asked, her expression dimming a bit.

"I want you too," he said, not wanting her to think he didn't, not even for a millisecond. "But I have a question."

She raised an eyebrow.

"Do you trust me?"

The slight smile on her face disappeared. "What does that have to do with anything?" she asked.

"I want more than just your body, Mo. I want *all* of you. And I suspect you've gone through the motions of making love in the past, while still holding the most important parts of yourself back. I want what you haven't given others. I want your hopes and dreams. Your fears. Your imperfections and your passion...just as I want to give you mine. Sex is great. But that's not all I want from you. I want everything."

Pid couldn't believe he was saying that. He should've been thrilled that Monica wanted to have sex. But if he wanted a superficial romp in the sack, he could have that any day of the week. He was getting too old for that nonsense. He wanted what Mustang had. What Midas and Aleck had. He wanted a connection with the woman he took to his bed. With *Monica*.

"I...you know I don't trust anyone," she replied quietly.

"I do," Pid said with a nod.

She looked away from him, and Pid waited with bated breath to see what she'd say next.

"Most men would jump at the chance to have sex," she grumbled.

"I'm not most men," Pid said.

"I know," Monica answered. Then she said in a whisper, "I can't...I can't risk it."

Disappointment hit Pid hard, but he kept his voice

gentle when he said, "You can with me. I know what a gift your trust is, and I'd never, *ever*, let you down the way others have."

"You don't understand," she said.

"You're right, I don't," Pid told her. "But I'm trying. Here's the thing: I'm falling for you, Monica. Do I want to slide inside your hot, wet body? Hell yes. But I want more than just something physical. I want long nights sitting on the back deck talking. I want more laughter and smiles and that adorable dimple in your cheek. I want to see you happy and relaxed after you spend some time with the other women. After a difficult mission, *you're* the one I want waiting at home for me. I want to go to sleep with you in my arms and wake up the same way. And, down the line, if we work out the way I think we could...I want to see you with our children. You'd be an amazing mother, Mo, and even though I haven't known you all that long, and I've never really thought about being a father, I know I want that. With you."

Her eyes filled with tears as she visibly struggled to contain her emotions.

"But I need you to want all that too. Not just be with me because you think you might like me a little bit. Or because being here is comfortable. I need you to trust me, Mo. I know that's asking a lot. And it's probably not fair of me to ask for it so soon in our relationship...but there it is."

"Stuart—" she began, her devastation clear in that single word.

"No." He shook his head. "Don't say you can't. I think you can. I *know* you can, because I know I'm worth your trust. I won't let you down, Mo. You just have to want all that as much as I do."

"That's not fair," she told him. "It's not that easy to just forget thirty years of conditioning."

"I know it's not," Pid told her. "And it'll be one of the hardest things you've done. But if you don't, you're letting him win. He's still controlling your life, even all these years later. You're letting your head get in the way of your heart. You *can* trust me, Mo. And when you figure that out, I promise you'll feel free. Free of that asshole who hurt you all those years ago and made you think leaning on someone else is a bad thing.

"You think you want *me*? You have no idea how hard it is for me not to haul you down the hall, throw you down on my bed, strip you naked and show you exactly how much I want *you*. And I will...when you can honestly say that you trust me to have your back. To have your best interests at heart at all times. To be your lover, your friend, and your protector. I know that's archaic, but I am who I am."

Pid stared at the woman in his arms and prayed she'd be able to break through everything she'd been taught by her sperm donor.

"I understand," she said finally.

Pid wiped away the few tears that had fallen from her eyes...and felt his heart breaking. He couldn't take back what he'd said, and he didn't want to. All of it had come from his heart. But he couldn't be with a woman who didn't trust him either.

Monica leaned forward and rested her cheek on his chest. Pid wanted to take it as a good sign that she hadn't pulled away and told him he was crazy. He held her close, marveling anew at how perfectly she fit against him.

Eventually, she pulled back, wiped her cheeks, and said, "We need to get going so you aren't too late."

Pid wanted to say to hell with work. Wanted to force her to talk to him so they could get past this, but he knew it wasn't that easy. Besides, he didn't want Monica just to tell him what he wanted to hear. It would tear him apart if she did, then he found out she'd lied just so he'd sleep with her.

It was a weird position to be in. One he'd never been in before. He was actually saying no to sex. But he truly felt if a long-term relationship with Monica was going to work out, he had to earn her trust.

"You okay?" he asked softly.

Monica nodded. "I get where you're coming from," she told him. "I'm just not sure I can get there."

"Do you want all that stuff I talked about?" Pid couldn't help but ask.

"Yes."

"That's all I need to hear. I'm patient, Mo. I can give you time."

"How will I know though?" she asked, sounding frustrated. "I've never trusted anyone before. I have no idea how I'll even know if I trust you."

"You'll know," Pid told her.

"You're kind of a pain," Monica retorted with a sigh.

Pid laughed. "Yeah. And, Mo?"

"What?"

"Just because I'm not ready for you to make love to me, doesn't mean I don't want to kiss you. And touch you."

She gave him a small smile. "Same."

"Glad we're on the same page with that at least," Pid said, leaning down.

They made out right there in the middle of the kitchen for what seemed like an eternity. When Pid finally pulled back, his cock was hard once again, and Monica was holding onto him as if she never wanted to let go. They were both breathing hard and her lips were swollen and red.

She was sexy as hell, and Pid nearly blurted that he was wrong. He didn't need to wait for her to trust him. But he held back, knowing if they were ever going to work out long-term, he needed to be strong for both of them.

"Now we're both going to be late," she said, not moving out of his embrace.

"Totally worth it," Pid said. "Besides, I can't tell you how many times Mustang, Midas, and Aleck have been late."

Monica giggled.

They left the house hand in hand, and while things had taken a strange turn that morning, Pid couldn't be upset about it. He felt good about where he and Monica stood. As he'd told her, he'd give her as much time as she needed to work through her feelings. He suspected she already trusted him to some extent, even if she didn't realize it. She wouldn't have agreed to stay with him if she didn't. It was just a matter of her coming to terms with her upbringing and overcoming the damage her father had done to her psyche.

Of course, that was easier said than done, and he could recommend some really good psychologists for her to talk to that might make it easier. He should've already brought it up, and he'd be sure to do it soon. Pid only wanted Monica to understand what an amazing woman she was. Exactly *as* she was. She didn't have to change in order to love and be loved.

\* \* \*

Monica thought about what Stuart had said all day as she interacted with the children at the Head Start Center. One thing stuck out like a bright neon blinking light.

He wanted kids.

With her.

She'd dreamed about having a family, but had frequently pushed the thought to the back of her head. She was too fucked up to get married. And while she knew she could have children without being married, she wouldn't want that for a child.

There was a part of her deep down inside that wanted what she read about in books and saw in movies. She wanted a husband who loved her unconditionally. Who'd be there when she needed him. Who'd be one hundred percent present when it came to raising their children. He'd go to ballet recitals and soccer games. He'd change diapers and help clean the house. He'd never freak out if someone broke something or made a mess.

She'd thought it was a pipe dream. The real world didn't work like that. So she'd thrown herself into being the best nanny she could be. Living vicariously through other people's children.

Then she'd met Stuart.

He wasn't perfect. He made more messes than some of the children she'd cared for, and was lax about keeping his house clean, although it was obvious he was trying harder now that she was there. He left the toilet seat up all the time. When they watched TV together, he tended to hog the remote. Surprisingly, he couldn't multitask. She'd assumed that a special forces operative would absolutely be able to do two things at once, but that wasn't the case with Stuart. At least not that Monica had seen.

But did any of that really matter in the long run? The

list of things that were amazing about him was four times as long as the little things that annoyed her. Starting with building her a freaking *safe room*. And letting her stay with him. And sharing his friends with her.

And now, he'd freely admitted that he wanted her to have his children.

Monica felt tears well up in her eyes once more, but blinked them back. She wanted children too. She just wasn't sure she could ever trust a man the way Stuart wanted her to trust him. And that sucked.

By the time he arrived to pick her up at the end of the day, she mostly had her emotions under control. It helped that he didn't act any different toward her than he normally did. After she'd gotten into his minivan—a *minivan*, for God's sake; he was already way more ready for kids than most men—he leaned over and pulled her into him and kissed her long, hot, and hard.

"What was that for?" she asked breathlessly.

"I missed you," he said. "I got used to seeing you whenever I wanted on the base. You have a good day?"

"Yeah. Sylvia asked if I'd filled out the application she emailed me," Monica admitted.

"And?"

"I've filled it out, but haven't submitted it," she said.

"It's a big decision," Stuart told her as he headed for his house. "I'm guessing it doesn't pay as well as what you were earning as a live-in nanny."

"It doesn't," Monica confirmed.

"And child care during the day isn't the same as being with someone full time," he said.

"No, it's not."

"And these kids are very different from the ones you're used to looking after," Stuart added.

"And?" Monica said a little defensively.

"And nothing, it's just an observation. Most of the children at Head Start are from disadvantaged parents, and you're used to nannying for ambassadors and other well-off families."

Monica wasn't sure nannying was a word, but that wasn't what bothered her about Stuart's observation. "Maybe these kids need me *more*," she said a little huffily. "The color of their skin doesn't make a difference to me. Or how much money their families have. Besides, that's all the more reason to work with them. To try to make up for any gaps they might have before they get into the public educational system. To put them on the same page as their peers."

Stuart was grinning as he drove, and that annoyed her further. "What are you smiling about?"

"You. I couldn't agree with you more. The kids here *do* need you, Mo."

She realized suddenly that somehow she'd gone from not being sure about turning in the application to advocating for working at Head Start rather than finding a job for another ambassador or another wealthy family. "You're impossible," she muttered.

Stuart only chuckled. "Hey, all I did was ask how your day was."

Monica had to concede his point. She'd been the one to bring up the application. "I should probably find my own place if I decide to stay," she said quietly, broaching a subject they'd touched on before.

"No."

Monica waited. He didn't say anything else. "No?"

He sighed. "You already know I like you in my house. *You* like it in my house. You've got your own room, I'm

239

doing my best not to be an asshole roommate. I told you once that I wouldn't rush you, and I'm telling you again. There's no reason for you to move out. If you want to prove that you can be independent, there's no need. I already know you can be. You're a grown woman and have done a damn good job of looking after yourself ever since you moved out of your parents' house when you were sixteen. I like hanging out with you and talking about our days. I like having someone to make breakfast for. I like everything about you, Mo. If there's anything I'm doing, or not doing, just say the word and I'll fix it."

"It's not you," she said automatically. But it *was* him. He confused her. Made her feel safe. Made her happy.

"Then stay," he cajoled. "If you need to feel more independent, we'll find you a reliable used car so you can have your own transportation. I just...don't want you to go," he finished softly.

It was hard for her to believe they were even having this conversation, but at least he was driving. That made it easier. Otherwise, he'd probably take her in his arms and kiss her like he had that morning, making her brain short circuit.

"Okay. I'll stay."

"Good. Now, what do you want for dinner?"

She had to admit she liked how he made intense topics seem not so...well...intense. "Hamburgers."

"Done," he said with a smile.

They drove a few miles before Monica tentatively asked, "Did they find him?"

Stuart knew who she was talking about. "Not yet," he said. "But they think they've nailed down a few of the aliases he's been using. It's only a matter of time," he said confidently.

Monica felt bad that she hadn't recognized Shane Beyer when she'd looked at his profile. But everyone had known it was a long shot. The man she'd seen had half his face covered and was twenty years older than the pictures she'd looked at. But that didn't assuage her guilt.

"Do they have any idea what his plans are?" she asked.

She didn't miss the concerned look Stuart shot her way.

"I know it's all probably being kept hush-hush, but this involves me, Stuart," she said earnestly.

Stuart sighed. "They don't. But now that Huttner knows who he's looking for, some of the letters and emails he's received make more sense."

"Like?" Monica asked when he didn't elaborate.

"Do you remember that picture of the murdered woman Huttner showed you when you first got to Hawaii?"

Monica couldn't forget it. The image of the poor woman bleeding out on her comforter, pretty pink flowers covered in blood spatter, was burned into her brain. That could've been her, if it hadn't been for the safe room in the ambassador's house. "Yes," she said simply.

"The note accompanying the picture was full of clues."

Monica racked her brain trying to remember what it said, but with no luck. She'd been too fixated on the picture. "What did it say?"

Stuart recited the note as easily as if it was something he'd read every day, emphasizing the important words.

*"I'd like you to **meat** my latest work of art. Pictures are better in the **raw**, I'm no **bull** in a china shop. I was taught by the best.*

*They said I was insane...does this look like the work of an insane man?"*

"Oh my God," Monica said.

"Yeah, he practically painted us a picture and no one caught on," Stuart said in disgust. "Spelling out m-e-a-t instead of m-e-e-t wasn't a mistake; Meat was Baker's nickname when he was on the teams. And the reference to Baker's last name, *Raw*lins, and Beyer's own nickname, weren't coincidences either. There are other messages Huttner received over the years that are similar in nature."

"So what now?" Monica asked, more shaken up than she wanted to admit.

"We're on this," Stuart said firmly. "And you can bet Baker is not a happy man right about now. Knowing someone he trusted and worked with has turned out to be downright psychotic isn't settling well. He knew the man needed help all those years ago, but this..." Stuart shook his head. "It's not good."

Monica wasn't sure she wanted to know the answer to her next question, but she asked it anyway. "Am I in danger? You know, because I saw him?"

"We don't think so," Stuart told her, holding out his hand.

Monica put hers in it without thought. She no longer worried about him holding her bad hand. He'd never indicated in any way that he was repulsed by it, and she'd gotten used to his touch.

"Bull seems more interested in making sure the Navy looks bad, and that the leaders understand he's only doing what he was taught as a SEAL."

"You've been taught to rape and murder women?" Monica blurted before she could think better of it.

"Hell no. But we *do* know how to get in and out of countries without being detected. And we do kill, but only those who are a threat to the security of our country. Baker was right all those years ago. Bull is definitely unstable."

"So why does he assume he won't come after me?" Monica asked.

"Because it's Baker he's most pissed at. After reading all the notes and letters, it's obvious his anger is focused on his former team leader. He blames him for getting kicked out of the Navy, and everything he's said puts the target directly on Baker's head."

"That's crazy," Monica said softly.

"Yeah. Huttner wanted to put Baker in protective custody."

Monica couldn't help it. She laughed.

"Right? That's about what Baker thought of that plan too. He's perfectly willing to use himself as bait if it means stopping Bull."

Monica sobered. "That's not good."

"No, it's not. But I trust Baker."

"He's not on your team," Monica pointed out.

"No, he's not. But he's a SEAL. I don't care if he's been retired for a decade or more. He's also assisted my team on more than one occasion. He's got more integrity in his little finger than Bull has in his entire body. Now that we know for sure it's Bull who you saw, and who's behind some of the mayhem in countries that don't need any more unrest, and who's been escalating by killing and raping women in those countries, he'll be found. If he dares come looking for Baker? It'll be the last thing he ever does."

Monica shivered. She didn't like this situation. Not at all. But she was relieved that she didn't seem to be the target of this Bull guy's wrath. Then something else occurred to her. "Is Jody safe?"

"Who?"

"The woman Baker likes."

"Oh. I'm sure she is. They aren't together, but there's no way Baker would let anyone touch a hair on her head. You've seen how protective he is of her."

She had, but if Bull really wanted revenge, going after the woman his nemesis was interested in would be a good way of doing it. She didn't voice her opinion. She wasn't the expert in this situation. Baker was. And Stuart. And his team and their superiors.

Stuart mumbled something under his breath that Monica didn't catch. "I'm sorry, what?"

"Nothing. I was just kicking myself in the ass for worrying you," Stuart said.

Monica squeezed his hand. "Don't. If you had blown off my questions and said everything's fine, I would've known you were lying. And that isn't exactly the way to get me to trust you."

She didn't mean to say that, but now that she had, she couldn't regret it.

"You're right. But, Mo, there will be times I can't tell you what's going on with me and work."

"I know. And honestly, I don't want to know every-thing. I know there's ugliness in the world. I experienced it firsthand. And I think if I knew about some of the things you do while on missions, it would eat at me."

It was Stuart's turn to squeeze *her* hand.

"But that doesn't mean that I want you to put a wall between us when it comes to your job," she said, knowing she was being contradictory, but struggling to explain herself.

"I get it," he said.

Of course he did.

"I promise to talk to you about what I can...things that won't make you uncomfortable. There are lots of good things that we see when we're deployed."

"Like?"

"Like the babies we've helped bring into the world. Like the stray dogs we've helped get into rescue groups. Like the citizens who thank us for what we're doing. Like the children we meet."

Monica smiled at that. "You have time to meet kids?"

"Sometimes, yeah. And play with them too. Soccer mostly. They kick our asses," Stuart said with a smile.

Monica could totally picture Stuart, Mustang, Midas, and the others out on a street kicking a ball around with the local children in their downtime.

"I'm proud of you," she said a little shyly. "Thank you for your service, Stuart."

"Those words usually don't mean much to me," he admitted. "But coming from you, they mean the world." He lifted their clasped hands and kissed the back of hers.

Monica sighed and closed her eyes as he continued to drive them home.

Home.

She wasn't sure when she'd begun to think of his house as home, but she did. And even scarier still, she wasn't freaked out about it.

She'd lived in huge mansions overseas, expensive homes provided to ambassadors by the government, but none had ever come close to being a home more than the small two-bedroom house she was living in with Stuart.

How the man sitting next to her had come to mean so much, Monica had no idea. One second he was the military man she was extremely wary of, and the next, he was the man she couldn't bear to leave.

It was confusing...but for once in her life, Monica decided to just roll with the punches. Maybe, just maybe, she'd get a break and things from here on out would be nice and boring.

# CHAPTER SIXTEEN

It was three days until Kenna and Aleck's wedding, and Monica's new friend was freaking out. She was constantly texting everyone in the group chat about how nothing was ready. They all knew for a fact that Robert had everything under control, because Kenna had told them more than once how amazing he was.

Both her parents and Aleck's folks had arrived in town. They'd had dinner last night and everyone had gotten along perfectly. The weather was supposed to be beautiful on the day of their wedding, and as far as Monica could tell, Kenna was freaking out over nothing.

Being privy to all the arrangements for their ceremony made Monica realize that she didn't want anything remotely similar. If she ever got married, she wanted to keep everything small and simple. No party favors. No huge catering details to work out. No cake. Just her and the man she loved, vowing to be together through thick and thin.

And thinking about weddings brought her thoughts back to Stuart.

Last night, they'd gone further physically than they ever had before. They'd been making out, and Monica had wanted so much more. *Needed* more. She'd pushed him back on the couch and lifted his shirt. One of his hands had cradled the back of her head as she'd kissed her way up his rock-hard abs. When she'd kissed one of his nipples, it had tightened under her lips.

Knowing she could affect him so much was a heady feeling. He was bigger, stronger, and most of the time seemed to have his shit together. But the moans that left his lips as she nibbled on his erect nipple made goose bumps race down her arms. She became a little too enthusiastic, sucking on the skin next to his nipple and giving him a hickey. But she didn't regret it. She liked seeing her mark on him. A lot.

Her hand had eased between his legs, and she'd felt his hard erection for a fleeting moment before he'd grabbed her hand and switched their positions before she even knew what he was doing. Then she was under him, more than ready for him to take her...but he just leaned down, kissed her so gently it made her want to cry, then sat up.

He was very serious about the damn trust thing. On one hand, it was irritating. Men were supposed to have no trouble jumping into bed with women. Figured she'd find the one who wouldn't. Monica *wanted* to tell him that she trusted him, but she just couldn't get the words out.

On the other hand, she couldn't deny that him not wanting to rush into bed made her feel special. Valued. It also said a lot about his character, and proved that he didn't want to sleep with her simply because she was handy.

So she'd gone to bed horny as hell. Getting herself off

wasn't as satisfying as she knew being with Stuart would be. This morning, she'd still been somewhat irritated with him when he'd taken her into his arms and held her gently, reverently, saying all the right words and making her believe that everything would be okay.

But would it?

Only if she somehow reprogrammed herself from thinking all men would turn on her in the end. She didn't think Stuart was like that, but all she had to do was look down at her hand for a harsh reminder of what could happen if she let down her guard.

At the end of the day, Elodie had been waiting for Monica outside the Head Start Center instead of Stuart.

"Is Stuart all right?" she blurted when she reached Mustang's beat-up truck that Elodie was driving.

"He's fine," Elodie said with a smile. "I guess the guys are still in some super important last-minute meeting, and he asked if I wouldn't mind picking you up and taking you home."

"Oh, well...thanks. I appreciate it. Is everything okay with the team?"

"I'm sure it is. The meeting could be nothing, or it could be about an upcoming mission they need to plan for."

"Do they get deployed a lot?" Monica asked. She hadn't had a chance to talk to any of the other women about life as the wife or girlfriend to a SEAL, and decided now was as good a time as any.

"Depends on what you think a lot is," Elodie said. "The hardest part isn't them leaving; it's not knowing when they'll be back. They could literally be gone for a few days or a few months."

"Yeah, that stinks," Monica agreed.

"But what keeps me going is knowing Scott is making the world a safer place," Elodie admitted. "That sounds cheesy as hell, but the Navy isn't sending the team off to have tea with exotic women or something. They're hunting terrorists. Or rescuing hostages. Or like you experienced, getting Americans out of trouble that's heading their way."

Monica liked thinking about Stuart's job like that.

"So, while I don't know what their meeting is about today, I know it's important. And that the guys will do what they have to in order to keep us all safe."

Monica nodded.

"Not to change the subject, but are you ready for the shindig this weekend?" Elodie asked.

Monica laughed. "I don't think anyone is."

"True. But it's gonna be so much fun!"

Monica couldn't help but agree.

The rest of the trip home was uneventful, except for a guy who seemed to be riding their ass on the Interstate. The car had windows tinted so dark, Monica couldn't see who was driving, but she glared back at whoever it was anyway.

"I hate driving," Elodie complained. "People are such maniacs on the road."

"And you still came to get me?" Monica asked as they got off the Interstate. Whoever had been following them so closely zoomed by.

"It's what friends do," Elodie said simply.

Monica almost cried at the simple statement. She was feeling extremely emotional lately, and she wasn't sure she liked it. When she had herself under control, she said, "Well, I appreciate it."

"I'm sure you'd do the same for me."

"I would," Monica said. "Although our men have questionable taste in vehicles."

Elodie laughed. "Right? Although, this pickup might look like shit, but it runs amazingly well. Now, Pid's minivan?" She giggled. "It's so...not cool. But at least he won't have to be convinced to get one when he has kids."

Monica couldn't help but smile. That was very true. Although she had a feeling that even if Stuart had a Mustang or something, he wouldn't hesitate to exchange it for a more family friendly vehicle.

Elodie pulled up outside Stuart's house and turned to Monica. "For the record...I'm really hoping you decide to stay."

Monica was surprised at her words.

"You're funny and nice, and even though you don't talk a lot when we all get together, I can tell you're interested in what we're saying. And you talk when you *do* have something to say. And you make Pid happy, and he's my friend, so that makes *me* happy. Not only that, but Theo hasn't stopped asking about you since he met you. Anyway...you fit here, Monica. I just wanted to make sure you knew that."

Once again, Monica had to fight back tears. "Thanks. I emailed Sylvia my application this morning."

Elodie beamed. "Awesome!"

"Yeah," Monica agreed. And she had to admit to feeling a bit of relief that she wouldn't be packing up and heading off to some other foreign country anytime soon.

"Text me when you get home," Monica ordered Elodie.

"I will. See you soon! You're coming to the penthouse on Saturday morning so we can help Kenna get ready, and we can all get our hair and makeup done, right?"

"I'm not sure I'll be much help," Monica said.

"Are you kidding? We need you there to make sure we don't drink too much! It wouldn't be cool for Kenna to be like the sister in the movie *Sixteen Candles* when she walks down the aisle."

Monica couldn't help but chuckle. "True."

"Great. See you there!"

"Bye." Monica waved as Elodie headed back down the driveway. She headed for the house and unlocked the door, making sure to bolt it after she was inside. She might feel safe here, but that didn't mean she was stupid. She was a woman alone in the house. Leaving the door unlocked was akin to leaving it wide open and inviting trouble in.

Monica changed out of her clothes into a pair of leggings and a T-shirt, then checked her email. Sylvia had already replied to the application email Monica had sent earlier that day with an enthusiastic note, including lots of exclamation points. She also opened an email from her boss at the nanny agency, accepting her official resignation —which she hadn't mentioned to Stuart. She hoped to surprise *him* this time. The woman had offered to give her a glowing reference and reassured her that if she ever wanted to come back, she was more than welcome.

Feeling positive about her future, and excited, Monica headed for the kitchen. She was standing in front of the refrigerator, staring into it and trying to figure out what she could make for dinner with what they had—they were definitely running low and needed to make a grocery run— when a noise off to the right caught her attention.

Glancing over to the door that led to the deck, Monica froze when she saw a man standing there.

Not just any man—but the same one she'd seen in Algiers.

For a second, she felt as if she was back there. Except this time, she knew the man's name...and how dangerous he really was.

Shane "Bull" Beyer tapped on the glass with the end of a thick steel baton. It looked like the kind the police wore on their belts.

"Remember me?" he asked in a singsong voice.

Monica didn't wait around to hear anything else.

Not even bothering to close the refrigerator door, she bolted for the hallway. Before she'd reached her room, the familiar sound of glass breaking echoed throughout the small house.

"You can't hide from me this time," Shane called out.

"The hell I can't," Monica muttered as she frantically tapped the switch that would open the false wall in her room. It seemed to open ten times slower than she knew it actually did. She practically threw herself inside—but when she turned to look behind her, she knew it was too late. The house was simply too small to give her time to hide, then escape out the outer door for help.

Shane was on her before she could do more than let out a frightened *eep*.

"Got ya," he said as he dragged her out of the room, forced her to her feet, then wrapped his arm around her from behind, putting her in a choke hold.

Monica fought harder than she'd ever fought before. Flashes of the woman he'd murdered swam in her brain. Visions of a knife sticking out of her chest made her claw at Shane with her right hand, desperate to get him to let go.

"Fuck, you're a wild one," Shane said.

It sounded like he was happy about that, which did nothing to help calm Monica.

He walked backward, dragging her kicking and screaming with him. But nothing she did made his hold loosen. He also wasn't exactly being gentle, not caring when her knee hit the doorjamb on the way out of the bedroom, or that when he turned them, her legs slammed into the wall. Her toes stung from the contact, since she wasn't wearing shoes, and the closer they got to the glass on the floor, the more scared Monica became.

But it was when he turned and threw her onto her back on the coffee table that Monica *really* began to panic.

She opened her mouth to scream, and Shane hit her. *Hard.*

Monica had been struck before. Her father loved to smack her around. But Shane meant business. He'd used a swift fist to the gut to shut her up, and it worked. Gasping for breath, trying to roll into a ball and failing because Shane was holding her down, all she could do was stare up at him in pain.

He hit her again. Monica suspected it was just because he wanted to that time, not because he was trying to keep her quiet. Her breath left her again. She wanted to fight back. Wanted to kick him in the balls and run screaming out of the house, but those punches *hurt*. She had a feeling that even if she managed to get to her feet, she probably wouldn't be able to get far before she collapsed.

Shane fumbled with something in his pocket for a moment before holding up a syringe. He had a small smile on his face. "You have two choices right now. Hold still while I inject you with this, or fight me. If you fight me, I'm still gonna put this in you, but I'll beat the shit out of you first, then rape you, *then* inject you. And I'll also wait around for your boyfriend to get home and put a bullet in his brain before he even knows what the hell is happening. Which will it be?"

Well, shit. She didn't like either of those choices. And she sure as hell didn't trust him. Even if she chose door number one and let him inject her with whatever the hell was in that syringe, there was no guarantee he still wouldn't rape her and kill Stuart.

But could she chance it? No.

So she remained silent on the table, staring up at him.

"Smart choice," he praised, flicking off the cap of the needle.

Monica closed her eyes as she felt the needle sink into the skin of her neck.

"Good girl," Shane crooned.

His voice made her sick, made her think about her father saying the same words when she did whatever insane thing he wanted her to do.

She opened her eyes, and as the drug he'd injected began to take effect, Monica mentally swore to do whatever it took to kill this man. She'd been taught by the best...and somehow, someway, she'd kill Shane Beyer—and not feel one ounce of guilt.

"That's it. Just relax. For the record, you're just a means to an end. I don't want you. I want Baker—and you're my ticket to getting him."

Monica had no idea what he was talking about. She'd only met Baker once; she was the worst person to use to try to lure the former SEAL into some crazy trap. But she couldn't find the words to tell him. She couldn't even keep her eyes open. Every muscle in her body felt as if it weighed a hundred pounds.

She felt herself being lifted and flung over Shane's

shoulder, but she couldn't do a damn thing to resist. She was boneless.

"It's just a bonus that your man will panic when he comes home and sees my handiwork," Shane said with a laugh.

It was the last thing she heard before succumbing to the drug racing through her veins.

# CHAPTER SEVENTEEN

Pid was exhausted by the time he pulled up to his house. It had been a long, stressful day. They were preparing to be sent on another mission, this time to Tajikistan. The country was just beyond Afghanistan's northern border, and they'd gotten word of a possible high-value Taliban target hiding there. The Tajikistan government asked for assistance in raiding the suspected hideout, so the SEAL team would be heading overseas fairly soon.

But details of the purported hiding place were sketchy, so they'd spent the day poring over reports and satellite images of the area. It wasn't anything Pid or the rest of the team hadn't done before, but Aleck was obviously stressed that they might be sent before his wedding and it would have to be postponed.

During a break, Jag had also admitted that he was more and more worried about Carly, and the fact that Luke Keyes was nowhere to be found. This was an island; it shouldn't be that hard to locate someone. And the fact that her ex's son had most likely been the one who was supposed to pick up his father and Carly the day of the attack at Duke's, and take them who-knows-where, was extremely concerning. Jag knew it. Carly knew it. And everyone was on edge about that situation.

Mustang and Midas were naturally always concerned about leaving Elodie and Lexie. Hell, even Slate wasn't as enthusiastic and impatient to leave for a mission. Pid knew it was because of Ashlyn. He worried about her almost as much as Jag worried about Carly. Ashlyn was outgoing and friendly and often didn't think twice about putting herself in questionable situations when it came to her safety.

And, of course, Pid was nervous about their pending departure because it would be the first time he'd been deployed since meeting Monica. He worried about her state of mind while he was away. He so desperately wanted her to trust him, but breaking down walls she'd spent years building to protect herself wasn't easy. And certainly wouldn't happen within the short time they'd known each other.

But he was chipping away at that wall every day. He could sense it. He wanted her like he'd never wanted another woman, but he was willing to wait until she believed he wasn't going to do *anything* to hurt her. Pid was well aware he had a hard road ahead of him, and it was likely Monica would need more therapy to help her get past what her asshole parents had done. But she was brave and capable.

Not thrilled about telling Monica that he was likely going to be deployed, but looking forward to seeing her, Pid unlocked the door to the house and called her name.

"Monica? I'm home."

The house was unnaturally quiet. Pid's well-honed instincts immediately kicked in, and he froze, listening.

For what, he wasn't sure. Some sound that the woman he was falling in love with was there. But he heard nothing.

Pid crept forward quietly, his head on a swivel, as he searched for some sort of clue as to what the hell felt so off. The second he stepped into his living room, he saw his refrigerator door standing open. Then he caught the scent of the plumeria tree in his backyard...

Looking at the sliding glass door that led to the deck, his entire body tensed as he realized it wasn't open—it was shattered. Glass littered the floor of his home, as well as the deck itself.

Without thinking, Pid spun around and ran toward the hallway and his guest room. The door was open, and he spotted the clothes he'd last seen Monica wearing in the laundry hamper in the corner. She was the neatest person ever, and if it had been any other day, he would've smiled at seeing the evidence of her tidiness. But the door to the safe room he'd built, standing open, had already drawn his attention.

He walked toward it, not sure what he'd find.

The area between the two walls was empty. The blanket he'd placed in the room was half inside and half outside the small space...as if it had been dragged out. The door that led out to the yard was still latched.

The possibilities of what could've happened ran through his head, and Pid felt sick. He hoped he was just being paranoid. Maybe she'd put something in the safe room and had forgotten to close it. Maybe she'd accidentally smashed the back door and had gone to a home store, hoping to fix it. Maybe this was a random break-in, and Monica didn't even know about it yet because she and Elodie had gone straight to Kenna's to help with wedding stuff.

But the second those possibilities went through his head, Pid dismissed them. He was one hundred percent sure Monica wouldn't leave without at least writing him a note or texting him to let him know what was going on, let alone leaving the fridge open. And if she'd broken the door, the *last* thing she'd do was leave the house unsecured with glass everywhere, even if she somehow hoped to replace it.

When Pid pulled out his phone, he realized that his hands were shaking. He hit Mustang's name and waited for his friend to pick up.

"Hey, what's up?" Mustang asked.

"Is Monica with Elodie?" Pid asked, knowing he was panicking, but not able to stop himself.

"No. Why? What's wrong?"

"I can't find her. She's gone. And my glass door is shattered. Someone took her." The last three words were almost whispered, as if by saying them out loud, it would make them true. But Pid knew in his gut that's what had happened.

"I'm on my way," Mustang said, and Pid had never been as grateful for his team leader and friend as he was right that second. "What do you see? Was she hurt? Do you see any evidence of blood?"

Pid almost stopped breathing. *Shit*—he hadn't even thought about that. His gaze flew over her bedroom, and he wasn't sure if he was relieved or not when he saw no evidence that Monica had been injured in whatever altercation had happened there. "None in her room. Hang on."

He struggled to focus. He'd been in the worst situations that anyone could imagine. He had to think on his feet all the time while doing his job. Many times, plans A and B turned into plans D, E, or F. And he'd always been able to pivot without any issues. But right now, Pid felt as if he were walking through a thick fog, trying to see more than five feet in front of him but not having any luck.

He stood at the edge of his living area and eyed the room. He looked for anything out of place. It was frustrating as hell when he didn't spot anything other than his broken door.

"No blood," Pid told Mustang. "The knives are all still in the block and nothing's knocked over. It's as if someone broke the door, walked in calmly, somehow subdued Monica, and walked out the way he came, cool as a cucumber and without disturbing anything else."

"Shit," Mustang muttered.

"What?" Pid asked, torn between wanting to know what his friend was thinking and absolutely *not* wanting to know.

"Could this be Bull?"

The four words made the hair on the back of Pid's neck stand up. "Fuck."

"I'm calling Huttner," Mustang said.

Pid nodded, not even caring that Mustang couldn't see him.

"Stay calm," Mustang ordered. "I'm already on my way. We're gonna find her."

Pid didn't respond.

"Pid?"

"Yeah?" he replied, already on the move toward his front door.

"Did you hear me? We're gonna find her."

"I heard you."

"Call Midas and Slate. After I talk to the commander, I'll call the others. Okay?"

"Okay," Pid said, his mind racing about where Bull could have taken her.

"Later."

Pid clicked off the phone as he walked out his front door, not even bothering to lock it behind him. If someone wanted to go into his house and take shit, let them. The most important thing in his life had already been stolen.

He strode toward his minivan, hating that it wasn't a faster, sleeker sports car that would get him to where he needed to be faster.

As he sat, he clicked on a name in his contact list. It wasn't Midas. Or Slate.

"Baker," the man's deep voice said through the phone connection.

"Bull's got Monica," Pid said in lieu of a greeting.

"What?" Baker asked.

Pid supposed he couldn't blame the man for being confused. It wasn't as if they talked a lot. And this was the first time Pid had ever called him, even though he'd had his number since he'd assisted with Elodie's situation.

"I came home and the back door's shattered, just like it was in Algeria. Monica's nowhere to be found. Bull's got her. I know it."

"*Fuck*," Baker said. "Where are you now?"

"I'm about to head north, toward you," Pid said. There was no way he could just hang around his house waiting for Mustang to get there. He needed to be *doing* something. And since Baker was the only person who knew Bull, really knew him, that was who he needed.

"No," Baker barked.

Pid tensed. If Baker refused to help, he was going to lose his shit.

"I'll come to you," Baker continued. "If I—" His words cut off abruptly. "Hang on, my other line is ringing."

Pid wanted to yell. Wanted to tell the former SEAL that if he took another call while Monica's life was in danger, he was an asshole, but he didn't get the chance before the line went silent. He sat in his vehicle and stewed. His adrenaline was so high, his entire body was shaking. He'd never felt like this before in his life. Ever.

He heard a click and then Baker was back.

"That was him. You're right. He's got your woman."

Pid's hold on his phone tightened so hard, he was afraid he was going to shatter the thing. "Where is he?" he asked. "And what does he want with Mo?"

"He doesn't want her," Baker bit out. "He wants *me*. She's bait."

Pid didn't know whether to be horrified or relieved.

"I'm on my way to you."

"It's gonna take too long to get here from the North Shore," Pid said.

"No, it won't. Trust me."

It was ironic that Baker used those words. And for the first time, Pid understood exactly how annoying they were. You couldn't just *tell* someone to trust you and have them immediately do so. He'd been saying the same thing to Monica ever since he met her, and now he had an idea how she must've felt. Pid was just as incapable of trusting her life to someone else, even a fellow SEAL like Baker, as Monica was of instantly trusting *him* for the same reason. It was a sobering thought. He prayed he'd have a chance to tell her that he understood how she'd felt every time he said those words.

At the moment, she was probably scared to death, and

there was no telling what a psychopath like Shane Beyer might be doing to her right this second.

"He wants me," Baker repeated, bringing Pid back to the present with a jerk. "He's hated me since I wrote him up and he got kicked out of the Navy after the subsequent eval. This is a game to him."

"This isn't a game," Pid growled.

"No, it fucking is not," Baker agreed. "I'll be there in an hour. Be ready to go."

"Go where?"

"To get your woman back."

* * *

Monica came to a couple of times, but each time she did, Shane injected her again and she fell back into unconsciousness.

When she woke up a third time, she slowly realized they were on a boat. If she'd been given the chance, she'd have told Shane that she suffered seasickness. Not that he'd have cared. It was probably a good thing she'd been drugged, otherwise the boat would have been puke central from the moment she got on.

Shane didn't drug her again when he realized she was awake. He simply smiled and asked how she was feeling. As if he was a friendly neighbor, looking out for her well-being.

She had no idea how long she'd been unconscious or where they were, but when she asked, Shane didn't reply. All Monica knew was that it was dark, she was scared, and she had a very bad feeling about how this was going to go for her...especially when Shane didn't pull into a marina.

He stopped the boat, hopped out, and held out his hand. "Time to go."

Monica didn't move from where she was lying in the bottom of the boat. She thought for a second about grabbing hold of the steering wheel, or helm, or whatever it was called on a boat, but Shane laughed.

"Don't even think about it. Now come on, before I lose my temper. I have a very important meeting to get to."

With no other ideas, Monica stood—and almost fell flat on her face. She reached out with a hand and caught herself on the side of the wheelhouse. The boat was small, but by the looks of the large engine on the back, it was powerful.

She tried to see something on the shore, but everything was pitch-black. There weren't any lights. No sign that anyone was nearby who might be able to help her.

"*Now*, bitch!"

The change in his voice was startling. As if he was two different people. Without a choice, Monica walked toward him. As soon as she was within reach, he grabbed her upper arm and yanked her toward him.

She would've fallen if it wasn't for his hold. The second she stepped onto the shore, she yelped in pain. Whatever she'd stepped on hurt. Bad.

Shane laughed again. "I forgot you don't have shoes on. You have two choices."

Monica was sick of him saying that. She never liked any of the choices he gave her.

"You can walk, or I can carry you."

"I'll walk," she said immediately, not wanting this guy's hands on her. Besides, if she walked, she might have a chance to get away at some point.

He smirked. "Right. Then let's go." He released her arm and turned his back, walking inland.

Monica took another step, and winced. Then another, crying out as a particularly sharp rock pierced the tender skin of her instep. There was no way she could walk on whatever rocks were under her without shoes. And there was zero chance she'd be able to make a run for it.

Shane turned back. "Change your mind?" he sneered.

"Where are we? Why can't you just leave me on the boat and go to your meeting without me?" she asked.

He stalked back toward her, but Monica refused to cower. "We're on Hawaii. The island, not the state, in case you were confused. The ground beneath your feet is lava. It's sharp as fuck when it hardens and cools. Kilauea started erupting again recently. Gave me the best idea. But, in order to put my plans in motion, I needed bait. And you, my dear, *are* that bait. No offense."

Monica stared at the man in confusion.

"I was going to grab one of the other women, but you and I have unfinished business. You got away from me once. I couldn't let it happen again. That would make me look bad." He laughed again, a sound that grated on Monica's nerves...and let her know that something definitely wasn't right in the man's head.

"Now, we don't have a lot of time to get to our rendezvous point. I've already called my friend, and I know he'll do whatever it takes to get here as fast as he can."

Then Shane moved, coming at her so fast, Monica didn't have a chance to retreat. Not that she'd be able to with the incredibly sharp lava under her feet.

He grabbed her wrist and roughly yanked her toward him. He moved his hold to her biceps and squeezed so hard, Monica knew she would have a nasty bruise. That was the least of her worries.

"Don't even think about trying to get away. There's nowhere to go, and the lava is flowing even faster and more widespread than it was a few years ago. There's no one around here, all the houses were overtaken by the lava from Kilauea. We're completely alone. The last thing you'd want is to find yourself in the dark, surrounded by lava, right?" Then he laughed again. "Now get on my back," Shane ordered.

Monica wanted to say no. Wanted to protest, to fight him, *something*. But he had the upper hand and they both knew it.

Feeling more frightened than she could ever remember being, even around her father, Monica awkwardly hopped onto Shane's back. It was so dark, there weren't any lights no matter which direction she looked. It almost felt as if they were on a different planet. A deserted one.

After clicking on a light he'd strapped around his head, he put his hands on her ass, which made her skin crawl, and headed off into the darkness.

Monica closed her eyes and prayed whoever he was going to meet in the middle of this literal hell might help her. But if he, or she, was someone Shane worked with, someone just as amoral and evil as he was, she was in deep shit.

Her thoughts turned to Stuart as they trudged farther and farther inland. She wondered what he'd thought when he came home and she wasn't there and his door was shattered. Would he be able to figure out who took her? Maybe...but the more depressing thought was that it was unlikely he'd be able to *find* her. Why would he ever think to look on a different Hawaiian island, in the middle of a lava flow?

It was clear she was on her own. She'd have to figure out a way to escape.

She *had* to survive—because she'd been given an amazing gift. And she hadn't realized it until this moment.

Stuart was one of the good guys. One of the best. He was nothing at all like her father. Nothing like her dad's military friends. Nothing like the evil man currently using her, a stranger, to get revenge on someone else.

She'd seen a few psychologists over the years, and they'd all told her exactly what Stuart had—she was letting her experiences as a child rule her life as an adult. But she'd refused to truly believe them. They hadn't suffered what *she* had. They could never understand.

But as she was carried over a frickin' *lava field*, everything they'd ever tried to impart finally sank in.

Life was short. Damn short. She could spend it closed off and bitter over the rough hand she'd been dealt...or she could make a conscious decision to be happy. To not let her father rule her life any more than he already had. To this day, she was giving him the power he'd always wanted.

Stuart had told her she could trust him time and time again, and she'd blown off his words. But now that she was in the hands of a madman, a man exactly like her father, she realized the one man she'd refused to trust—despite his patience, kindness, and generosity—was her best chance of being saved.

She had a lot of regrets about her life, but not trusting Stuart was right there at the top.

No. Stuart wasn't anything like her father. And everyone she'd met because of him was just as honorable. Just as kind. Being in the military didn't make someone a monster. She'd painted all soldiers and sailors with the same tainted brush. It sucked that it had taken something like this happening to make her realize how much she loved Stuart.

And that she truly did trust him.

Monica had no idea how this would end, but she hoped she'd have a chance to see Stuart one more time. To tell him how much she cared about him. That she knew he was a good man, and she trusted him with everything in her.

Closing her eyes, she held onto her kidnapper and prayed whatever he had planned, for her *and* for his mysterious friend, didn't end in both their deaths.

* * *

Shane "Bull" Beyer smiled as he walked over the barren landscape. He'd waited years for this moment. He replayed his short phone call with his former team leader in his head. Meat had been *pissed*; it was easy to hear it in his voice. Said that if Bull hurt Monica, there'd be hell to pay.

Bull had laughed. Meat wasn't in charge anymore. He no longer had the power to order him around; nothing he said could change what Bull was going to do. There was little doubt the asshole would do exactly as he'd been ordered and come to the coordinates Bull had given him. Meat was a pussy and a pushover. Always had been.

Even when they were on missions back in the day, Meat refused to hurt women or children. Bull had argued with him more than once, swearing the dumb bitches were just as deadly as the men. Meat hadn't listened.

But he was listening now.

Thanks to Monica, Meat would join them soon for a

little chat. Of course, Bull didn't want to talk. He didn't want to hear *anything* Meat had to say. No. He just wanted to kill his former team leader, then get rid of the bitch. The lava would cover his tracks and vaporize the bodies.

And Bull would disappear once more, free to live off the money he'd amassed throughout the last decade.

Smiling wider, almost giddy knowing revenge was finally within reach, Bull walked faster. The bitch was heavier than she looked for someone so short, but he was getting close to the rendezvous point. He'd picked an area that had been decimated a few years ago by the lava flow. Completely deserted, with zero chance anyone would interrupt.

Not only that...the lava was headed for the same area it had overtaken before.

Bull laughed out loud this time and felt the woman on his back stiffen. Good. He hoped she was scared to death. She was a means to an end, collateral damage, and he felt no remorse whatsoever for what was about to happen. Her death was Meat's fault. *Everything* was his fault. If he'd been a better man, a s*marter* man all those years ago, and had seen Bull for what he was—an asset to the Navy and a damn good SEAL—none of this would've happened.

Anticipation flowed through Bull's veins. He couldn't wait to see Baker "Meat" Rawlins again. Then watch as he died a slow, painful death.

# CHAPTER EIGHTEEN

Pid paced his yard while his team did their best to try to figure out where Bull would take Monica. Commander Huttner was pulling all the strings he could to track the man down. He'd apparently arrived in Hawaii using another one of his aliases. No one had known he was here. Which was fucking embarrassing. The United States Navy was supposed to be the best of the best, and yet they couldn't track down one man? It was bad enough it took so long to figure out who was causing so many problems for so many years. But the fact that it had turned out to be one their own? A man they'd spent a large amount of money and time training? It was like a punch to the gut.

But Pid didn't care about any of that, all he cared about was finding Monica. It had been fifty-three and a half minutes exactly since he'd spoken to Baker, and he hadn't heard another word from the man. There was no way he'd be able to get to his house in an hour unless—

His thoughts were broken off when a very familiar sound reached his ears. Even though it was dark, he looked up at the sky as the light from a helicopter got closer and closer. It wasn't a military chopper, but rather one that took tourists up for aerial tours of the island.

The noise had all of his teammates looking upward as the chopper began to descend. Luckily, the property Pid lived on was largely a wide-open space. The landlord was probably wondering what in the hell a helicopter was doing landing in his field, but Pid didn't spare that more than a thought.

The second the skids came to rest on the ground, Pid and his team were running toward the helicopter. The door opened and Baker stuck his head out.

"You!" he yelled over the noise of the blades, pointing at Pid. "Get in."

Pid continued toward the chopper, but Midas grabbed hold of his arm, forcing him to wait. "Talk to us, Baker. What the fuck is going on?"

This wasn't the time for a conversation. Monica was out there somewhere with Bull, and every second she was with him was one more second she could be hurt.

"Bull wants me. Says he'll kill Monica if I don't show up at the coordinates he gave me."

"Where?" Jag asked.

"Leilani Estates!" Baker yelled.

"Fuck. On the Big Island?" Midas asked.

Baker nodded. "There's only room for one of you," he said. "Bull said to come alone, but if it was *my* woman, there's no way in hell that would happen."

"Damn straight," Pid growled.

"I'll call Huttner," Mustang said. "See if we can't get a second chopper in the air to have your back."

"If you get too close, he'll kill her," Baker warned. He looked each one of the SEALs in the eye before he said, "Let me handle it. I'm gonna take care of him once and for all. Bull's a menace to society, a fucking psycho, and he'll continue to kill. This ends now."

"Go," Mustang told Pid, letting go of his arm, giving him a small shove toward the helicopter.

Pid climbed into the chopper with Baker's assistance. He had no idea what the plan was, but one thing was for sure—he wasn't going to come home without Monica. He wasn't going to lose her. Especially not to a rogue SEAL. He had no idea if she'd want anything to do with him afterward. She'd lived her entire life being afraid of military men, and now here she was, in a deadly situation because of yet another.

Even before he was settled, Pid felt the chopper lift off. He put on the pair of headphones Baker handed him and didn't waste time. "What's really going on, Baker?"

"Bull's fucking lost it, that's what," Baker said. "Not that we had any doubt before now. He brought her to the middle of Kilauea's hot zone. The coordinates he gave me lead right to the middle of a section that was overtaken by lava a few years ago. The same place the lava is headed for again."

"Shit!"

"Yeah. And like I said, he told me to come alone, so you'll have to stay out of sight."

"Where'd you get the chopper?" Pid asked.

Baker merely shrugged. "I called in a favor."

It must've been a hell of a favor. Glancing at the pilot, Pid saw the man was focused on flying, showing no interest in their conversation. He'd bet his life the man was former military of some sort, but at the moment, Pid was just grateful Baker had been able to secure the perfect mode of transportation to get to the other island so quickly.

"What's the plan?"

"We'll be dropped off as close as we can get to the coordinates. It'll depend on the lava flow and how hot things are in the area. I'll go meet with Bull, kill him, get your woman, and we'll get the hell out of there."

It wasn't much of a plan, and both men were well aware of all the things that could go wrong, but without knowing what kind of situation they were headed into, they couldn't actually strategize.

"Monica's life comes first," Pid felt obligated to say. "I know you and your former teammate have bad blood, but if it comes down to it, Monica's life comes before revenge. If Bull escapes, he escapes."

Baker eyed Pid with irritation. "You really think I'd sacrifice your woman for revenge?"

Pid didn't flinch from the ire he saw in the other man's eyes. Baker had scary connections and might exude some pretty serious killer vibes, but with the way Pid was feeling, *he* was the man Bull should be worried about right now, not his former team leader. He maintained his silence and didn't answer Baker's question.

"The objective of this mission is to find Monica and get her the hell out of there," Baker finally concurred. "But if I get the opportunity, Bull's a dead man."

Pid nodded. That was more than fine with him. The last thing any of them wanted was to have to worry about him coming back for a second chance to hurt someone close to Baker.

The two men fell silent as the chopper made its way across the ocean toward the Big Island.

\* \* \*

Monica yelped in pain as Shane stopped abruptly and shrugged her off his back. She barely managed not to fall on her ass, but the sharp lava rocks under her feet hurt like hell.

"We're here," he announced with glee.

Looking around, she couldn't make out much beyond the light on Shane's headlamp. She couldn't see any stars or the moon, figuring clouds must be obscuring the night sky. She hadn't seen any other illumination the entire time they'd been moving. Not only that, but the heat around them had increased as Bull walked. She'd caught glimpses of the roofs of cars and other signs of civilization that had been swallowed by the lava flow a few years ago.

Shane bent over and picked up a lava rock, throwing it in the air before catching it once again. He smiled as he turned toward her.

Monica winced and shielded her gaze from the head-lamp shining in her eyes.

"Sorry," Shane said, as if they were two friends out on a nighttime pleasure hike. He took off the headlamp and looked around. Then he walked over to a pile of rocks and propped up the light, illuminating the area around them. "There," he said in satisfaction.

He picked up another rock and twirled it around his fingers, before putting it in his pocket.

"That's bad luck," Monica blurted before she could think better of it.

He merely laughed. "I don't believe in luck," he said. "I've studied long and hard to be as good as I am at what I do. Luck has nothing to do with it."

"What about Pele's Curse?" Monica asked. "Any visitor who takes sand or rocks off the islands will have bad luck until they return the pilfered objects."

Shane shook his head. "It's bullshit. That story was made up by a disgruntled park ranger who was angry so many rocks were being taken from his park. You're stupid if you believe that garbage. Besides, I want a souvenir. To remember the night I finally exacted revenge on the man who fucked up my life."

So he was meeting Baker. Hopefully Shane didn't have an accomplice on the way. She'd bet on Baker over this psycho asshole any day. Monica wanted to tell Shane that the only person who'd fucked up his life was himself, but she decided that probably wasn't a good idea right now.

As her eyes adjusted, she looked around again, realizing it wasn't quite pitch dark out here—wherever here was—after all. Off in the distance, there were odd bright flashes here and there...and after a moment, Monica realized she was seeing red-hot lava as it ever so slowly rolled closer. Small flares winked brightly when something caught on fire, before being smothered by the lava.

She'd watched a documentary about lava once, intrigued by how it was black on top from the cooler air, while viscous and absolutely deadly underneath to anything in its path. At the time, she'd found it fascinating and almost beautiful in its own way.

Right now, it was anything but. It was fucking *terrifying* to think of that same two-thousand-degree molten lava moving steadily toward her. Even from a decent distance, she was beginning to sweat from the intense heat. She saw more flashes of the yellowish-red flow moving steadily toward them. She wanted to flee. To get away. But she had no idea which way to go, and she wouldn't get far without shoes. She was well and truly stuck. She just had to hope Baker arrived soon...and somehow got them both out of this.

On the heels of that thought, she suddenly had no doubt whatsoever that Stuart would accompany his friend. He wouldn't let Bull kidnap her, then sit back and do nothing while Baker did all the work.

As if her thoughts had summoned it, the sound of a helicopter cut through the quiet of the night.

"He's here," Shane said with a smile. "The fun's about to start."

Monica wanted to puke. Wanted to scream. But instead, all she did was stand as still as possible and pray.

Pid watched as Baker slid out of the chopper and down the rope to the ground. Because this was a civilian helicopter, they didn't have any of the rescue gear they might've had if they were in a military chopper.

They were about one click, or a kilometer, away from the coordinates Bull had given Baker. He had to have heard them, but there was no need for silence. Bull knew Baker would come, insisted on it; it was just a matter of what would happen when they came face-to-face.

Pid was about to put aside his headphones to fast-rope out of the chopper when the pilot caught his attention. "Hey! The heat from the lava is pretty intense. I can get to the coordinates you gave me, but obviously I can't land, and I can't get as close to the ground as we are right now. With the way that lava's moving, the coordinates are going to be surrounded within a few minutes. New vents are opening up all around us, must be another eruption forcing the lava up through new fissures. The only way out is up."

Nodding, Pid turned to look at the man. "I'll radio

when we're ready. Baker might've called in the favor, but I owe you."

"You don't owe me shit," the man said. "The man's got a beef with Baker, he should've taken it up with *him*. Not involved an innocent woman. I take personal offense to that. No one owes me anything."

There would be time later to argue about who owed who a boon. For now, Pid had his woman to rescue. He took off the headphones, grabbed the rope, and stepped out of the chopper. The news about the lava surrounding them wasn't good, and it would be difficult to get Monica back up in the chopper without a rope ladder, stokes basket, harness, or any other type of rescue gear. But no matter what, they'd figure out a way for all of them to get the fuck out of the middle of this hell.

Landing, he radioed the pilot and let him know he was clear of the dangling rope, and he and Baker watched as the chopper flew off. It wouldn't go far, as the pilot was waiting for the signal to come back and pick them up.

"Stay out of sight," Baker warned unnecessarily. "Bull won't hesitate to kill Monica if he even *thinks* anyone else is here. He's not an idiot, I'm sure he expects it, but he's conceited enough to believe that it won't matter. He'll use any excuse to kill her, just because he knows it'll make you suffer and piss me off."

In his frustration and anger, Pid wanted to lash out at the other man, tell him that he wasn't a rookie, that he knew what he needed to do. But that wouldn't help anyone —least of all Monica. He simply nodded tersely. "We don't have a lot of time."

"Understood. This is gonna be over soon," Baker promised, then he turned and without another word, headed in the direction his former teammate had indicated he would be waiting.

Pid followed as best he could. He stumbled several times, but nothing slowed him down. When they got close to the coordinates, he fell back. Not being in the thick of what was about to happen was intensely difficult, but he knew it was in Monica's best interest. She was the only thing that mattered right now.

He heard Bull shout Baker's name, and Pid dropped to a crouch. The only weapon he had was a pistol, which wasn't effective at long ranges. By the time he got to where Baker and Bull were, it would be too late. He had to trust Baker to do what he came to do...and keep Monica safe in the process.

There was that word again...trust. He'd been such an idiot. Harping on Monica to trust him, like it was something she could just turn on and off. In reality, it was perhaps one of the most difficult emotions you could develop for someone else, especially when it was a matter of life or death.

When Monica was safely home, he needed to have a long heartfelt talk with her. A confession, really. He didn't need her trust—he just needed *her*. He'd take her any way he could get her. She was worth it...worth everything.

Light from what he assumed was a flashlight of some sort lit the area where Bull and Monica stood, casting them as silhouettes. Pid shook his head in stupefaction. Bull, a former SEAL, should know that light put him at a disadvantage. Seemed Baker was right. The man was overconfident and conceited enough to think that it wouldn't matter.

Pid didn't waste time wondering what the fuck Bull was thinking, he was just grateful the light would allow him to get closer than he would've been able to otherwise. He got down on his belly, ignoring the way the sharp lava rocks bit into his skin even through his clothes. He crawled forward, changing direction to avoid the forward-facing light, approaching from the side and getting as close to the action as possible.

He stopped when he found a good vantage point behind a large hump of hardened lava still a good twenty-five yards away. He pulled out his pistol, knowing at this distance, it still wasn't going to be very effective, but there was no way he could just lie there unarmed, not ready for anything. Propping himself up with his arms outstretched and the sight fixed on Bull, Pid waited.

The second Bull saw Baker appear out of the darkness, he reached down and pulled out a pistol. No—two of them. He pointed one at Monica and the other at Baker.

"I knew you'd come," he called out.

Pid could feel the adrenaline coursing through his veins. He wanted nothing more than to shoot this asshole. He dared threaten the woman he loved. That was unacceptable. But he forced himself to take a deep breath and control his fury. He knew Baker wouldn't drag this out. The second he had an opening, he'd take it.

"Hang on, Mo," Pid muttered in a toneless whisper.

\* \* \*

Monica jerked in surprise when Shane said, "I knew you'd come."

She turned and saw a man walking into the small circle of light from the headlamp. For a second, she thought it was Stuart, then realized it was Baker. He'd shown up, just as Shane wanted.

By the time she glanced back at Shane, she was surprised to be looking down the barrel of a gun. She had no idea where he'd gotten it, but she should've expected it.

"I'd say it's good to see you again, Bull," Baker drawled, "but that would be a lie."

Shane chuckled. "Same, asshole. Same. Stand over there," he ordered, gesturing to a spot to his left.

"No."

That was it. Just no.

Monica held her breath. Baker stood casually, looking for all the world as if he were out for a pleasure stroll through the devastated landscape that used to be a beautiful Hawaiian subdivision, now a bleak, depressing swatch of black rock as far as the eye could see. Well...that they could see if it wasn't the middle of the night.

"You'd better be alone," Shane said.

"I am," Baker told him.

"You always were a fucking liar," he retorted without any humor. "I *know* you aren't alone."

"Cut the shit, Bull. *You've* always been so fucking dramatic. This little scene isn't any different. Let's get on with it. If you're gonna shoot me, shoot me," Baker said, sounding unconcerned that he was baiting a crazy man to violence.

"You aren't in control here."

"And you think *you* are?" Baker barked a humorless laugh. "Look behind you, asshole."

"Right. Like I'm gonna fall for that," Shane scoffed.

Baker held his hands out to his sides. "I'm unarmed. And seriously—look. I don't know what you had planned for this little outing, but I'm guessing getting swallowed up by that encroaching lava flow wasn't it."

Monica swallowed hard and looked past Shane, seeing

what Baker meant. The lava that she'd thought was a fairly safe distance away was now almost upon them. The extremely hot and deadly flow wasn't gushing like it would from an exploding volcano, but it wasn't taking its time either.

The second Shane turned his head to take a quick glance behind him, Baker moved.

The man might not have held a weapon in his hands, but that didn't mean he was unarmed. He executed some sort of swift, complicated move, spinning around with his leg flying out to knock one of the guns out of Shane's hand.

Almost at the same time, the other weapon went off.

Monica let out a shriek, but before she could think of something to do to help Baker, someone grabbed her from behind, hauling her off her feet. She flailed and fought frantically, but it was no use. Whoever had her wasn't letting go.

Just as she opened her mouth to scream bloody murder, a familiar voice spoke in her ear.

"It's me."

Every muscle in Monica's tense body relaxed. Stuart. She'd never been so happy to see someone in her life. He pulled her backward, farther away from the two men wrestling over the other gun still in Shane's hand.

Even as she watched, another shot rang out, and Stuart dropped to the ground. He still held Monica tightly, but now his entire body was curled around hers, attempting to protect her.

Her heart was beating so hard in her chest, it almost hurt. Partly from fear, partly because yet again, Stuart was putting himself between her and a bullet, just as he had in Algiers.

"Go help Baker!" she pleaded, trying to wiggle out of his arms.

But he only tightened his hold. "Baker's got this," he said with the utmost confidence. The trust Stuart had for his fellow SEAL wasn't lost on Monica. If he could trust his friend, when all of their lives literally depended on him overpowering Shane...so could she.

She held her breath as the two men continued to fight viciously. Eerily, they didn't speak, didn't yell...only small grunts punctuating the silence as each man put all of his efforts into overpowering the other. It was hard to see who was who in the dark, and after what seemed like several minutes—but was probably only ten to fifteen seconds—another shot echoed through the unnervingly dark night.

Monica jerked at the sound, then looked around Stuart's arm, holding her even tighter...to see Baker standing over Shane. The headlamp had been knocked off the rocks in the fight and was lying nearby, illuminating the scene. A dark stain was spreading on Shane's thigh, obviously from a gunshot wound.

"Such a waste," Baker said with a shake of his head.

"Fuck you!" Shane bit out.

"No, fuck *you*," he retorted. "You were one of the best on the team. But I saw concerning signs early on. You liked killing a little too much. Liked hurting our targets to get info, even when they cooperated. I tried to get you help, man...but like usual, you thought you were smarter than everyone else. Tonight just proves how fucking stupid you *really* are. Taking a SEAL's woman wasn't smart, Bull. In fact, it was downright moronic."

"You ruined me!" Shane seethed. "And—"

But Baker didn't give him a chance to say more. "Wrong. You ruined yourself. I had nothing to do with it."

"Are you okay, Mo?" Stuart asked, taking her attention away from Baker and Shane.

She nodded jerkily, even as she began to shake from the adrenaline coursing through her veins.

"This isn't over, asshole!" Shane swore. "I don't care how long it takes, who I have to bribe, how much it'll cost me—I'm gonna make you suffer. I'll kill everyone you care about. Your SEAL pals? They're dead! Their women? I'll pay extra to have them raped and tortured before *they're* dead. You'll never be free of me. *Ever!*"

Monica shivered at the deranged venom in his voice.

To her surprise, Stuart's arms loosened around her and he stood. Then he was moving away from her, toward Baker and Shane.

She watched as the man she loved more than she ever thought she could love another human being walked up to Shane, pointed a gun she didn't know he had, and pulled the trigger.

Shane howled in agony. Monica wanted to look away, but couldn't. She watched in morbid fascination, needing to know what was happening, that she was safe.

Shane was writhing on the ground, holding one of his knees.

Baker lifted his hand and aimed the gun he was holding.

She wasn't as surprised by the loud noise this time.

They'd shot both of Shane's kneecaps. There was no way he was getting up anytime soon. He was effectively out of commission, though the shots hadn't been lethal.

"Radio the pilot," Baker ordered Stuart, then he squatted down near Shane, lowering his voice. Monica couldn't hear what was being said.

"Pid here. We're ready," Stuart said, walking back

toward her as he spoke to someone through a very sophisticated-looking headset.

"Hang in there, Mo, we'll be out of here in no time," he said in a low voice as he knelt next to her.

Monica supposed she should be leery of Stuart. He'd just shot someone point-blank, illustrating a ruthlessness that was eerily similar to her father's. The difference was, her father would have enjoyed it...and it was clear Stuart hadn't taken any pleasure in what he'd done. Also, her father would never have done something like what Stuart had in order to protect *her*. Besides, after what Shane had said? She'd wanted to shoot him herself.

Monica wanted to feel relieved. Baker and Stuart had prevailed. They'd prevented Shane from hurting her and had effectively ended any immediate threat to anyone else. But even in the short amount of time it had taken to defeat him, the heat from the nearby lava had increased tenfold. Monica could feel sweat rolling down the sides of her face. Stuart was also sweating, but he looked otherwise calm, as if he stood in the middle of a lava field every day.

"You can't leave me here!" Shane cried out.

Monica turned her attention back to the other men. Baker was now standing again.

"Why not? It's what you had planned for me and Miss Collins, wasn't it?"

"A SEAL never leaves a SEAL behind!" Shane shouted desperately.

Baker shook his head. "The only SEALs I see here are me and Pid. The first time you used your training against us, you stopped being a SEAL and became a terrorist. And that reign of terror stops here. You've been a bully for the last time. If I were you, I'd start trying to make my peace with God."

Then he holstered his weapon behind his back and headed toward Monica and Stuart.

"The pilot comin'?" Baker asked.

Before Stuart could reply, the sound of a helicopter gave Baker the answer to his question.

"Seriously—help me!" Shane begged.

"We need to get away from that approaching lava," Baker said calmly, ignoring his former teammate.

Monica felt a little sick, knowing what was about to happen to her kidnapper. But considering what Shane had said, how he'd planned to terrorize Baker and kill everyone he knew and loved, including her and Stuart, she couldn't feel sorry for the man. For every home he'd looted, for every man, woman, and child he'd killed. For every act of terrorism against his country...he was reaping what he'd sown.

She instinctively took a step away from where Shane was lying, still begging for his life, and couldn't stop the small sound of pain that escaped.

"What? What's wrong?" Stuart asked immediately.

"My feet," Monica said. "I'm not wearing shoes and the rocks freaking hurt."

Even before she'd gotten the last word out, Monica was being lifted. Stuart held her securely in his arms. She relaxed and put her head on his shoulder as she clung to him. Amazingly, she felt not one twinge of fear in his arms. Stuart would never drop her. Ever. She knew that without a doubt.

He carried her about forty feet from where they'd left Shane. He was still screeching behind them, his begging turning to anger. He was using some swear words Monica had never heard before, screaming at Baker that he was basically a piece of shit. She stared at him as the glowing red-hot lava got closer and closer to where he lay.

Stuart turned away from the injured man to try to prevent her from seeing what was about to happen. "Don't watch," he told her.

"I don't want to...but I need to," Monica said, not sure she could really explain why she had to see such a gruesome sight.

"Fuck. I'm calling a psychologist first thing when we get home," Stuart muttered, but he turned back around.

Monica would have laughed but it definitely wasn't a time for humor. Her gaze returned to Shane, frantically attempting to crawl away from the molten lava. The headlamp on the ground gave her just enough light to witness his end.

The second the lava touched his boot, a flare of fire burst upward as the rubber sole immediately caught fire.

Shane screamed then...a sound so piercing and gut wrenching, Monica knew she would never forget it.

Almost as soon as the sound started, it stopped. She watched in fascinated horror as the lava steadily flowed over his feet...his calves...his thighs...

Within seconds, Shane "Bull" Beyer was no more. He was instantly cremated.

Monica couldn't help but think of Pele's Curse. As far as she was concerned, it was definitely a real thing.

Her hair whipped around her face, and Monica realized as she'd been staring at a man burning to death, a helicopter had arrived high above their heads.

"I'll go up first," Stuart told Baker, loud enough to be heard over the rotor blades of the chopper. "I'll make a loop with the rope."

Baker nodded and held out his arms.

Stuart looked down at her for a moment. "This is almost over, Mo. Just hang on for a little longer, okay?"

She nodded. What else could she do? A tantrum wouldn't help right now, neither would crying or freaking out. All she could do was go with her newfound trust in Stuart. She'd had an epiphany earlier; now was no time to question it.

Stuart kissed her hard and fast, then transferred her into Baker's arms. Monica watched as Stuart grabbed hold of a rope swinging wildly in the wind of the blades and began to climb. He made it look so easy, but having tried to do the exact same thing on her dad's obstacle course, Monica knew it was anything but.

"I'm okay. You can put me down, Baker," she said, turning her attention to the man.

"No," he replied simply, not taking his eyes off Stuart, still climbing above their heads.

With no choice but to stay where she was, Monica tightened her hold around Baker's neck as she craned her neck back and followed Stuart's progress. It didn't occur to her until he was over halfway up that if he fell, he'd most certainly die. It was impossible for anyone to survive a fall from that height. Not to mention the lava that was all around them.

"He's fine. He'll make it," Baker said, yet another SEAL who could seemingly read her mind.

Monica held her breath anyway, relieved when Stuart reached the skids of the chopper. He let go of the rope with one hand, reaching for the skid. She gasped as he let go of the rope entirely and dangled there for a long moment, before using his incredible strength to pull himself up and stand on the skid, then climb through the open door of the helicopter.

"Holy shit," she breathed. She didn't think she was loud enough to be heard over the chopper, until she felt Baker's laughter shaking her lightly.

"You ready for a ride?" he asked.

Monica looked at him skeptically. "Um...you guys *do* know there's no way I can climb that, right?"

"Yup. Which is why all you have to do is hold on. Pid'll pull you up once you're secured to the rope."

Monica wasn't sure that sounded much better, but she pressed her lips together and looked upward once more.

Stuart had hauled the rope into the helicopter, where she could see him fiddling with it.

"Head's up," Baker said, stepping backward.

The rope appeared about ten feet above their heads once more, but this time there was a large loop in the end.

Monica heard Baker talking to the pilot, directing him to come lower. As soon as the rope was within reach, Baker slowly lowered her feet to the rocky ground. She managed to hold back a wince when her already bruised and probably bleeding feet touched down. Baker kept one arm around her, holding her steady as he grabbed the rope and, without a word, looped it over her head and under her arms. He wrapped her palms around the coarse rope and said, "No matter what, do not let go, understand?"

Monica wanted to roll her eyes. There was no way she was letting go of that rope.

"The ride won't be that comfortable, but Pid'll have you inside with him in a blink."

Then he stepped back, waved his hand in a circle, and Monica felt tension on the rope. Suddenly her feet were off the ground and she was airborne.

Gasping in shock as the rope tightened uncomfortably around her back and under her arms, she did her best not to completely panic. Still, looking down, she realized how precarious their situation was for the first time. The light that Shane had brought with him was no longer in sight, having been swallowed by the same lava that had burned him alive. But she didn't need the light to know Baker was in deep shit.

The lava was slowly but surely closing in on him. It seemed to be bubbling more aggressively than it had when she and Shane arrived. Monica wasn't sure why; maybe another vent had opened nearby? Or the entire ground under them was about to open up? She didn't know. She only knew there was nowhere for Baker to go because he was surrounded by the deadly lava. If Stuart didn't get her into the helicopter quickly and lower the rope for his friend, Baker would certainly suffer the same fate as his ex-teammate.

Deciding looking up was preferable to watching the lava creep closer to Baker, Monica tilted her chin. The chopper looked so far away, but she was indeed being pulled upward at an extremely fast rate. Pid had to be tired after climbing up himself, but she'd never have guessed. She felt the rapid jerks of the rope every time he pulled.

Before she knew it, she was approaching the skids. Just when she thought she was going to hit her head on them, she stopped. Her body was being buffeted back and forth from the power of the blades, and as she spun in a circle, she wondered how in the hell she was going to get inside the cabin of the chopper.

Then she nearly had a heart attack when Stuart climbed from the cabin and straddled one of the skids. She couldn't see any safety harness around him either. He leaned down, keeping a firm grip on the doorjamb and held his other hand out to her.

Their gazes met, and Monica saw nothing but confidence in his. He seemed to know exactly what he was doing. Even though they were who-the-hell-knew-how-far above an active lava field, his friend was minutes away from burning to death, and Stuart was literally straddling a freaking helicopter skid far, he looked calm and composed.

For a split second, a familiar memory flashed through Monica's mind yet again. Struggling to climb that wall when she was little, her dad impatiently waiting for her at the top. She'd asked for help and he'd lowered his hand, just as Stuart was doing now. What followed was the most pain she'd ever experienced in her life. Even now, her left hand tingled as if in warning.

*Trust no one but yourself.*

Her father's words echoed in her head. Monica froze as she stared at the fingers reaching for her. Then her gaze moved up the hand, up the arm, and locked onto his face once more.

This wasn't her father.

It was Stuart. A man who'd proven time and time again that he wouldn't hurt her. That she could trust him. And she *did* trust him. With her life.

And if she didn't make a move right this second, Baker would die. She wasn't going to let that happen.

Without another thought, Monica let go of the rope with her right hand and reached upward. Within seconds, she felt Stuart's strong fingers around hers.

"I've got you!" he yelled.

And he did.

Stuart pulled her up using nothing but brute strength. Once she was kneeling on the skid, he maneuvered himself back up inside the cabin of the helicopter, without once letting go of her hand. Then she was inside too, in his arms, holding onto him and never wanting to let go.

But she had to. Baker was still in danger. She couldn't be all needy when he was about to be swallowed by lava.

Monica forced herself to let go of Stuart. He stared at her for a split second with a look she couldn't interpret, then quickly and efficiently removed the rope from around her. He turned back to the open door and dropped it once more.

Monica scooted backward until she was clear of the door. The last thing she wanted was to get in the way of Baker being able to get inside. She felt the chopper move, and panicked for a second because Baker wasn't inside yet.

Stuart, as if feeling her apprehension, turned to her and yelled, "He's on the rope, we just have to move because of the heat!"

Monica nodded and took a deep breath. She was safe. They were *all* safe.

She felt the difference when they were no longer over the lava field, the temperature in the air dropping considerably. Within seconds, Baker's head appeared in the doorway. He climbed inside and moved forward on his hands and knees. He nodded at Stuart, who shut the door. Immediately, the noise inside the cabin dropped by half. It was still too loud to have any kind of conversation, but talking wasn't high on her list of things to do right now.

As soon as the door was secured, Stuart came toward her. He dropped on his ass next to her and Monica immediately snuggled into him. As he pulled her onto his lap, she closed her eyes, sighing in contentment, every bone in her body relaxed. She was safe now. Stuart had her.

# CHAPTER NINETEEN

The ride back to Oahu went by quickly. Pid couldn't make himself let go of Monica long enough to make sure she was unhurt. He had no idea what Bull had done to her in the hours he'd had her alone. The thought of him even touching her made Pid want to go back and kill him all over again.

It helped that his death hadn't been easy. It had been a bit too fast for Pid's peace of mind, but at least no one had to worry about him popping up in the future. There would be a lot of meetings he'd have to attend, a lot of explaining he and Baker would have to do, but for now, all he cared about was that Monica was alive and in his arms.

Getting her inside the chopper had been tricky. Pid knew reaching for her hand would possibly be a trigger. But he hadn't had a choice, and while he'd seen the panic and flashback in her eyes, he'd never been more proud than when she'd overcome her fear and reached for his hand.

Pid felt a tap on his leg and turned to see Baker pointing at the ground, then lifting one finger. He hadn't bothered to put on a headset, needing to hold Monica more than he wanted to communicate with the pilot or his friend.

Nodding to show he understood, Pid tightened his arms around Mo. She'd been boneless from the moment he'd pulled her onto his lap. After a brief panic attack, during which he'd thought she'd passed out—then being relieved he was wrong—Pid had just held her.

The landing was nothing but a small bump, then the pilot immediately shut down the engine.

Monica lifted her head and stared at him. "It's over," she said.

"Yeah."

The door to the chopper opened, and Pid wasn't surprised to see Mustang and Slate standing there. Behind them were Midas, Aleck, and Jag.

"She okay?" Mustang asked, the stress clear in his voice.

"Not sure," Pid answered. At the same time Monica said, "Yes."

She tried to get off his lap, but Pid couldn't let her go just yet. Not after the scare he'd just had. "Easy, Mo. I've got you."

To his relief, she relaxed against him immediately.

Mustang jumped into the cabin and reached for one of his arms, as Baker gripped the other. Between the three of them, Pid stood without having to let go of Monica. When he got to the door, Slate and Aleck helped him climb out, again without jostling Mo too much in the process.

When Pid's feet were on the ground, he was only slightly surprised to see he was back on his property. The pilot had brought him straight home.

Turning, Pid met Baker's eyes. "Thank you."

Baker nodded.

Pid turned to go, but Monica stopped him. "Wait!"

He immediately halted.

"Baker?" she said tentatively.

"Yeah, darlin'?" Baker asked.

"I'm sorry about your friend."

"He wasn't my friend," he said, his voice low and harsh. "No friend of mine would *ever* do what he did. He deserved what he got—don't for a second think otherwise."

"I'm still sorry."

"I know you are. Because you're a good person, Mo." Baker turned to climb back into the helicopter when Monica called out once more.

"Baker?"

He sighed as if annoyed when he turned back around, giving her an amused look. "What?"

"I'm glad it was me and not Jody," she said softly.

Baker swallowed. Hard. Then, holding Monica's gaze, he walked toward them.

Pid expected her to tense, especially considering the look on Baker's face, but he didn't feel her so much as twitch as the man stopped before them.

He lifted a hand and cupped her cheek. Leaning forward, he kissed the top of her head, then stared at her for a long moment before turning and heading back to the helicopter without a word.

The SEAL team all stood back as the pilot started up the engine once more. Pid was sure his nearest neighbors would be pissed since it was so damn late—or early, depending on how one looked at it—but at the moment he didn't particularly care.

Without waiting for the helicopter to take off, he

headed for his house. He wanted to get a good look at Monica's feet. She'd had to walk on that lava rock too damn far, and he wanted to make sure they were cleaned and disinfected.

He pushed open his front door and wasn't surprised to see that his teammates had cleaned up the broken glass. They'd also boarded up the back door, and he didn't doubt they'd already arranged for someone to come and replace it tomorrow.

He set Monica on his kitchen table and framed her face with his hands. He stared at her for a long moment, drinking in the fact that she was here, back in his house, and that she seemed to be all right.

"I'm okay," she confirmed, gripping his wrists.

Pid couldn't seem to speak past the lump in his throat.

"Pid?" Aleck asked from next to him. "Where is she hurt?"

He swallowed hard and found his voice. "Her feet. The bastard made her walk on the lava rock without shoes." He wanted to check them, but Pid literally couldn't make himself let go of her. Everything that could've happened kept running through his mind in a horrible, unending loop.

Aleck seemed to know how he was feeling, and he nudged him to the side gently.

Pid grabbed hold of Monica's left hand and gripped it hard as Aleck knelt down and took a foot in his hand. He examined both her feet, then stood.

"She's got some cuts and scrapes, but nothing major. I think a good long soak will fix her up. Where else do you hurt?" he asked Monica.

"Nowhere. Just my feet."

"Now's not the time to be a hero," Pid chided gently. "Whatever he did, we'll deal with it."

Monica reached up and palmed the side of Pid's face. He felt her touch down to his soul. "I'm fine. I mean, he hurt me, hit me a few times, but I was out of it for most of the boat ride to the other island. He kept me drugged, which was probably a good thing because given how choppy it was, I probably would've puked my guts out," she said. "He pulled up to the shore fairly close to where you found us. He carried me most of the way, then we waited for you to show up."

Pid closed his eyes in relief. It would have killed him to know Bull had assaulted her, but it wouldn't have changed how he felt about her. Not in the least.

"If you're sure you're okay, we'll go," Mustang said. "If you need anything, you know all you have to do is ask. I'm sure El is going to want to come check on you guys tomorrow."

"Same for Lexie," Midas said.

"And Kenna," Aleck added.

"I wouldn't be surprised if Ashlyn found her way over here," Slate threw in.

Pid was grateful for the support, but the last thing he wanted was for Monica to have to entertain everyone so soon after what happened. He opened his mouth to tell them but Monica beat him to it.

"I appreciate that so much. And I'll text them tomorrow, but can you maybe...would they be offended if I asked for a day before they came over?" Monica said. "I think Stuart needs some time."

Pid jerked in surprise. His friends smirked.

"Of course. But when Elodie gets stressed, she cooks.

Would you object to us dropping something off?" Mustang asked.

"Of course not."

"Lexie will be fine with that as long as you text her," Midas told her.

"And as long as you're still coming to the wedding this weekend, Kenna'll be cool," Aleck said. "You *are* still coming, right?"

"We wouldn't miss it," Monica said.

Pid knew he should be the one reassuring his friends, but he was too raw right now. He'd almost lost Mo before he'd really even had her. Monica was exactly right—he did need some time.

"I'm thinking Huttner's going to want to talk to you both ASAP," Mustang said. "But I'll see if I can buy you a short break. You might need to come to the base to talk to him tomorrow afternoon."

Pid nodded. He didn't like it, but he knew he needed to talk to his commander. They both did. Baker would most certainly be in touch with Huttner, letting him know what happened to Bull, but both he and Monica would need to add their account of what happened as well. If nothing else, to protect Baker.

"Glad you guys are all right," Slate said, clasping Pid on the shoulder before he headed for the door.

"Same," Aleck said. "But I'm not surprised. Your woman is tough as shit."

Each of his teammates added their agreement to Aleck's comment before they all headed out, finally leaving Pid alone with Monica.

He put his arms under her and lifted, heading for her bedroom. Putting her down on her bed, he ordered, "Stay."

She smiled, and that dimple in her cheek nearly brought him to his knees. He'd come too close to never seeing it again.

"What am I, a dog?"

"No," Pid said seriously. "You're mine."

Then he turned before he blurted something else she wasn't ready to hear, heading for the bathroom. By the time he'd prepared a bowl of warm, soapy water and a washcloth and returned to her room, she was standing by the dresser, having already changed clothes.

He wanted to scold her for standing on her injured feet, but he couldn't. Not when she'd put on one of his T-shirts...and from what he could tell, nothing else.

"I hope you don't mind. I kinda stole this the other day when I did laundry. Your shirts are more comfortable to sleep in than the pajama set I bought."

Pid cleared his throat before saying, "I don't mind. Anytime you want to steal my clothes, feel free."

She smiled at him again. "I'm not sure anything else will really fit."

Pid put the bowl of water on the floor and held out his hand. She took it without hesitation, and once more his heart nearly melted. He urged her to sit on the bed and, once she was settled, he ever so gently cleaned her feet.

Aleck had been right, there weren't any deep cuts on her soles, thank goodness. Mostly just scrapes. She'd been lucky—very lucky. If she'd had to run from Bull or walk any distance on the sharp lava, it would've been a different story.

He dried her feet and remained kneeling in front of her.

"Stuart?" she asked a little uncertainly.

"You did good out there," he blurted. "There wasn't

time to really explain what was happening, but you didn't panic. Especially with the rope-and-helicopter thing."

She blew his mind with her next words. "I was scared, but I knew you wouldn't let anything happen to me. I trusted you to find me and get me out of there."

"You trusted me?" Pid croaked.

"Yes. I admit that for a second, when I was dangling on that rope like a fish on the end of a line, and you reached out, I had a hard time seeing anything but my past. But then I realized where I was, and whose hand was reaching for me. You told me that before we could move our relationship forward, physically, I had to trust you. I didn't think that was possible...but when push came to shove out there, I realized that I've trusted you for a while."

"Mo," Pid said, his voice reverent.

"You're a good man, Stuart," Monica said. "And you're nothing like my father or the military men I grew up around. I trust you. One hundred percent."

Pid stood and slowly climbed onto the bed with her. She scooted backward, then sighed when he put his arms around her and lay back.

She immediately snuggled into him, and Pid couldn't remember a time when he'd been as content as he was right that second. They lay there in each other's arms for a long moment before she spoke, mumbling into his chest. "Stay?"

Wild horses couldn't tear him away from her. He nodded and kissed her temple.

"Stuart?"

"Yeah, Mo?"

"I think I'm too tired right now to do more than this... but I expect you to live up to my fantasies tomorrow. You know...now that I trust you and all."

Pid laughed. He couldn't help it. "There's no rush."

Monica pushed up on an elbow. "Wrong. I want you, Stuart. And you promised."

He kind of liked this aggressive side of her.

"Unless you've changed your mind," she said a little uncertainly.

In response, Pid pulled her down and covered her lips with his own. He was a little aggressive, but he couldn't help it. He hated that Monica was unsure about his feelings for even a second.

After several minutes of kissing, he pulled back just enough so they could both breathe. His nose brushed hers as he said, "I love you, Monica Collins. I hadn't realized how much until you were almost taken from me. I want you to stay with me. In Hawaii. You can accept that job at Head Start we both know Sylvia's gonna offer you and we'll get married. Then we'll have all the kids you want."

She smiled. "Yeah?"

"Yeah."

"Okay."

"Okay?" he asked, knowing he'd been a little presumptuous. Okay, a lot presumptuous.

"Uh-huh."

He waited for a second, then added, "And we'll make this the master, because it's got the safe room. Even though it's smaller, we don't need a big bed...not when you're gonna sleep just like this every night."

She chuckled. "You might want to wait on that decision. I could be a horrible sleeper. Always shifting and moving, kicking you. A king-size bed might be the better option."

"Never," he vowed.

"This is weird," she mused. "Us talking about marriage

and kids when we haven't slept in the same bed even one night together."

"Fine. I'll bring it up again in the morning, after we've slept together."

Monica laughed. Then sobered. "Are you sure you wouldn't mind making this the master?"

"I wouldn't have suggested it if I did," Pid assured her.

"I didn't make it in time...when he showed up," Monica said quietly.

Hating that she was still thinking about that asshole, but knowing what happened would haunt her for a while, Pid tucked her head into the crook of his neck, sifting his fingers through her silky hair. He didn't know what to say to make her feel better, so he didn't say anything, just held her.

He felt her sigh, then lift her head. "I'm okay," she said firmly. "He can't hurt anyone else again."

"No, he can't."

Monica put her head back down and stroked his chest with her left hand. Then she held it up and studied it. "I used to hate this hand," she said. "I thought it was hideous, and it reminded me of the pain that I went through when it got smashed. Every time I saw it, I'd think of my father and what he'd done. What he'd taught me. But you know what?"

"What, love?"

"It's just a hand."

Pid grabbed it and kissed the palm before pressing it to his heart. "It's *your* hand. That makes it beautiful."

He felt her snort against him, and he smiled.

"I love you, Stuart. Saying that scares me to death, but I know I wouldn't trust you if I didn't love you. And I wouldn't love you if I didn't trust you. For me, they go hand in hand. I just...I wanted you to know."

Pid thought his heart was going to burst out of his chest. "I love you too. Tomorrow, when we're both rested, and everything that happened tonight isn't so fresh, I'll show you how much."

"Maybe I'll show *you*," she countered.

Pid loved this feisty side of Monica. He hadn't seen much of it. "Deal," he said. "Now sleep."

"The light's on," she said.

"Yup."

"It's not going to bother you?" she asked.

"No. You?"

"No, it's fine. After everything that happened, I think I like it on. At least for tonight."

Pid made a mental note to get a nightlight, pronto. Maybe he'd text Mustang and ask him to get one and bring it over when he and Elodie dropped off whatever dish she made for them.

He felt and heard Monica sigh, and then she melted even further into him.

He thought he'd lie awake reliving everything that happened, but as soon as he heard her deep breaths and felt the warm puffs of air against his neck, Pid relaxed completely and let himself fall into a deep, healing slumber.

# CHAPTER TWENTY

Monica woke slowly, feeling better than she could remember feeling in a very long time. It wasn't until she felt someone's hand caressing her thigh that she realized she wasn't alone, and everything came back in a rush.

Shane. The boat. Baker showing up. Shane being burned alive by lava. Stuart. The ride up to the chopper. Grabbing Stuart's hand.

Him saying he loved her, and Monica returning the words.

Opening her eyes, she looked over at the clock. It was almost eleven. She never slept this late, but then again, she hadn't fallen asleep until almost daybreak.

"Good morning," Stuart said in a deep, rumbly voice.

"Morning," Monica said, stretching experimentally. Yup, she felt surprisingly good, considering all that had happened. Her movements jostled Stuart's hand, and she felt his fingertips against her sensitive inner thigh.

"You feel okay? How are your feet?"

It was hard to take stock of her body with Stuart touching her like he was, but she did her best to concentrate. She was a little sore, but her feet felt all right. "I'm great," she told him. "And lying here, my feet feel fine. Ask me again once I'm upright."

He nodded, and his hand shifted once more, sliding between her legs, almost touching her where she needed him most.

"Stuart?"

"Hmmmm?" he murmured.

When his fingers only teased, and his thumb caressed her inner thigh, Monica shifted impatiently. "Are you gonna touch me already or what?"

His gaze came up to meet hers. "You want that?"

"Yes." Her answer was short and to the point.

"I love you," he said, his gaze pinning her in place.

"I love you too," she told him. The words fell off her lips without hesitation.

The small smile that crossed his face was worth all the angst she'd been through recently. Her world had transformed in a way she never could've predicted, but she wouldn't change anything about what had happened to her if it meant she'd end up right here, right now, with Stuart.

Without breaking eye contact, his hand finally moved to where she wanted it. His fingertips brushed lightly over her sex, but the barrier of her underwear kept her from feeling too much.

Without a word, she reached down and pushed the elastic over her hips, lifting her ass off the bed and doing her best to shove the material down. Stuart was no help whatsoever. He just watched as she struggled to take off her underwear.

"Some help here?" she asked.

His hands brushed hers away and he ever so slowly peeled the cotton down her legs, never once taking his eyes off hers. It was startlingly seductive, and by the time she kicked her panties off, Stuart's hand was back between her legs.

The T-shirt she was wearing was rucked up around her waist, leaving her bare and open to his fingers. He shifted, moving down her body until he was lying between her legs. His gaze was no longer fixed on her face—it was now entirely focused on her pussy.

For some reason, Monica thought Stuart would be gentle, especially the first time they made love. She hadn't even expected him to go down on her, but she definitely wasn't going to complain.

When he grabbed her thighs and roughly shoved them open, Monica couldn't help but gasp.

That got his attention. His fingers squeezed her bare thighs for a moment before she saw his jaw tighten. "Sorry," he muttered, his thumbs brushing back and forth over her sensitive skin as if in apology.

"You just surprised me," she said.

Stuart took a deep breath, then said, "I'm so turned on, I'm not sure how gentle I can be."

With any other man, Monica might pull back, try to slow things down. But this was Stuart—and she trusted him. It was a heady feeling. She reached down and ran her fingers through his hair. "I don't need gentle. I won't break."

As if her words were all he needed to hear, his hands tightened around her thighs once more and he scooted forward a little, putting his mouth right over her soaking-wet pussy. "If it gets to be too much, all you have to do is tell me," Stuart said.

Monica nodded and opened her mouth to tell him that she trusted him, but she never got the chance. All that came out was a strangled *umph*, because he'd dropped his head and was eating her out as if she were a four-course meal—and he was ravenous.

He held her pussy lips open with his thumbs and proceeded to drive her crazy. He was rough, frenzied, but she felt every single lick down to her toes. When he latched his mouth over her clit and sucked, she almost came off the bed.

"Stuart!" she cried, latching onto his hair. She felt him smile against her sensitive skin, but he didn't stop what he was doing. His hands stroked her thighs as he feasted. That was the only word Monica could find to describe how enthusiastically and energetically he was eating her out.

It wasn't long before she felt an orgasm welling up inside her. But then he moved his mouth from her clit to tongue her opening. It felt good, but she was still disappointed. She groaned. "I was so close," she complained breathily.

"I know," Stuart said. She heard the humor in his voice.

"Stuart," she complained.

"Patience," he said, his warm breath against skin that didn't often see the light of day making her shiver. "I'm gonna make you come, Mo. I can't wait to see you explode in my arms."

He shifted one hand so his fingertip brushed over her clit. She jolted at even that light touch.

"So sensitive," he murmured. Then his finger dropped lower, and instead of gently easing it inside, he thrust into her quickly.

Monica couldn't stop the way her body rocked, tightening around the intrusion.

"Fuck yeah, just like that," Stuart said. Then he

proceeded to fuck her with that one finger. It felt good but wasn't nearly enough.

"More," Monica pleaded.

This time, he didn't deny her. He added another finger and continued to fuck her. Monica's hips came up to meet his hand each time, and she could hear how wet she was as his fingers entered and retreated from her body.

Then he stopped moving, letting his fingers still inside her. Monica squirmed, still wanting more. But Stuart seemed to know what she needed better than she did. He leaned down and placed his mouth over her clit.

Again, he didn't start out easy; he sucked hard. Monica bucked and writhed, but he held her easily with his free hand as he very quickly brought her to the brink.

"I'm close!" she gasped, not sure why she was telling him. He had to know; her legs were shaking and it felt like every muscle in her body tensed as she neared the precipice.

Stuart didn't respond verbally, but she felt the fingers inside her flex. This was the most intimate she'd ever been with a man. The most vulnerable. But instead of feeling uncomfortable, she felt...free. She could let herself go and not worry about how she looked, how she sounded, what Stuart might think of her...

The second that thought went through her brain, Monica was coming. She bucked up violently, her ass coming off the mattress, and felt as if she'd exploded from the inside out.

She was still coming when Stuart lifted his head, removed his fingers, and crawled toward her on his hands and knees. He wore a pair of sweats—he must've changed sometime before she woke—and he merely shoved the elastic down over his incredibly hard erection, leaning over to the table next to the bed. Just as Monica had stopped shaking from the most intense orgasm she'd ever had, Stuart finished rolling a condom over his cock and was reaching for her.

Once again, she expected him to be gentle, since this was their first time. But he was anything but as he braced himself with one hand, shoved her thighs apart again, then guided his cock between her legs.

Still feeling extremely sensitive, she opened her legs even wider, welcoming him.

With one long thrust, Stuart buried himself inside her.

A small twinge of pain registered before blooming into intense pleasure.

Stuart grunted and braced his other hand next to her shoulder. He loomed over her, his eyes nearly black from the way his pupils were dilated with lust.

"Holy shit," he breathed, before pulling back and thrusting inside her once more.

It wasn't terribly romantic, but Monica smiled up at him anyway.

"Fuck, that dimple's gonna kill me," Stuart told her.

Her smile widened.

He began pounding into her in earnest, each thrust feeling better than the last, her breasts bouncing from the impact. She was soaking wet from her orgasm, and he seemed to fill every last empty spot inside her.

"Feel. So. Good," he said, timing his quick words with his thrusts.

"So do you," she assured him, grabbing hold of his biceps and digging her fingernails in as he fucked her. Monica closed her eyes as sensation nearly overwhelmed her.

"No. Don't. Look at me," Stuart ordered.

Monica never would've guessed he could be like this. So bossy. Demanding. He'd been nothing but gentle and patient in the past. But she liked it. A hell of a lot. Her eyes opened and she stared into the face of the man she loved as he fucked her into oblivion.

Any other time, she would've been embarrassed at the sounds of their rough sex, but he was making her feel so good, she didn't care. He was still mostly dressed in a T-shirt and sweats, and she still wore his pilfered shirt. This wasn't the slow and gentle lovemaking she thought she wanted. It was intense and overwhelming and frantic...and it was the best sex she'd ever had. She tightened her inner muscles around him and was rewarded with a groan.

He shifted above her, straightening to his knees and putting a hand under her ass, holding her tightly against him as he thrust even faster, harder. Monica gasped when he reached between them and thumbed her clit.

Once again, he didn't ask if that was all right. Didn't flick her clit gently. He took her exactly as he wanted, and it felt amazing.

Her orgasm rose swiftly, exploding with no warning. She shook as her inner walls clenched around him.

"Fuck, you're so tight!" he hissed between clenched teeth as he continued to fuck her. All Monica could do was hold on. If she didn't, she felt as if she'd break apart and fly away.

Stuart's thrusts were almost frenzied, and he resumed his attention to her clit. It was too much, she was too sensitive—but unbelievably, she felt another small orgasm roll through her.

Finally, Stuart grunted as he slammed inside her as far as he could get, holding her to him with both hands under her ass now, groaning long and low.

Monica could feel his cock twitching inside her as he came. She'd never seen anything as beautiful as the expression on his face. If she didn't know better, she'd think he was in pain by the tight grimace. But as she watched, the grimace relaxed incrementally, morphing into a satisfied smile.

She let out a small screech as he dropped his hands from her ass and swiftly came down over her, making sure not to crush her under his weight.

She felt surrounded by him. He was still lodged inside her body, and there was no way she could ever push him off. But Monica wasn't scared. Wasn't even the least bit concerned. She loved having him right where he was. She felt protected.

"Damn, woman," Stuart said as he slowly eased to the side, taking her with him.

Monica snuggled into him, wishing she could feel his bare skin against hers. "We're overdressed," she mumbled.

"Sorry. Couldn't wait," he said.

"Yeah, me either."

"Mo?"

"Yeah?"

"Are you...was that okay?"

She lifted her head and met his gaze. "Are you kidding right now?"

"No. I was...I didn't mean to be so..."

"Amazing? Perfect?" Monica asked, trying to find a word to finish his sentence.

She was rewarded with his smile. "I was going to say *forceful*. You taste so good, and when you came around my fingers, my brain kind of short-circuited. I couldn't wait to feel you squeeze my cock the same way."

Monica lifted her hand and ran it through his hair. "I

won't deny that you morphing into some sort of alpha dom was a bit surprising, but not in a bad way. I should've expected it. I mean, you're a SEAL. You're used to being obeyed. To being in charge. I...I liked it," she said shyly.

She could feel his tense muscles relax at hearing her admission. "Next time will be better," he promised.

"Better?" she said. "You almost killed me *this* time, Stuart."

He chuckled. Then got serious. "You're so beautiful, Mo. I'm the luckiest damn man in the world, and I'm gonna do everything within my power to try not to fuck up this relationship."

"Me too," Monica said. "I love you, Stuart. And I trust you."

"I'll never do anything to make you lose that trust," he told her. "It's the greatest gift I've ever received, and I'll defend and protect it with everything I have."

Leave it to Stuart to realize that her trust was more of a gift than her love. The words "I love you" were easy to say. Trust? Not nearly as easy for her.

His cock softened enough to finally slip out of her body, and they both moaned at the loss.

"Thank you for putting on a condom," she said. "Things went pretty fast there. Protection was the last thing on my mind."

"I want kids with you, Mo," Stuart said in response. "I want to see your belly get round with my child in there. I want to watch you nurture and love our kids. But I want *you* to want that too. And I'm selfish enough to want a little bit of time with just you first. I'll always protect you, even from myself."

Monica wanted to melt into a puddle right there on the mattress. This man. God, was he even real? First he built her a safe room, then offered to move into this smaller room so she could be comfortable. Then he wore a condom without complaint. And hearing him say he'd protect her no matter what? She was never letting him go. Ever.

"I want kids," she said. "Not in nine months though." She paused, then took a deep breath and said, "Maybe a year."

Stuart nodded—then froze. "You mean...get *pregnant* in a year?" he asked.

Monica grinned. "Have a baby in a year," she clarified.

"In three months, we're getting married," Stuart declared. "On our wedding night, I'm gonna fuck you without a condom, over and over, and hopefully knock you up. One year. You said it. I'm not letting you take it back."

There was that dominant alpha again. "I don't want to take it back."

At her words, Stuart practically leaped out of the bed. He shoved his sweats down his legs and tore off his T-shirt. He removed the used condom right there, without bothering to go into the bathroom for privacy.

Monica blushed, not used to that kind of intimacy, but she didn't look away from him. Stuart reached toward the table and, after stroking his cock a few times, was already hard again. He rolled the second condom down his length and got back on the bed. He reached for the hem of her T-shirt, and Monica helped him remove it.

She didn't feel the least bit shy being completely naked with him. Somehow, Stuart made everything that was awkward for her in the past feel natural and right.

He reached between her legs and lightly fingered her once more. He didn't ask if she was sore. Didn't ask if she was ready. Once he realized she was still soaking wet, he pushed his hard cock back inside her.

Monica sighed when he was seated as deep as he could go.

"I can't wait to do this bare. To feel your hot, wet body welcome me without any kind of barrier between us," he said.

"Same," Monica said.

"Slow and gentle this time," Stuart said, more to himself than to her, as if he was reminding himself.

Monica had a feeling they'd always have a hard time with slow and gentle, but she nodded anyway as her man began to rock forward and back.

Fifteen short minutes later, she lay boneless on top of the man she loved and trusted, completely exhausted.

Slow and gentle had lasted for about a minute before Stuart lost control and began fucking her hard once more. Then he rolled them over so she was on top, and she fucked *him*. He played with her tits as they bounced, and she pinched his nipples in return. He flicked her clit as she rode him, until all she could do was grind down on his cock and shake as she came. Then he lifted her hips slightly and used his incredible core strength to fuck her from below.

It was the hottest experience Monica had ever had, and she'd never felt more cherished.

This time when his cock slipped out of her body, he headed out of the room, returning a minute later with a hot washcloth. He cleaned her reverently, then lay back down, taking her in his arms once more.

"We should get up," Monica said—then yawned huge.

"Later."

"But Elodie and Mustang will probably come by," she protested.

"They already did," Stuart said nonchalantly.

"What?" Monica asked, coming up on an elbow.

He gently forced her to put her head back on his shoulder and hugged her. "I heard them when you were still sleeping. Mustang texted, and I told him to use his key to come in and put whatever deliciousness Elodie made in our fridge."

"Well...all right then."

"So you can nap."

Monica snorted. "Napping right after I woke up from sleeping all night. Right."

"All night is a bit of a stretch. And anyway, I just want to lie here and hold you."

How could she say no to that? "Okay."

"We're going to need a bigger house."

Monica blinked at the change in topic. "Um, why?"

"There are only two rooms. And we need at least one or two more bathrooms. I'm not sharing a bathroom with our kids." He shuddered.

A wave of contentment flowed through Monica. "Yeah," she agreed. "There's no rush," she told him.

Stuart hugged her hard and kissed the top of her head. "This is going to work," he said almost forcefully.

"This?" she asked.

"Us," he clarified. "We're gonna get married, have babies, and live happily ever after. Being in a relationship with a military man isn't easy, and being with a SEAL has its own special challenges, but I'm going to bend over backward to make sure you don't regret staying here with me."

"Okay. I know I have a lot to learn about the military

—or a lot of stuff my father taught me to *un-learn*. But I'm going to do my best to be the kind of woman you can be proud of."

"You already are."

Three simple words. That was all it took to make tears well up in Monica's eyes. She hid them from Stuart by keeping her head on his shoulder. "I love you," she managed to say.

"And I love you. Sleep. I'll be here, watching over you."

"Thanks for finding me last night," she said. "And coming so fast."

"Nothing would've kept me away," Stuart said in a tone that at one time might've frightened Monica, but now it made her feel warm and fuzzy inside.

She wanted to ask about Baker, if he was all right. Wanted to ask about Huttner and about the meeting they might have to go to later that afternoon. But her eyes were heavy, she was sated and warm, and being in Stuart's arms was the most comforting feeling she'd had in a very long time.

So she closed her eyes and relaxed, trusting Stuart to keep her safe as she slept.

# CHAPTER TWENTY-ONE

Pid ran his thumb back and forth over Monica's hand as Kenna walked down the sandy swatch of beach toward her soon-to-be husband.

The last few days had been hectic. Between meetings on the base about Bull and what had happened the other night, and meetings with the team about what was happening in Tajikistan and making plans to deploy, Pid rarely had a moment to relax.

But today was for Kenna and Aleck. Both sets of their parents were there, and everyone had met up at Duke's last night for a dinner party. The only person who hadn't attended was Carly. Kenna had been disappointed, as had Jag, but at least she showed up today for the actual wedding.

Robert, the concierge at Coral Springs, had outdone himself. There was a pig roasting in the ground not too far from the ceremony for the wedding feast afterward, hula dancers were at the ready to entertain the guests, and there was enough food to feed five hundred people, which was far more than were actually attending the ceremony.

But any uneaten food wouldn't go to waste. The caterers were going to package it up and Lexie and Elodie would bring it to Food For All on Sunday to share with their patrons.

Looking over at Monica, Pid grinned. Theo was sitting on her other side, holding her right hand and smiling excitedly. He guessed the man had probably never been to a wedding. He'd been thrilled to be invited to this one, and even more happy when he spotted Monica.

All things considered, they'd been lucky. Bull could've assaulted and killed Monica before he called Baker. He could've shot her when Baker showed up. Hell, Baker could've been killed as well. Bull had been seriously unstable and disturbed. Pid wasn't upset the man had died a horrific death. He was just relieved he was gone and wouldn't be a problem any longer.

Baker hadn't shown up for the ceremony, but no one was too surprised. He wasn't exactly social, even though he'd bent over backward to help the SEAL team's women time and again.

Kenna and Aleck had decided not to have a wedding party, so they stood in front of the rows of chairs by themselves. Monica squeezed his hand when Kenna reached Aleck and their friend wasn't able to keep from pulling his almost-wife into an embrace and kissing her. Hard.

"The kissing's supposed to happen after I pronounce you man and wife," the officiant said with a chuckle.

Without missing a beat, Aleck said, "I haven't seen her all day, and to see her looking like this? So damn beautiful she makes my eyes hurt? No way I *wasn't* kissing her."

Everyone chuckled.

"Right, so let's get on with this so you don't make any other faux pas."

Pid tuned out the ceremony and looked over at Monica yet again. Yes, Kenna looked pretty today—of course she did, it was her wedding day. But in Pid's mind, she didn't hold a candle to his woman.

She'd spent the morning in Aleck and Kenna's penthouse with the other women, getting ready for the ceremony. A stylist had swept her blonde hair into a dramatic updo, which the ocean breeze was slowly and steadily destroying. Wisps of hair blew across her face, and because both her hands were occupied, Pid gladly helped her out by reaching over and smoothing the strands behind her ear.

Monica wore a simple blue sundress with spaghetti straps. It came down to her knees and had some sort of built-in bra that showed off some impressive cleavage. She had on a bit more makeup than usual, but neither was the reason Pid's gaze kept straying back to her.

It was the smile that had been plastered on her face since he'd arrived to escort her to the beach. She smiled all the time now, her dimple regularly making him weak in the knees. It was hard to even remember how closed off she'd been when they'd first met. Serious and wary of anyone and everyone she came into contact with.

Before leaving that morning to meet the other women at Aleck's, she'd woken him by taking his cock into her mouth and giving him the most memorable blowjob he'd ever received. It was obvious she didn't have a lot of experience sucking cock, which just turned him on even more.

And when she'd looked up, attempting to smile with her lips stretched around him, that adorable dimple in full view, he'd almost lost it right then and there. He wasn't proud that he'd grabbed her way more roughly than he'd ever wanted to touch her and thrown her on her back.

He'd rolled a condom down his length in record time and was balls deep inside her before he'd even realized what he'd done.

And throughout it all, no matter how rough he was, Monica's smile never dimmed. Her dimple winked at him, letting him know she loved his rough touch. He'd fucked her hard and fast, like always, and she'd taken every inch of his length, grinning the entire time.

"You're supposed to be looking at them, not me," Monica whispered.

Pid wasn't ashamed in the least to have been caught staring. He couldn't help but lean in and kiss the dimple that he loved so much. "I love you," he whispered.

Before she could respond, Theo shushed him.

Nodding to the other man apologetically, Pid squeezed Monica's hand. She smiled and mouthed "I love you" back to him.

Sitting back, Pid realized he'd never felt as relaxed as he did at that moment. His adult life had been spent mostly on his toes. Watching for trouble everywhere he went. It was ingrained in him...thanks to the Navy.

Normally right before a mission, he was even more hyper alert. But even knowing the team would be heading overseas soon, he was calm. And it was all because of the woman at his side. Knowing she loved and trusted him was enough to ease his soul.

Tonight was a night to celebrate that love. And the love Aleck and Kenna had for each other. They'd stay up late on the beach, laughing and having the time of their lives. Deployment would come soon enough. For now, they would enjoy all the good things they had in their lives.

\* \* \*

"Stay," Jag urged Carly after Aleck and Kenna had been pronounced man and wife. The Coral Springs staff was moving the chairs from the ceremony, placing them around the tables that had been brought in for the Hawaiian luau feast. A stage had been erected a little farther down the beach for the dancers' performance scheduled after dinner.

It had been extremely difficult to convince Carly to come to the wedding. The longer it took to find Luke Keyes, the son of her abusive ex-boyfriend, the more Carly became a shell of the woman she once was.

When Jag had first met her, she still smiled, was friendly and outgoing. But now her shoulders were constantly hunched, as if that might protect her from anyone who wanted to hurt her. Her eyes continually scanned her surroundings, probably looking for Luke.

Jag hated seeing her this way. She should be laughing and joking with her friends, not scared out of her mind every time she was out of her apartment.

"I need to go home," Carly insisted.

"No, you need to stop letting your ex and his son win," Jag couldn't help saying.

He'd been supportive. He'd been patient. He hadn't pushed her in any way. But it was time for her to begin taking her life back. She could remain cautious. But she couldn't stay holed up in her apartment forever. She needed to live.

Carly looked up at him, and Jag was fucking thrilled to see anger in her eyes. She'd been going through the motions of living since the night her ex had gone to Duke's to confront her with a bomb strapped to his chest. He'd planned on making her suffer, but she'd gone home early that night because she hadn't been feeling well. Instead, he'd grabbed Kenna.

"You don't understand," she said through gritted teeth.

"Don't understand what?" he asked, not backing down.

She stared at him for a long moment before blurting, "How it feels to be vulnerable! You're a *SEAL*. You're the best of the best. You run *toward* bullets instead of away from them. You have no idea what I'm feeling!"

She was so wrong, it wasn't even funny. But this wasn't the time or place to get into his past and what he'd survived. Jag took a step closer, reaching out and tugging her toward him with a hand at the back of her neck.

Her eyes widened in surprise, her hands landing on his chest as she stared up at him.

"I know you're scared out of your mind," Jag said quietly. "You're terrified of what Luke will do if he catches you unaware. But what you don't understand is, I've got your back. I can't guarantee that asshole won't try something—in fact, he probably will, especially since he was willing to drive the getaway boat your ex was going to use to kidnap you. But I'm telling you here and now, there's *nowhere* he can take you that I won't find you, Carly. And do you think for one second Kenna's husband will sit back and do nothing if he comes after you? Or Mustang? Or Midas? Hell, Pid or Slate as well? Not to mention Baker Rawlins.

"You're forgetting you have an *entire* SEAL team on your side. Hiding isn't going to make your problem go away. Facing it, facing *him*, would probably be more effective. I'm thinking Luke is getting off on seeing how scared you are. You need to start living your life again."

She snorted, but wasn't struggling to get out of his

hold. "You think me prancing around as if I didn't have a care in the world is gonna keep him from coming for me?"

"No," Jag told her honestly. "Which is my point. If he's going to try to get revenge for the death of his father, he's going to do it whether you're cowering in your apartment or not."

She glared at him. "I'm not cowering in my apartment."

Jag didn't dignify her denial with a response.

"I just..." Carly sighed. "Kenna almost *died* because of me," she whispered.

"But she didn't," Jag replied. "You can't think about the what-ifs. If you do, they'll drive you crazy."

Neither spoke for a long moment, simply stared at each other.

Then Carly's eyes dropped and she said softly, "I need to go home."

He sighed. He'd thought for a moment he'd gotten through. That Carly would take a chance and actually attempt to relax for the first time in months. But even though she'd ultimately fallen back on the routine she thought was working for her—namely, hiding out in her apartment—he'd seen a spark of...something...in her eyes. She didn't like missing out on her friends' activities. She didn't like sitting at home being scared.

After his mission to Tajikistan, once he was back home, he was done letting her hide away.

Jag brushed a thumb along the side of her neck and was rewarded with a small shiver. This woman had gotten under his skin, and he was conceited enough to think he'd gotten under hers too. But if he wanted what his team-mates had, clearly he was going to have to fight for it. And he was more than ready to do just that.

\* \* \*

Carly's gonna be stubborn...but I have a feeling she's met her match! Get *Finding Carly* now to find out how it plays out!

*Want to talk to other Susan Stoker fans? Join my reader group, Susan Stoker's Stalkers, on Facebook!*

## *Also by Susan Stoker*

### SEAL Team Hawaii Series
*Finding Elodie*
*Finding Lexie*
*Finding Kenna*
*Finding Monica (May 2022)*
*Finding Carly (Oct 2022)*
*Finding Ashlyn (TBA)*
*Finding Jodelle (TBA)*

### Eagle Point Search & Rescue
*Searching for Lilly (Mar 2022)*
*Searching for Elsie (Jun 2022)*
*Searching for Bristol (Nov 2022)*
*Searching for Caryn (TBA)*
*Searching for Finley (TBA)*
*Searching for Heather (TBA)*
*Searching for Khloe (TBA)*

### The Refuge Series
*Deserving Alaska (Aug 2022)*
*Deserving Henley (Jan 2023)*
*Deserving Reese (TBA)*
*Deserving Cora (TBA)*
*Deserving Lara (TBA)*
*Deserving Maisy (TBA)*
*Deserving Ryleigh (TBA)*

### SEAL of Protection Series
*Protecting Caroline*
*Protecting Alabama*

*Protecting Fiona*
*Marrying Caroline (novella)*
*Protecting Summer*
*Protecting Cheyenne*
*Protecting Jessyka*
*Protecting Julie (novella)*
*Protecting Melody*
*Protecting the Future*
*Protecting Kiera (novella)*
*Protecting Alabama's Kids (novella)*
*Protecting Dakota*

## SEAL of Protection: Legacy Series

*Securing Caite*
*Securing Brenae (novella)*
*Securing Sidney*
*Securing Piper*
*Securing Zoey*
*Securing Avery*
*Securing Kalee*
*Securing Jane*

## Delta Force Heroes Series

*Rescuing Rayne*
*Rescuing Aimee (novella)*
*Rescuing Emily*
*Rescuing Harley*
*Marrying Emily (novella)*
*Rescuing Kassie*
*Rescuing Bryn*
*Rescuing Casey*
*Rescuing Sadie (novella)*
*Rescuing Wendy*

*Rescuing Mary*
*Rescuing Macie (novella)*
*Rescuing Annie (Feb 2022)*

## Delta Team Two Series

*Shielding Gillian*
*Shielding Kinley*
*Shielding Aspen*
*Shielding Jayme (novella)*
*Shielding Riley*
*Shielding Devyn*
*Shielding Ember*
*Shielding Sierra (Jan 2022)*

## Badge of Honor: Texas Heroes Series

*Justice for Mackenzie*
*Justice for Mickie*
*Justice for Corrie*
*Justice for Laine (novella)*
*Shelter for Elizabeth*
*Justice for Boone*
*Shelter for Adeline*
*Shelter for Sophie*
*Justice for Erin*
*Justice for Milena*
*Shelter for Blythe*
*Justice for Hope*
*Shelter for Quinn*
*Shelter for Koren*
*Shelter for Penelope*

## Ace Security Series

*Claiming Grace*

*Outback Hearts*
*Flaming Hearts*
*Frozen Hearts*

**Writing as Annie George:**
*Stepbrother Virgin (erotic novella)*

# ABOUT THE AUTHOR

*New York Times*, *USA Today* and *Wall Street Journal* Best-selling Author Susan Stoker has a heart as big as the state of Tennessee where she lives, but this all American girl has also spent the last fourteen years living in Missouri, California, Colorado, Indiana, and Texas. She's married to a retired Army man who now gets to follow *her* around the country.

She debuted her first series in 2014 and quickly followed that up with the SEAL of Protection Series, which solidified her love of writing and creating stories readers can get lost in.

If you enjoyed this book, or any book, please consider leaving a review. It's appreciated by authors more than you'll know.

www.stokeraces.com
www.AcesPress.com
susan@stokeraces.com

facebook.com/authorsusanstoker

twitter.com/Susan_Stoker

instagram.com/authorsusanstoker

goodreads.com/SusanStoker

bookbub.com/authors/susan-stoker

amazon.com/author/susanstoker